'Til There
Was U

'Til There Was U

Dianne Castell

BRAVA

KENSINGTON PUBLISHING CORP.
http://www.kensingtonbooks.com

BRAVA BOOKS are published by

Kensington Publishing Corp.
850 Third Avenue
New York, NY 10022

All Kensington titles, imprints and distributed lines are available at special quantity discounts for bulk purchases for sales promotion, premiums, fundraising, educational or institutional use.

Special book excerpts or customized printings can also be created to fit specific needs. For details, write or phone the office of the Kensington Special Sales Manager: Kensington Publishing Corp., 850 Third Avenue, New York, NY 10022. Attn. Special Sales Department. Phone: 1-800-221-2647.

Brava and the B logo Reg. U.S. Pat. & TM Off.

ISBN 0-7582-1005-1

First Kensington Trade Paperback Printing: November 2005
10 9 8 7 6 5 4 3 2 1

Printed in the United States of America

To my son David,
part computer guru, part Mama Jillin
and totally fabulous guy.

Chapter 1

Sweat beaded across Ryan O'Fallon's upper lip as he stood in the middle of his California office, gripped the phone tighter and said to the reporter on the other end, "That grandbaby my father's showing off around O'Fallon's Landing is not mine, no matter what he says."

Ryan disconnected, turned and collided with Effie Wilson, coworker, competitor and all-around hot babe. "Dear God, Ryan, you have a baby?"

"No!" He raked his hair with shaky fingers as he stared out the floor-to-ceiling windows of Designs Unlimited to the clear blue sky. He could feel Effie watching him. Well, she was entitled since he'd discreetly ogled her blond hair, green eyes, slender build—what he could see of it hidden under those damn business suits—every chance he'd gotten for the last eighteen months.

He pointed to the phone. "That reporter from the *Landing Times* got things screwed up. He should have said uncle. I have two brothers. Must be Keefe's baby or Quade's. I'm Uncle Ryan."

Effie sat in the chair by his desk and studied the folder in her lap. "Right. Just an uncle. Whatever you say. Now, about this mall in La Jolla that we're redesigning, I—"

"Why would any baby of mine be in Tennessee when I'm here? That makes no sense. Besides, I would never be that irresponsible," he said in explanation to himself as much as Effie.

He paced. He always paced, and he always, always used protection. But sometimes things happened. What if this was one of those times? He counted backward on his fingers, checking off the months and women—Maria, Jennifer, Lucy, Honey, Monica.

"Need a calculator?" Effie offered, a smart-ass edge to her voice. She held it up as if knowing exactly what he was doing.

"No!" Ryan considered the number of relationships he'd gone through in the last twelve months. Not exactly a surprise. He wasn't into any permanence, except with his job. Didn't have time and he always made that clear.

He added, "If it is my baby, why wouldn't the mother just tell me? Bring the baby to me here instead of going to Tennessee? She didn't do either of those things. How can it be mine? It's a mistake."

"Of course it is."

Did her brow just arch? Her eyes roll? "Okay, Ms. Know-it-all, you've obviously got some opinion brewing in that brain of yours. Spill it."

"I think we could win an Architectural Environmental Beautification Award if we utilize solar energy and water conservation facilities. Water's already the theme with fountains and still pools. You'll have to refigure the infrastructure, but it'll mean our names in *Architectural Digest*, a plaque. My name first, *E* before *R* and—"

"No way are you changing the subject and weaseling out of this, Wilson. You're talking mall and thinking baby. And you've got that shame-on-you look on your face, and I sure as hell don't want to deal with that all day."

Her spine stiffened, and she stared straight at him. "I do not have a look like that."

He stuffed his hands in his pockets. "Like hell."

She let out a deep breath and tilted her head. "You're sure you want to hear my opinion?"

"Shoot. Clear the air and then get back to the mall project."

This was the very reason he'd never persued getting it on with Effie Wilson in the first place. Work and personal lives were a bad mix, especially since his relationships always ended badly. No need to put his job or hers in jeopardy over some wild temporary fling involving hormones on a rampage and not much else. "And my name goes first on any plaques; O is before W."

"First names first on awards." She folded her hands over the papers. "As for the baby issue . . . How did you break up with whomever you were dating at the appropriate time for this baby to be yours?"

Lousy! Damn lousy! A year ago he was dating Monica. She hated his guts now. Wouldn't trust him with so much as a dust mite. Starting relationships was no problem, but ending them . . . Hell, how did any man end a relationship? Piss-poor! "You know for a fact I was dating someone a year ago?"

"Monica. The lunchroom knows all. You're on the fast track for partner, some consider you handsome and you're always dating, but it doesn't last longer than four months. The average is ten weeks and two days."

For the second time in less than ten minutes he felt as if he'd been smacked by a two-by-four. "You keep track?"

"Every woman in the building keeps track." She smiled sweetly. "I won the last two pools." She held up her foot and wiggled it back and forth. "Bought these with my winnings. They're Italian and go great with my Gucci purse from the last pool."

She gave him a superior wink. "I just nominated you for Mr. Sexy San Diego. After you win, I should clean up; you'll have more flavors-of-the-month than Baskin Robbins. I know you well, Ryan O'Fallon. So many women, so little time. I'll make a killing."

He sank into the chair. "There's a lunchroom pool on my dating habits?"

"It's this way: guys do football games, women do—"

"My relationships?"

"Known around here as bedroom bingo."

His eyes squinted, and he glared at her.

"That International House of Pancakes T-shirt you gave me for my birthday . . . The Ihop logo has nothing to do with me loving pancakes, does it?" He picked the coffee mug up off his desk and read, "Architects know all the angles. You gave me this for Christmas. It's not referring to my design abilities."

"Sort of. Maybe. It was kind of a multipurpose gift. But the point is, leaving the baby with your family makes more sense than giving the baby to you. Consider the fact that you had to think who the mother might be. Not exactly a sign of responsible parenthood. You're not up to raising a baby, anyone can tell that. Want me to leave you alone for a few minutes so you can make some phone calls and check on . . . things?"

"No, dammit. We're going to clear this up right now. I am not the father of this baby, and I can prove it with one phone call."

"I'll come back later." She closed her portfolio, stood and headed for the door.

"Sit." He pointed to the chair she'd just vacated, stopping her mid-stride.

"This is none of my business, O'Fallon, and I do not take orders from you."

"You started this. Who's wearing Italian shoes? My

business is damn-well your business, and I want to set the record straight right now before this goes any further and we never get this damn mall finished on time."

She reluctantly parked herself in the chair, and he snatched up the phone. "I'm calling my father. He'll know the whole story. I'm an uncle, just an uncle, and the *Landing Times* is fishing for gossip."

He hit speed dial for Rory O'Fallon. And two minutes later he disconnected more confused than ever. Rory had told him to forget the newspaper and stay where he was and keep his mouth shut. He had everything under control.

What kind of answer was forget the newspaper?

"Well?" asked Effie as Ryan stared at the phone for the second time today. This was not his favorite pastime. She added, "I didn't get much from this side of the conversation except 'but ... but ... but.'"

He cut his gaze to the flat landscape dotted with pristine modern office buildings and perfectly manicured grass. Even the trees in the business complex looked computer generated. He liked things precise and organized and wanted to stay right where he was, doing what he did best, building things his way, being a success in his own right in San Diego and not just Rory O'Fallon's son back at the Landing, but ... There was that word again.

Something was going on with his father and this baby. Rory O'Fallon was a man who told it like it was. He didn't hedge on the truth or dodge the issues ... 'til now. "I've got to go to O'Fallon's Landing."

He turned, catching one of her dazzling smiles. "Family restaurant here in town? Think they'll know what's going on?"

"Family business on the Mississippi and I'm sure they know what this is all about. I'm leaving for Memphis tomorrow."

Effie's eyes shot wide open, and she stared at him. "You can't do that. Out of the question. We are armpit-deep in plans for renovating this mall. The estimates are already running late. What'll we do? You work on half of the mall there and I work on the other half here and we glue the plans together in the middle? That's no way to win an award!"

He took her folder. "I'm the senior designer. I'll finish the plans at the Landing."

She stood and grabbed the other end. "And let you take credit for all my ideas? Over my dead body, O'Fallon." Her eyes blazed. Hot, sensual, sexy as hell.

She continued, "I'll finish up things here. You're the one taking off. I get the project." She pulled the folder her way.

He pulled back. "And you take credit for all my work? Not in this lifetime. I'll only be gone a week."

"We don't have a week."

"Then you're coming with me. I got you Italian shoes, dammit, you owe me. And it'll keep you from setting up some kind of father-of-the-baby pool or entering me in any more contests to embellish your wardrobe."

She let go of the folder. "Me? Go? The Mississippi River? I . . . I have dry cleaning to pick up on Friday, pilates on Saturday. I have a cat. What do I do with Wally? What if I don't want to go?"

"Then stay. Works for me."

She threw her hands in the air. "I'm a California girl. I'll lose my tan. There's not even a beach. What about sushi? I love sushi. I don't belong in Tennessee. I'm not all that sure where Tennessee is."

"Get a map." This time he gave her a superior look. "Unless you don't think you're up to a trip to rural America, you being a California girl and all."

"Staying here will kill my career." Her brow furrowed, and she glared while pointing at her chest. Least now he had an excuse to look at her boobs. "I intend to be the youngest partner this firm's ever had, and that means this project gets done on time and with my name attached. I'm up to anything you are, O'Fallon. When do we leave?"

Ryan drove the rental, and Effie read aloud the specs for the mall's parking lot as Rod Stewart sang "Mandy" softly in the background. She looked up. "We've been over the back roads of the world for an hour now. I feel like Daniel Boone."

"Except he didn't have to listen to Rod Stewart. And for the record, Daniel Boone belongs to Kentucky. We got Elvis and Jack Daniels."

And Ryan O'Fallon, Effie thought as she gazed at his sandy hair, broad shoulders, determined chin and sleeves rolled back exposing strong forearms. It was hard enough to ignore the San Diego Stud at the office where she could bury herself in work and go home at night. Now they'd be together nonstop for a week. That was not good and the real reason she hadn't wanted to come along.

She needed some sort of a diversion while they were here. That's what the Ryan O'Fallon Date Survivor Pool was all about, kept her focused on why she shouldn't like the man when every inch of her liked him a whole lot.

"Why'd you stop reading?"

"I'm thinking. So, what is a landing, anyway? Isn't that what our plane just did back in Memphis?"

"It's like a dock area on the river. Think later, read now."

"Always business. Business, business, business."

"Me? I'm not the one who named their cat Wall Street."

They turned onto another road, this one narrower with more bends. "Everything's so green."

"Around here we don't get three hundred and sixty days of sunshine. We get about half that in rain, and when it mixes with the blazing sun you get instant sauna and spontaneous mold. Be sure to wash between your toes."

The road curved right to a wide stretch, past two schools, a grocery store, a bank, two churches, a doctor's office with the *Landing Times* above, Burgers-n-Bait—she hoped they kept them separate—and a weathered clapboard building called Slim's that advertised cold beer, Memphis-style barbecue and Delta Blues. "Who's Slim?"

"Does the best barbecue in the northern hemisphere. We need to make the mall's parking lot larger or add a garage."

"Where are we?"

"You just read about dimensions of sidewalks and went on to parking—"

"Not that." She did a mental eye roll. "I mean, where are we on earth right now?"

"Small town on the lower part of the Mississippi River just above Memphis and the Wolf River."

She craned her neck around. "That was a town? There wasn't even one Starbucks. It looks kind of rundown."

"That's the town part of O'Fallon's Landing. The Landing itself is just down over the bluff with the docks and fifteen or so towboats. I'm not sure how many Dad has these days. The town grew up from people working the river over the years. They're not rich; they do what they can."

"What do these towboats tow?"

"Push barges up and down the Mississippi."

She put down the papers and turned sideways to face him. Blue eyes, capable hands, great butt. Some things she'd committed to memory. "Okay, if they push, why do they call them tows? I don't get it."

A flash of red sports car tore by them. "What the heck was that? Or more accurately, who was that?"

My guess is Conrad Hastings. His family owns the marine repair dry docks just down the river, though he's all that's left of the family."

"Well, business must be booming. That was a Ferrari and not an old one."

"Doesn't matter if business is good or not for Conrad. He was the Hastingses' only child, and they spoiled him rotten. He never outgrew either and is now mostly a forty-something conceited ass."

Ryan nodded back to the papers in Effie's lap. "If we add those solar panels, we need to reinforce the roof. Better make a note."

She made sketches in the margin as he turned, sending her pencil bouncing over the page. Gravel crunched under the tires as the car slowed, then stopped.

"Well, here we are," Ryan said, sounding only marginally less bored than a few minutes ago.

She looked up. "We'll justify the added expense in construction with the savings in electricity and . . ." The rest of her thoughts vanished as she gazed around. It was more of a gawk, and she never gawked, except at Ryan's butt when he wasn't looking, and since his eyes were on the front of his head that let her gawk a lot.

She threw open the car door and stepped onto the circular drive that separated a rambling white frame house with wraparound porch and baskets of Boston ferns swaying in the hot July breeze from the expanse of lawn and Mississippi River beyond. Oak trees formed a green canopy over everything, flowerpots overflowed with pink and white blooms, and a yellow dog bounded toward them with a ball in his mouth.

"This is *Gone With the Wind* meets *Old Yeller*."

Ryan remained in the car, door open, studying the plans. "*Gone With the Wind* is on a plantation in Georgia. This is just a river house, but the *Old Yeller* fits, least on a smaller scale. Meet Max of indiscriminate parentage. Is this scribble you just made supposed to be a tree? What's it doing on the roof? We should fax these changes to the client, without the tree, tonight. I wonder if Dad has a fax machine."

"I can't believe you grew up here. I grew up in a condo. I live in a condo. My first word was condo. But my grandparents lived in upstate Washington, in a place half this size on a little river. We caught trout, picked apples, played Parcheesi. I'd forgotten all about it . . . 'til now."

A smile crept across her face. "I used to make mud pies, run barefoot. I remember stepping on a bee and yelling my head off."

He got out of the car and leaned against it as he gazed around. "I spent my whole life getting to the big city, to the action, making my own way. Not much happening on the banks of the Mississippi. You can make a hell of a lot of mud pies, but that's about it. Hope Dad has high-speed Internet."

The front door suddenly flew open, framing a middle-aged woman with brown hair pulled back into a ponytail. She wore a blue blouse over a white T-shirt and jeans. She craned her neck, her eyes suddenly rounding as if not believing what she saw. She laughed, her whole face happy, while stepping around a stroller on the porch, then running down the steps with the enthusiasm of a teenager. "Ryan? My stars! Is that really you? Well, color me happy."

Before he could answer she stood on tiptoes, wrapped her arms around him and kissed him on the cheek, then stepped back, taking him in head to toe. "What in heaven's name are you doing here? Why aren't you in California building stuff like you always are? And you brought a . . . friend."

The woman's expression slipped a notch. It slipped several more as she glanced at Effie. California girl makes bad first impression on Tennessee woman. She continued, "I ought to be mad as a hornet that you haven't been home in two years, but I'm so all-fired glad you're here, I can't be mad at all."

Ryan grinned and took a little box from his pants pocket and handed it to her. "I missed your birthday."

She tossed her head and tried to look perturbed. "And I'm supposed to just up and forgive you for not getting here more often, is that it?" She lifted the lid, and her eyes widened as she held up a gold bracelet. "Honey, you are so forgiven." She laughed and kissed Ryan again.

Ryan O'Fallon remembered a birthday? This from the man who came to work on Thanksgiving because he forgot it was Thanksgiving? Of course the reason she knew he was there was because she was there, too.

"So, what's going on, Thelma?" Ryan asked. "And don't say nothing's going on, because there's a baby in that house"—he nodded in that direction—"and I'm supposed to be the father, right?"

She looked from the bracelet to Ryan. "I'm thinking this is a bribe more than a present."

"When I called, Dad wouldn't talk about the baby. Told me to stay where I was. Seems a little strange since she's my offspring."

"Well, you should have done what he said, but it's too late now." Thelma let out a deep breath and nodded at the river. "Better go see your daddy before things get any more complicated, as if they could. That man's got his hands full."

"Meaning . . . ?"

"Meaning you best be seeing him alone. He's down at the docks, wrestling with barge schedules. I'll take care of your girlfriend 'til you get back."

Girlfriend? "I'm Effie Wilson." Effie held out her hand. "Ryan and I work together, just work."

Thelma's eyes brightened, and she chuckled as she shook Effie's hand in a friendly grip. "And not his girl-friend? Well, that sure does help some. Glad to meet you. I'm the chief cook and bottle washer around here. Have been since Ryan and his two brothers were whiny pups."

Ryan opened his mouth, but Thelma waved her hand at him as if shooing a fly. "You best be finding Rory. He's going to be surprised to the bottom of his toes to see you, that much I know for sure." She wagged her head slowly. "You should have stayed in California."

"With my daughter being here? Who brought her here, Thelma? Who's the mother? Where is she now? Why didn't she hang around or at least call me? Why didn't you all call me? Hell, I'm the father. Right?"

"Go find your daddy. He's the man with the answers."

Chapter 2

Which meant what? Ryan wondered while walking across the grass to the road that led down to the dock. The deep resonating sound of an idling towboat drifted his way, and he looked out onto the rolling Mississippi, spying a line hauler sitting in the channel. It gleamed crisp and white in the afternoon sun. *River Rat* on the name board across the upper deck in red, O'Fallon Transport underneath in the same color and the O'Fallon flag of four red stars, one for each of the O'Fallon men, on a yellow field flying from the top just under the stars-and-stripes.

A hundred and fifty feet of boat was one hell of a lot of boat. Probably here to change crews and take on fuel and provisions, the only reasons these workhorses stopped. Too big an investment to let sit idle.

The humidity of summer on the river settled in around him, gluing his shirt to his skin. Maple and poplar trees hugged the slopes, air hung heavy and still, and dragonflies darted low over the muddy banks. A turtle rested on a chunk of driftwood, and an egret stood in the shallows watching for dinner. Sweat slithered between Ryan's shoulder blades as the landing did a slow bake in the sweltering sun.

He walked onto the solid concrete-and-steel dock anchored to the bottom of the river and started for the houseboat at the end that served as the offices for O'Fallon Transport.

"Hey, Ryan," came a voice from behind him. Ryan turned and faced Deek Prescott. They had graduated high school together but weren't exactly friends. Deek grinned and held out his hand. "Long time no see. You sure got a cute baby. What's she doing here without you?" His grin broadened. "Bet that's some good story."

"Yeah, damn terrific." Ryan shook hands and hurried on down the dock, not wanting to answer questions until he had some answers himself. He walked past reels of cable used to lash barges together, coils of thick dock line, steel drums and a forklift. Everything neat and tidy. A disorganized dock was a deadly dock.

He spied Rory down at the far end where a harbor tug powered up for work, its engines vibrating the concrete and metal into his shoes and penetrating his very bones. He knew the feeling well; he'd worked the docks half his life and run barges the other half . . . 'til he moved to San Diego. He caught his father's eye and waved.

Rory O'Fallon dropped his clipboard, stared, blinked and nearly walked off the end of the dock. His father did not walk off docks. There was a hell of a lot more going on here than Ryan O'Fallon, missing daddy.

Ryan pointed toward the office. They couldn't talk out on the landing with the racket. Besides, everybody and their grandmother would be watching.

He followed his dad inside, past empty desks, the workday nearly over. Air-conditioning along with the blue-tinted windows offered a bit of heaven against the brutal sun. Still not saying a word, they headed straight into Rory's office, and he closed the door behind them. His craggy brows pulled together in one line, his blue eyes tired, his face drawn. "What the hell are you doing here, boy? You don't show up for two whole years, and then when I want you to stay put, you come. What the hell's that? Kids! Do they ever do what you want 'em to? Shit-fire no!"

Ryan laughed. "Hello to you, too."

Rory raked his hand through his hair, and his face relaxed. "Didn't expect to see you."

"Did you really think I'd stay away after that phone call yesterday?"

"Hell, yes. Everything's fine and dandy here, so why don't you just get yourself on back to Calif—"

"Dad, talk to me."

"Balls of fire, what do you think I'm doing! You being here is just making things worse than they already are and getting more people involved. That's not good for anybody. I can handle this."

Ryan pointed to his dad. "You're going to handle my baby?"

"Your baby? Ha!" Rory kicked his trash can across his office. It ricocheted off the wall, tipped over, scattering paper across the floor. He snagged a picture off his desk and thrust it at Ryan. "Bonnie's not your baby; she's mine, dammit. I just can't let anyone know. There, now you found out the big secret and you can go back where you came from and I'll take it from here. But keep your mouth shut, you hear. I was doing just fine 'til that reporter got his nose into this, making a big mess."

Ryan felt the air go right out of his lungs, the same reaction he'd had yesterday when he got that call from the

Landing Times. He plopped down in a chair. "What are you talking about!"

"I know, I know. There's no excuse for not claiming your offspring, but there's a damn good reason here or I wouldn't have gotten you involved and—"

"You're fathering children at your age?"

Rory's head snapped back as if he'd been doused with cold water. "My age! What's wrong with my age?" He peered at Ryan through slitty eyes and pointed at him as he had when he was ready to skin him alive when he was a kid. "I'll have you know that fifty-two is not one foot in the grave. I cannot only father children, I can care for Bonnie and—"

"But you are fifty-two, for godsake."

"I just said that, and you're thirty-one. So what's your point?"

"You have a . . . I have a . . . What the hell's happening around here!"

Ryan felt his brain roll around in his head like a rock in a box as his dad said, "Daughter and sister? Are those the words you're looking for?"

"Where's the mother? Why are you passing me off as the father?"

Rory sat down in the chair behind his desk and gazed out the big windows to the river, the sun sinking toward the horizon setting the sky afire with pinks and red. "There's the rub. I need for everyone to think Bonnie is yours. Couldn't pass Bonnie off as Keefe's baby. Him being a soap opera star, the publicity would be all over the place in no time. Reporters will dig and dig, tormenting the piss out of everyone to get the truth and splashing Bonnie's name everywhere. Quaid was in that isolated station in Kodiak, Alaska, doing search-and-rescue with twenty other Coast Guard guys for company for two months. He sent E-mails back to the school kids here for their social studies class, so everyone knows he can't possibly be the daddy."

"So the honor fell to me."

Rory stood and did the O'Fallon pace—ten steps across, three up, ten back and three to complete the rectangle. Rugs in the house had been worn threadbare with this pattern.

"Mimi DuPont's the mother and—"

"Wasn't she your office manager about a year ago?"

Rory paced a little faster. "And she's in some kind of trouble or she never would have up and left here one night without so much as a see-you-around. Then she came back in the middle of the night and dropped Bonnie off on the screened-in porch without any explanation. If whoever is after Mimi thinks Bonnie is her baby, it might put the baby in harm's way, least that's the way Thelma and I see the situation."

"Where the hell is Mimi now?"

"Damned if I know. I have a PI turning up the countryside for her right now. Bonnie arrived on our doorstep in the middle of the night with the gold four-leaf clover necklace I'd given to Mimi. I know her, and the only way that woman would part with her baby, our baby, was if there was a big problem she couldn't handle alone and wanted Bonnie safe."

Rory ran his hand over his face which had suddenly paled. "I just wish she'd trust me enough to let me help her, too," he said as much to himself as Ryan.

Ryan studied the baby picture on his dad's desk. "She's got our eyes."

A slow grin split Rory's face, and his color returned. He looked vibrant and proud now. "And she's got the O'Fallon temper, a yard long and a mile wide."

Ryan laughed. "Poor Bonnie."

"Christ-in-a-sidecar, boy. It's poor us! Wait 'til she cries . . . not that she does much of that with Thelma and me around. But she sure can cut loose and rattle the windows when she wants something. She's O'Fallon clear to the bone. A mind of her own and Mississippi River water in her veins like the rest of us."

Ryan stood and put his hand on his dad's shoulder. "I'm going to help you with this as long as it takes. I brought another architect with me, we're working on a project together, but I'll send her back to San Diego tomorrow and get her out of the way. Then I'm hanging out here 'til we get this cleared up and you find Mimi. Besides, it won't look too convincing that Bonnie's mine if I go trotting off to California and not take her back with me."

Rory let out a tired sigh. "I know you don't like it here much, never did, and you got your career to consider. But I do appreciate you staying on. With a little luck this will all be taken care of in a week or two, and you can be on your merry way."

"Have any idea what kind of trouble Mimi's in?"

Rory sat on the edge of his worn desk, carved wood heron perched on one side and the salvaged bell from the *Bootsie B* on the other. "Not the foggiest. I'm guessing Mimi's not even her real name. She came here looking for work, and we needed some filing done, no need to check references for that. But the woman's a managing wizard and got this whole damn office humming along like a well-tuned fiddle in no time. We spent time together, got real close."

He wagged his head and looked at Ryan. "This wasn't just some fling with Mimi, I want you to know that. I planned on marrying her, and she accepted. Then something happened and she took off. If I could just find out where the hell she is, I could make everything right."

"She'll turn up. Whatever it takes we'll find her. But for right now why don't you introduce me to my daughter."

Rory's eyes met Ryan's, and Ryan noticed a spark behind the cloud of worry. His dad loved Mimi and Bonnie. They were his family every bit as much as he, Quaid, Keefe and Thelma.

"I'd like nothing more than for you to meet Bonnie. You just wait, she's a real charmer."

"Hey, she's an O'Fallon." Ryan shared a chuckle with his dad as they left the building. The tows were gone now; the only sound was the hum of insects and water lapping the shore. "Nothing like the river," Rory said as they turned up the road, and saw Max coming down to greet them.

"How many times do you think you've said that over the years?"

Rory patted Max. "Couple million, I suppose. Hope Thelma's got some iced tea waiting. It's hotter than blazes and hinges on Hades out here."

"And pecan pie," Ryan added. "I have dreams about that pie."

They passed under the maple tree that had been at the bend in the gravel road as long as Ryan could remember. Rory said, "Seems to me somebody your age should be dreaming about other things than pie."

"Yeah, well, right now, after the baby scare, pie is just fine by me."

"That's because you haven't met the right woman." They turned off the road that continued on into town and walked across the grass under the oaks toward the house.

"How do you know, Dad. How do you know when you've met the right one?"

"When you do, you won't be asking me that question. You'll be telling me to set another place at the table 'cause this here is the gal for you." He nodded ahead. "Who's that by the white car?"

A woman in shorts, white blouse, barefoot and with a big purse slung over her shoulder was pulling something from the backseat. "The car's my rental, but I don't know who . . . Holy cow! Effie?"

"Who's Effie?"

"I . . . I'm not sure," he said to Rory as much as to himself as he took her in. Golden hair hanging free instead of bound up in some business do, a flimsy little blouse and . . . lots and lots of bare legs. No wonder she didn't want to lose her tan. Ryan ran his hand around the back of his neck. "I'm not sure at all and that's not good."

"I don't know who you're looking at, boy, but that gal is mighty fine."

California Effie he could handle, but this? Who the hell was this? She gave a final tug, the suitcase sliding all the way out, making her stumble backward and fall on the ground, the luggage landing on top of her.

Ryan rushed across the grass and picked up the luggage. Rory took Effie's arm and helped her up. "Are you okay, little lady? You should have waited for someone to help you with that thing. Could have squashed you flatter than a frog on the freeway."

"I'm fine, thank you," she said to Rory with a genuine smile, making Ryan suddenly want her to smile at him like that. "The porter at the airport must have jammed that suitcase in the back. Like a size twelve foot in a size nine shoe."

Rory's eyes twinkled. "Well, I'll be. Haven't heard that expression in a coon's age. A real country girl."

Effie laughed, and Ryan's insides did a little flip. She'd never laughed open and carefree like that before either. She said, "Born and raised in San Diego, but my grandparents lived on a farm. This place reminds me of it, sort of brings out that country girl you mentioned."

Ryan nudged the suitcase. "What the hell's in this thing? And where'd you get those clothes? You never dress like this."

She turned his way. "I only packed slacks. I hadn't planned on the blast furnace you all call the weather around here and being out in it. Thelma lent me clothes." Effie smoothed the blouse and shorts. "Wasn't that nice of her?"

"Thelma does not own short-shorts." Did she just say 'you all'?

"Rolled them up. And as for the luggage, I packed a fax machine and printer along with toner and paper so I can set up an office in the dining room. Thelma said it was okay with her and—"

"You packed office equipment?" Ryan watched a hint of breeze tease the wisps of blond hair curling in the humidity at her temples.

"You're the one who said the Landing was nothing like our office, that this place was rural."

"I didn't say they used stone tablets and smoke signals."

"Well, that's what you implied. All I know about Tennessee is that it has mountains and they filter whiskey through ten feet of sugar-maple charcoal." Effie shrugged. "One of my old boyfriends was a whiskey snob."

"I'm Rory O'Fallon," Rory said on a chuckle as he nodded at Ryan. "His daddy and happy as all get-out to meet you. The two of you together is damn interesting, I'll tell you that." He held out his hand to Effie.

Ryan felt as if he were seeing Effie for the first time, like when she'd come into his office all those months ago and knocked him on his ear. Trouble was, she was more beautiful now than then. He was certainly seeing parts of her he'd never seen before. Bare legs, bare arms, buttons open down the front of her blouse hinting at delectable cleavage where he suddenly wanted to bury his face. Shit!

Why couldn't he work with the big fat guy down the hall and have him along now? Because the big fat guy wasn't half the architect Effie Wilson was.

Rory hitched his chin toward the river. "We've got whatever office equipment you need right down at the landing. Help yourself anytime, though cell phones don't work for spit in these parts." He grinned. "The crew will sure appreciate having you around, give them something nice and pretty to look at and brighten their day. Hope you don't mind a wolf whistle or two. They don't mean nothing by it, just a little appreciation for the finer things in life."

Did Effie blush? Ryan had never seen her do that. Made her eyes greener, her hair blonder, her skin shimmer. No way was he letting her go to any damn docks.

Okay, this great idea to bring her along so they could work together was not his best lifetime idea. In fact, it sucked. He'd thought things would be the same as in the office; he could handle Effie in a suit and buttoned up. Except she sure as hell wasn't buttoned up now. He had to get rid of her, just like he told Rory he would. "Afraid she won't get that far, Dad. Effie's leaving in the morning."

"I am?"

"There's no need for you to be here. I've reconsidered."

She folded her arms and glared at him. "Well, bully for you."

"I can take care of everything."

"Like designing the mall by yourself." Her foot nudged the luggage by his feet. Cute toes with dark red painted toenails. "I don't think so, and I didn't haul all this crap across the continent to just pack it up again and leave without using it."

She tied together her shirttails with a decisive yank, showing her narrow waist and giving Ryan a quick peek at her navel—her navel pierced by a little gold ring—as she made the knot.

His mouth went dry; his head wobbled on his neck. He had to swallow before he could speak. How could she make a baggy shirt of Thelma's look like this? "What happened to 'I'm a businesswoman, a California girl?' What about your cat and sushi?"

"What happened to me owing you for the shoes and the mall plans?"

Rory's eyes widened a fraction. "Ryan, this Ryan, bought you shoes?"

Effie nodded and did a mischievous wiggle with her eyebrows. "And they're Italian."

Thank God she didn't wiggle anything else.

"My mom has Wally, so the cat issue is solved. I met Bonnie and she's darling." Effie grinned at Rory. "She looks like you. She has your dimple. She definitely has Ryan's temper." She turned her attention back to him. "I can get along without sushi while I'm here." She smiled hugely. "Thelma introduced me to her pecan pie."

"Pie?" Dread raced up Ryan's spine, competing with basic lust. "You had pie?"

"Last two pieces. You can have some tomorrow, when she bakes another one."

Ryan's stomach growled in protest, and Rory laughed deep in his throat. He slapped Ryan on the back and said to Effie, "Oh, I'm thinking you should definitely stay at the Landing, Effie Wilson. I could stand a little fun about now, and I think you're just the ticket to stir things up."

"Effie is not fun," Ryan called after Rory as he ambled his way toward the house. At least for him she wasn't. Suddenly she was a tempting delectable morsel driving him more nuts than ever before. "She's an employee, a working partner. She can be a real pain in the butt, Dad." Like now!

Effie tossed her head. "I am so fun, and I am not a pain in the ass. That would be you."

"You can get a flight out tomorrow. I'll work on the plans here, and you can set up dates with the contractors."

She gave him a bug-eyed look. "I can't do anything with contractors 'til the plans are approved, and we both need to work on them, like we agreed. You're not thinking too clearly. What happened? Did you get some bad peanuts on the plane?"

He ignored her because he didn't have an answer. He just wanted her gone so he could regain his sanity. That gold ring made him a little loony. He said, "I have to stay here, and it's going to be a longer visit than I'd planned. I can use the office equipment you brought, and we can fax plans back and forth and work off each other's ideas."

He rushed on before she could protest again. "Dad and I talked. I am Bonnie's father." He held up his hands to stop her from interrupting. Best to get this over with all at once and get rid of her. "I know I said I wasn't, but I was wrong and I can't just up and leave now. I've got to take care of things here."

She studied him for a moment. "Oh, really." Her forehead wrinkled. "Tell me, who's Bonnie's mother?"

Uh oh. Maybe he should have planned this better before he opened his big mouth. "I'm not sure." He couldn't implicate anyone or this scheme could blow up in his face. "She just dropped off the baby and left."

"And I suppose she just left a note to you saying you were the father?"

Okay, that sounded pretty good. Believable. Why not? "Yeah, that's exactly what happened."

She pursed her lips as if she knew something he didn't, making a twinge of apprehension snake up his spine. "You're no more Bonnie O'Fallon's father than I am, so now tell me what's really going on around here."

Chapter 3

Conrad Hastings pulled the Ferrari to a tire-screeching stop in front of the home that had been in the Hastings family for the last one hundred and fifty years. The stately columns on the front porch never ceased to impress him. No one else on the Landing had a house as impressive as Hastings House.

Seemed a pity he was the only one left to enjoy the place, but that's the way it was and not likely to change since bachelorhood suited him to a tee. In his estimation it was the quintessential lifestyle for a male, and he lived it to the fullest.

He grinned as he slid from behind the wheel, thinking how he'd passed that white car a few moments ago as if it were standing dead still. A Chevy was no match for a Ferrari.

"Arthur," he said as he strode into the living room and headed for the mahogany sideboard for a drink. "What an unexpected pleasure. A visit from my favorite attorney."

Conrad splashed whiskey into a crystal glass and nodded to the drink already in Arthur's hand. "I see Denise has taken good care of you."

"Your housekeeper is most efficient. And sometimes I think she's the only one in this house who is."

"Arthur, Arthur, Arthur," Conrad said on a low chuckle. "You worry too much. Life is meant to be enjoyed." Conrad saluted his friend in greeting and sipped. "To what do I owe the pleasure of your visit? Need my membership to the country club to take a client golfing? No problem."

Arthur wagged his head and sighed. "Conrad, old friend, you have great whiskey, flawless manners, superb taste in women and cars and you're broke as a virgin whore."

Conrad's stomach clenched, and a bead of sweat popped out across his upper lip. He knew things were . . . tight, just not this tight. Keeping his composure—Hastingses were very good at that—Conrad sat in the wing chair next to Arthur's and leaned slightly forward. "What the hell do you mean, I'm broke?"

So much for the Hastings' composure.

Arthur Billings nodded to a folder on the antique cherry table beside them. "As in no money, as in you've maxed out three credit cards, as in Hastings Dry-dock can no longer support you in the style to which you've become accustomed. As in—"

"Okay, okay, I get the picture." Conrad stood and walked to the window, peering beyond the white-columned porch and his car to the perfectly landscaped yard and Mississippi River rolling beyond. "What the hell happened?"

"Nothing. And that's the problem. You can't keep taking from a business and not put back into it. You've bled the place dry, Conrad, and now it's on the verge of bankruptcy."

Conrad downed his whiskey in one gulp, not his style at all, and faced Arthur. "I hired managers."

"You hired your friends, and they don't know the bottom line from a fishing line. You hired your gambling buddies and paid them too much to do nothing except run up expense accounts and take boondoggles to Vegas. There is no tugboat business in Vegas, Conrad. It's a damn desert."

Conrad went to the sideboard and poured himself a third whiskey. "Fine. I'll sell the damn company."

"Who the hell's going to buy it? It's in downright pitiful circumstances. The buildings are falling apart; the machinery is unsafe. No welder worth diddly-damn's going to work under those conditions."

Conrad gave his friend a mock salute with his whiskey. "Thank you very much, Mr. Optimist."

But Arthur didn't look chagrined. In fact, he suddenly looked smug and a bit pleased with himself. Conrad asked, "There's more?"

"I think I may have a way out. But you might not like it much."

He arched his brow and leaned against the sideboard. "If it's better than living on the streets, I'm going to like it plenty."

Arthur crossed his legs, ankle to knee, not a hint of bare skin in sight. His damn dress socks must have gone clear up to his armpits.

"Well, there's the obvious solution. You could work. You have an Ivy League education. Engineering and business, I believe."

"Christ Almighty, that's your great idea?"

"Actually, it's not. We're friends, so I know you pretty well. Work is a nasty four-letter word that doesn't suit you, but I thought it worth a try. People do change."

"Hell, man, not that much."

"You'd be surprised. But I do have another idea that's more up your alley. Marry for money. Women do it all the time." He shrugged his slim shoulders under his polo shirt. "Actually, men do too, they just don't admit it."

"M . . . Me married?" Conrad coughed and felt shaky. The thought made it hard to breathe, and more sweat formed across his lip. "Fuck-a-duck, Arthur, that's worse than working. Well, not really but sure-as-hell damn close. Not only is marriage something that doesn't appeal to me at all, but can you say prenuptial agreement? Any rich woman and her merry band of attorneys will insist on that. And even if I agree and resign myself to just living off her, these same attorneys will investigate, know I'm butt-ugly broke and bet I'm up to something."

He ran his hand through his flawless hair, knowing the perfect hundred-dollar cut would fall back into place as if never touched. "I'm a forty-eight-year-old self-proclaimed playboy and proud of it. Why would I suddenly marry now unless it's for money? Everyone will know what I'm up to."

Arthur tossed back the rest of his drink. "Unless you found the perfect pigeon. Someone who's inherited a nice tidy sum and doesn't know it yet. That's the key. You marry her before she finds out about the inheritance. No one suspects you of gold-digging, and you automatically get half at the divorce. But you have to play your cards right and charm the pants off her—so to speak—and get her to put the money in joint accounts right away. If she keeps it separate, you're finished." Arthur winked. "We're talking two million bucks here."

Conrad put his glass on the sideboard and cocked his head. "Two million is a lot of charm."

"Not if the pigeon isn't all that bright and, most important, has never been married and the only time she was in love she got dumped. Wooing her would be a snap for a man of your expertise. Wine her, dine her and she's yours."

"And this pigeon would be . . . ?"

"Thelma McAllister."

Conrad scoffed. "The heat's done broiled your brain like a big old peanut, boy. The woman's destitute. If it wasn't for the O'Fallons' taking her in and giving her a job helping with the twins when they were babies and keeping her on, she'd be a bag-lady somewhere. Her family's nothing but drunken river trash. And how do you know she got dumped."

"'Cause my cousins did the dumping. Like you said, she's river trash. But there's another side. Who does everyone around here call to help them out if they get sick or have a crabby baby that needs tending or to look in on an ageing parent? Thelma McAllister, that's who. She even looked in on Clyde Pierce these last three or so years. Fixed his food and tended his needs."

"So what. Clyde Pierce was a penniless old hermit who lived in a shanty, and if Thelma took care of him, she's as stupid as he is . . . was. And how do you know about that anyway?"

"Clyde Pierce was a multimillionaire recluse who left his money to Thelma. And the kicker is she doesn't know it yet because the old goat wrote his will in his own hand and the will's being authenticated as we speak before it becomes public."

Conrad slowly righted himself, taking in this last bit of information. He pulled his monogrammed handkerchief from his pocket and dabbed his upper lip. "And just how do you know all this?"

Arthur's smug look deepened. "I've been seeing this friend in Memphis, a legal aide for—"

"You've been stepping out on Dolores?"

"Dolores plays bridge on Tuesdays and Thursdays. I play something else. Anyway, this friend told me about an eccentric client of theirs who died and happened to live in my neck of the woods."

"Well, I'll be damned," Conrad said in a low, good-old-boy Tennessee drawl as he gave his attorney a slow grin. "And your reason for telling me this is . . . friendship?"

"And I get a cut of your take when you divorce. All you have to do is lure Thelma, get your name on that inheritance, then kick her to the curb. In one year you get a cool mil. Not a bad salary for something that's second nature to you, and it sure as hell beats working for a living."

"Not bad, not bad at all." Conrad winked at Arthur. "You're right. I could turn this marrying-for-money idea into a career. Do it for a couple of years and retire. Fact is, this is one profession I might actually be good at."

Arthur chuckled. "No one will suspect a thing because you're marrying before she inherits. Then after you have the money, no one will suspect you're just marrying for more. For Thelma you'll have to make it seem as if you've changed your ways, your taste in women, and suddenly realized what you've been missing by not settling down and blah, blah, blah. You can figure it out. But you've got to do it quick and you've got to be convincing. The handwriting experts should take about ten days or so, and after that the cat's out of the bag and it's too late. Someone will suspect what you're up to."

Conrad studied his reflection in the mirror and smoothed back his hair. "Thelma McAllister? She's such a nothing. 'Course the O'Fallons think she's Mother Theresa, but they're a bunch of goody-two-shoes, what would you expect?"

"They're not all that goody. Ryan's got himself a baby with no mother and no marriage license."

Conrad pulled in a deep breath and scoffed, "That's plenty true enough. But right now I have my own problems. I guess the question is can I really marry Thelma McAllister?"

"The question is, old boy, can you afford not to? And there's another hitch."

Conrad cut his eyes back to Arthur. "Good Lord, now what?"

"You'll have to add some money to the joint account you two open from the get-go. You have to do this for two reasons. First, when she gets the money she'll be inclined to put it in joint name just like you did. The second reason is that the more you intermingle your monies, the more inclined the divorce court is to split the assets down the middle. Buy stocks in joint name, real estate in joint name, cars. Whatever."

"But you just said I was broke. Where the hell's this joint money supposed to . . ."

Arthur nodded out the window, and Conrad's eyes bulged as he shook his head hard. "Not the Ferrari. I'm not selling it for some bag lady. I love my Ferrari."

"Bet you like eating three square meals a day more. Also, if you get rid of it and go for a Ford, it will—"

"A Ford? Dear God in heaven, Arthur. You really expect me to drive a Ford?"

"It will add to your sincerity of changing your ways, seeing the light, wanting to settle down and get married. That you're maturing."

"I don't want to mature. I want my Ferrari."

"It's a car, Conrad. Get over it."

He leveled his friend a narrow-eyed look. "A Ferrari is not just a car."

"You're such a snob."

"I know, and I like it that way. I work hard at it." He brushed a nonexistent piece of lint from his shirt. "A Hastings and a McAllister? My father will be flipping in his grave."

"What he's flipping over is you ruining his company that he and his daddy and his daddy before him worked their asses off to build."

"So I'm better at spending money than making it."

Arthur grinned. "Until now. Come on, you can do this. Buck up. Think of it as a new profession. And just because you marry a rich woman . . . or rich women . . . that doesn't mean you can't fool around a little on the side."

"That's true enough." Conrad felt marginally heartened. "You have your gal, and I never would have expected that."

"Who said it was a gal?"

Conrad's gaze fused with Arthur's, and Conrad dropped back down into the wing chair, nearly knocking it over. He couldn't speak. Hell, what would he say if he could?

"There are all kinds of changes, Conrad." Arthur stood and splashed whiskey into his empty glass, then Conrad's. He sat and handed Conrad his glass, then tapped it with his own. "To marriage and joint accounts."

Conrad shook his head. "To change?"

Arthur grinned. "Works for me." They downed the whiskey, and Arthur stood and placed his empty glass back on the sideboard, then headed for the front door. "You have less than two weeks, Conrad." He nodded to the folder of papers on the table. "And put those financial reports away. We don't need anyone suspecting anything 'til you've bagged your pigeon."

"Got it," Conrad managed to get out. He followed Arthur to the door as his lawyer said, "I'll be in touch."

"Arthur," Conrad said, putting his hand on his friend's shoulder. "Maybe you ought to tell Dolores. She's been a good wife to you. She deserves that much."

Arthur gave a rueful smile. "She already knows. I think she knew before I did."

Conrad watched Arthur drive off, then looked out to the Mississippi. He felt as if he were caught in one of those tacky glass globes that have sand and trinkets and you shake it and everything winds up in a different place than before. In the last half hour his whole life had changed like that.

Christ almighty! He, Conrad Hastings, was going to marry a ragamuffin raised in a river shack, and his best friend was gay. He looked longingly at the whiskey decanter. God, could he use a drink right now. But he couldn't. He had to captivate Thelma McAllister and get her to marry him. Both things were virgin territory, but Hastings rose to the challenge. They were survivors. His way might not be his granddaddy's way or his daddy's, but surviving was surviving. He could do this. He could go into the O'Fallon den and face them all. Hell, what other choices did he have?

Thelma gazed out the side kitchen window at Effie and Ryan arguing in the driveway. They hadn't been at the Landing much over an hour and had done battle royal for more than half that time. How'd those two get anything done back in California? Then again, the Landing was not California. Emotions flowed a little faster, a bit hotter, a little closer to the surface. Maybe it was the heat that brought it out of a person or being by the water itself.

She spied a red Ferrari zooming into the drive, coming to a gravel-spitting halt behind Ryan and Effie. Only one of those fancy cars around these parts. What in blazes did Conrad Hastings want here, of all places? The O'Fallon house was not his usual stomping ground. The Landing in general wasn't good enough for him. The highbrows of Memphis were where he spent most of his time, in and out of bed, and they were welcome to him.

Conrad slid from his car, grabbed a basket off the front

seat, waved to Ryan, gave Effie a quick once-over that hinted approval and headed for the front door as Ryan scowled after him.

Heavenly days, if he rang the bell, he'd wake Bonnie, and Rory was putting her down for a nap right this very minute. Thelma dried her hands on her apron as she tore for the front door. She yanked it open and snatched Conrad's finger just before it made the feared jab. "Don't do that!"

Conrad looked startled; Thelma let out a relieved sigh. "You'll wake the baby, and once she starts hollering we're all doomed 'til she falls back to sleep, and heaven knows how long that'll take." Thelma forced a hospitable smile as she let go of his hand. "What can I do for you, Mr. Hastings?"

He flashed a teeth-whitened smile that would do any dentist proud. "Aren't you going to ask me in, and since when do you call me Mr. Hastings."

Since always, she thought to herself. And that he didn't remember what she called him didn't surprise her one bit. Conrad Hastings looked right through her no matter where they ran into each other—the market, the bank, just passing on the street. She simply didn't exist to him. He always seemed to be too busy searching for someone far more important to bother with than the likes of Thelma McAllister. She didn't mind that he pulled that on her, but when he did it to half the people on the Landing, people she cared about, that pissed her off big time. Damn his pompous hide!

Well, he was on her turf now, and she did not have to put up with his attitude. Here he was just some guy. Handsome, for sure, a smooth talker, most definitely, but just a guy at the door, and that's just how she intended to treat him. Well, maybe not that good but she'd treat him all right.

Thelma stepped aside. "Please, come on in, but make sure you wipe your feet and no loud noises unless you fancy walking the floor with a howling baby in your arms who tends to spit up formula when she's agitated."

Conrad's grin slipped a notch as he stepped over the threshold, and Thelma bit back a laugh. The thought of a baby in Conrad's arms and puke on his shirt was enough to make any smile slip, especially his own. She eyed a covered basket in his hand. "A picnic?"

His perfect smile returned. "Actually, it is. I was wondering if . . . "

"Effie would go on a picnic with you?" Thelma put her hand to her hip while saying, "You are one fast worker, even faster than your reputation. Thought you'd broaden your horizons with a California girl, did you?"

"California? Well, I—"

"Ryan might have something to say about that." She hitched her chin to the driveway. "Those two look like they're arguing, but truth be told I think they're doing a whole lot more. But you can ask them yourself because they're headed this way."

Conrad shook his head. "Thelma, my dear, you've got this all wrong."

"You mean you're here to ask Ryan on a picnic. Well, la-de-da, now that could be interesting."

Conrad's jaw sagged. "R-Ryan? Trust me, I am not here for—"

"This here is Conrad Hastings," Thelma said to Effie as she came onto the porch. "He's wanting to take you on a picnic this afternoon."

"You are?" Ryan said, looking none too happy and a bit threatening. Not only was Ryan O'Fallon getting real territorial all of a sudden, but Conrad was completely dumbfounded. Well, good. He had it coming. He'd made enough people feel uneasy over the years. Maybe now he'd think twice about doing it.

Thelma offered, "Conrad's here to come calling on Effie. He's what we call a fast operator in these parts."

Conrad shook his head again. "I'm not here to see Lettie. I'm here to see—"

"It's Effie," Ryan said, his brow furrowing.

Thelma said, "If you don't want to go out with Effie, why else would you bring food into this house? You think I can't cook?" She caught Ryan's eye for a second and winked.

Ryan pointed to Thelma. "You don't think Thelma's a good cook? Needs help to feed her guests? Thelma's a great cook."

"Have you ever had her pecan pie?" Effie chimed in.

"No, I haven't but—"

"Someone's spreading rumors I can't cook, and you brought Effie food to impress her? Is that why you're here?" Thelma deepened her frown.

"Not at all," Conrad said to Thelma, his voice raising an octave, looking a bit frazzled. "I'm sure your cooking is superb and your pie is beyond compare but—"

"Why in the world would you care if I can cook and feel the need to head over here with a basket of vittles to rescue everyone?"

"I'm not rescuing—"

"I've got a good mind to get the shotgun, and you can tell whoever put you up to this that their little joke back-fired and—"

"Wait!" Conrad sliced his hand through the air as if cutting a big chunk out of it, bringing everyone to a standstill. He slapped a smile on his face that looked forced. "No one told me anything, and I am not here for Lettie."

"Effie," Ryan corrected.

"Thank you." Conrad pulled in a deep breath. "I'm here for Thelma and"— he faced her, rushing on before she could stop him—"it has nothing to do with your cooking. I just thought you and I could go on an evening picnic. And not because you can't cook but because it might be enjoyable for both of us to spend some time together on a beautiful summer night."

He pulled back the red-and-white-checked cloth that covered the basket. "I hoped I might tempt you with some unusual cheeses I picked up in Memphis and a pate and some Italian bread I'm fond of. And a '96 Merlot, of course. Can't have Gouda and Saga without a '96 Merlot."

Thelma considered her Gap T-shirt, her baggie denim capri pants that she'd splashed bleach on and had white steaks across the front and her hair that was held on top of her head in a ragged twist by a pencil she'd found in the drawer when she'd needed to get her hair out of her face. She looked at Conrad, his perfectly creased khakis, royal blue Ralph Lauren polo shirt, sophisticated look of self-importance. She laughed.

Ryan stood between her and Conrad. "Who put you up to this, Hastings?"

Conrad held his hand out, palm up. "No one. I've always admired Thelma, and I've decided to act on it. That's why I'm here."

Ryan's face tightened into a no-nonsense look, and Conrad rushed on with, "I know it didn't seem that way before now, but I wanted to make sure of my feelings before I pursued her."

Thelma felt her eyes widen by half. "You . . . You're pursuing me?"

Conrad did an elegant bow. "If you'd permit me the honor of your company. Why else would I be here if I wasn't sincere about my intentions toward you, my dear? You're looking at a changed man."

My dear? Thelma couldn't have been more surprised if the grandfather clock in the hallway had suddenly come to life and done a jig. "You're here to ask me . . . out?"

"I know you don't think much of me right now, but I intend to fix that if you would simply allow me the chance to do so. I've reflected on my life and found it wanting and am here to court Thelma if she'll have me."

And, oddly enough, the man did look sincere about what he said. And unbelievably handsome while saying it.

Ryan stuffed his hands in his pockets and rocked back on his heels. "It's up to you, Thelma, but something's going on. I know this guy."

Thelma shrugged. "I can't go out. I have Bonnie to take care of and—"

Effie said, "Ryan and I can help Rory with the baby. Don't let that be what's stopping you from going out. Besides, I bet you haven't had any time off since Bonnie got here, and babies are so demanding. You're due, and now that the real father's here he can do his share."

Conrad chimed in with, "I've come to make amends, Thelma. I've suddenly realized there's more to life than gallivanting around the world with no purpose or anyone special to share it with." He took her hand and stared into her eyes. "I want to get to know you and for you to know the real me. All I'm asking for is a date, an opportunity for us to spend time together because I admire the person you are."

Effie gave Thelma a why-the-heck-not look, then added, "You can stay here and make formula, or go on an evening picnic with a very handsome man and watch the sun set over the Mississippi."

Conrad nodded to Effie. "I thank you for that kind compliment."

Okay, there must be a glitch in the universe. Conrad Hastings was on her porch, complimenting her and everyone else. This was not like him at all. But, she did love wine and cheese, and she could jolly-well use a break. "Why not. Sure, Conrad, I'd love to go on a picnic."

"Wonderful." He beamed, and he looked relieved, as if he'd been afraid she'd say no and he really wanted her to say yes. Yep, the universe was really screwed up today.

She tucked an unruly strand of hair behind her ear and said to Conrad, "If you wouldn't mind waiting a few minutes, I'd like to put on something a bit more appropriate for our evening picnic."

"By all means." Conrad nodded.

Ryan scowled, and Effie said, "Perhaps Conrad would like a glass of lemonade while he's waiting."

"That would be delightful." Then he winked at Thelma, and she nearly passed out right there in the hallway. He turned and followed Effie back out onto the porch to a wicker chair. Ryan walked with Thelma to the stairs, stopping her before she went up. "I don't know what's going on with that guy, but be damn careful."

"You mean why would someone like the sophisticated Conrad Hastings be attracted to someone like me? Now that's a very good question."

Ryan held her hand. "That's not it at all. You're worth a million Conrads, but this visit is out of the blue. Take care of yourself. Take your cell phone. Keep your finger on speed-dial for home, pray for a decent connection for once. I think Effie has pepper spray in her purse. God knows she has everything else in there. Take that, too."

He grasped her hand tighter. "I don't want anyone playing fast and loose with my favorite girl."

Thelma giggled and kissed Ryan on the cheek. "You're so full of beans. I'm not a teenager, you know. I'm forty-seven, but I do appreciate you fretting over me. Now I better get a move on. I have a man waiting for me on the front porch." She smiled and twitched her hips.

Ryan made a sour face. "I just wish it wasn't that man."

Thelma tisked. "The food and wine look yummy, and I really haven't been out of the house for a while. If nothing else, tonight should be interesting."

"You really think Conrad's changed? That he's telling the truth?"

She bit back a laugh. "When the Mississippi dries up and the catfish say meow. That's when I'll know Conrad Hastings has changed."

Chapter 4

Effie leaned back in the white wicker rocker on the O'Fallons' front porch and listened to Conrad Hastings talk about the Landing, the Blues—though a man who drove a Ferrari couldn't know zip about the Blues—and Memphis-style barbecue as he waited for Thelma.

It wasn't that Effie liked spending time with this guy, but someone had to entertain him while Thelma changed. And it gave Effie a chance to deal with the idea of Bonnie being Rory's daughter, not Ryan's, and Ryan pretending to be the father to protect the child.

This was not the Ryan O'Fallon she knew back in San Diego. That Ryan never had time for anything but work . . . and a boatload of haphazard relationships. This Ryan put work on hold to help his father. That was good because he was a better person than she realized, and it was bad because she liked him all the more for it.

Blast, why couldn't he come here and kick a dog or something! Then she could hate his guts. But no, she had hunky Ryan O'Fallon all-around good son and protective big brother to deal with.

Effie nodded every once in a while to keep the conversation with Conrad going. Now this was a guy she could learn to dislike. Maybe she shouldn't have encouraged Thelma to go out with him, no matter how much the woman needed a break from the dirty diaper and formula routine.

Effie knew the Conrad type. Heck, she'd dated the Conrad type. Always after something—sex or money or sex or prestige or sex and getting made partner in her father's accounting firm. Except Thelma had no money or position, and no one had said anything about her father being an accountant.

So what was Conrad Hastings doing on the O'Fallons' front porch waiting for their nanny/housekeeper/family friend?

His little speech about changing was so much bull crap. She knew because she'd been fed that particular line on more than one ill-fated occasion. Oh, Effie, darling, I've changed. I won't—here she could fill in the blank with whatever he'd been caught at—again. Yeah, right!

Ryan came onto the porch, and she grabbed his arm. His turn to be polite to the guest, except she suddenly wasn't thinking about polite but about her hand on solid muscle. In all the time they'd been together she'd never actually on purpose touched him. Oh, they'd brushed past each other or skimmed each other's hands but not connected on purpose.

And she should have kept it that way.

She let go and stood. "I'll check on Thelma." She was amazed her befuddled brain could put words together. "I'll leave you two to catch up on old times."

Ryan gave her a look that suggested he'd rather eat nails than be with Conrad, and Conrad's expression was the same. Not exactly male-bonding time on the shores of the

Mississippi. More like gentlemen take your pistols, walk twenty paces and fire at will.

She went inside. The polished dark oak felt cool against her bare feet. She needed something cool after the Ryan encounter. Fishing from the company pier was a very bad idea, something she'd managed to avoid for eighteen months at Designs Unlimited. All she had to do was keep it up. When they got back to San Diego Ryan would be his old womanizing self, and she'd be back to liking him only on a physical level. That was a lot easier to resist than Ryan good guy.

She knocked on Thelma's door, hoping she wasn't intruding. Thelma threw open the door, eyes huge, jaw clenched. "I can cook, clean, nanny all at the same time, but I can't do this." She nodded downstairs. "I haven't dated in . . . Well, let's just say I haven't been twenty for a long time, and that was the beginning and end of my dating career."

She pointed at the two dresses on the bed. "This is it. The wardrobe from Prairie Home Companion. It's all I've got. That Donna Karen person would have a stroke."

Effie took in the two floral-print dresses and one blue polyester suit on the bed.

"My Sunday best," Thelma said. "What do I wear? The suit is out for a picnic, but the dresses kind of work. Not that I care what Conrad thinks, since I don't even like the man and never intend to go out with him again as long as I live. But a woman's got to look nice on a date or people talk. I don't need people talking."

She lowered her voice. "I'm just using Conrad to get out of this house. I figure he owes me that much for all the times he's snubbed me."

"Snubbed you? How could Conrad do such a thing? Though I do know the type."

"For him I think it comes natural, but his mama and daddy were never that way." Thelma nodded at the dress with blue roses. "Okay, pick."

Thelma was medium height, maybe a size sixteen, wild brown curly hair, light blue eyes, effervescence oozing from every pore. If Effie Wilson could spruce up malls, Thelma would be a snap.

Effie said, "Let's make Conrad Hastings sit up and take notice. Let's make him so sorry he ever snubbed you and make him cry himself to sleep tonight repenting the errors of his ways for not taking notice of you before. We're going to make him salivate when he sees you, physically pant. We're going to get even."

Effie grinned. "We're going to make Conrad Hastings drool."

Thelma pushed Effie into a chair. "Honey, I believe the Mississippi humidity has surely muddled your California brain. You're delusional. I'm nearly fifty. The only time a man drools my way is when he sees me with a double-dip of rocky-road. My drooling days are over, or closer to the truth, I never had them in the first place."

"Just you wait." Effie stood and called over her shoulder as she left the room. "Find some slacks and a T-shirt. Do you have an old pair of heels?"

"Not a problem. Everything I have is old. Hey, don't leave. I'm desperate here."

Effie went to her room and snagged her Gucci bag and headed back to Thelma. She dumped her purse upside down on the bed. Utility knife, markers, chalk, tape, scissors, measuring tape, camera, orange material for the top of survey stakes, a note pad, PDA, hair stuff, makeup stuff, sneakers.

Thelma stared, mouth open. "What is all that?"

"You've heard of bed-in-a-bag, this is career-in-a-bag. I don't leave home without it." She held up the pair of

Thelma's black slacks. "We can cut these and make capris. We can fold the ends into cuffs, put a vee in your white T-shirt and tuck in the ends to show off your cleavage—if that doesn't make Conrad drool, he's stone dead—and pull your hair back with the orange surveyor ribbons for color. We'll snip the backs off the white shoes to make slides and marker in black polka dots to pull the outfit together. If you have an old white handbag, we'll add the dots to that, too."

Thelma gave her a deer-in-the-headlights look.

"Or not." Effie held her hands. "Look, I'm sorry, I don't mean to take over your life, and I'm usually not this forward. Well, actually I am this forward, basically pushy, especially in my job because I want to get ahead, but—"

"How'd you do that? How'd you make a neat wardrobe out of nothing?"

"You like it?"

Thelma hugged her, and Effie felt as if she'd just designed a gown for the Oscars. "After living with men all these years I didn't know having a woman around this house could be so much fun."

"And after living with only men all these years you deserve fun and a whole lot more. Like sainthood, a footnote in the history books for still being sane."

Ryan sat on one side of the porch, Conrad on the other, dead silence between them. Ryan eyed the doorway, wishing Thelma to appear. What in the world could she be doing? How long did it take to put on a dress and—
"Holy cow! Thelma?" Ryan said as she came into the doorway making him sit up straight.

Thelma blushed as she stepped onto the porch, looking . . . hot? And not from the heat! Conrad seemed as dumbstruck as Ryan felt. Probably the first thing they'd ever had in common.

Conrad stood, his gaze not leaving Thelma. "You look wonderful."

She smiled, her whole face lighting up. "Why, thank you, Conrad. So nice of you to notice."

Conrad took Thelma's hand, reluctantly at first, then as if he meant it. They started down the front steps. Effie snatched the picnic basket and ran after them. She handed it to Conrad, who was still not looking himself at all.

"What do you think of Thelma?" Effie asked as she drew up next to Ryan and they watched the couple drive off in the low rumble of an expensive motor followed by a sudden streak of red.

"Were those surveyor flags I saw in her hair and tied around her middle as a belt?"

"Added color to the black-and-white scheme, a shabby chic look. I have to get my things out of Thelma's room. I left it a mess. I'll be back in a minute. She said I could borrow her copy of *Huck Finn* to read while I'm here, get me in a Mississippi River kind of mood. And don't go away. We need to talk."

Talk? When a woman said let's talk it was never to the man's advantage. "You're going back to San Diego; that's all there is to it."

She peered at him, a defiant tilt to her chin. That was never good for a guy either. "They need the preliminary ideas for the mall in ten days, and I don't want you to have all the credit. And you have the same feeling about me, especially when we're so close to finalizing our ideas. So we're stuck here together."

She turned away, and he caught a glimpse of that little gold ring at her navel. His muscles went as rigid as the posts holding up the front porch. Damn!

Rory came out of the door as Effie went in, and he said, "Give him hell, girl."

She laughed and flashed him a big smile. Ryan sighed.

He wasn't sure if it came from the hopeless arguing, or Effie again not giving him that smile. "Thanks for the support, Dad."

Rory slapped his son on the back. "If you had an ounce of sense, you'd know when to let a pretty girl have her way and just sit back and enjoy the ride." He glanced around. "Where the hell's Thelma? Thought I heard her voice out here. I need her to watch Bonnie while I go pick up an engine part at a dock in Fulton. Hastings Dry-dock used to carry anything I needed, but Conrad's let the place go to ruin. What a dumbass."

Ryan put his hand on his dad's shoulder. "You're going to love this. Thelma's on a date with Mr. Dumbass. Just left."

Rory stared at Ryan as if he'd sprouted another head. "Why the hell would she go and do a damn-fool thing like that? She doesn't even like that man. Nobody around here likes that man. What's to like?"

"He caught her at a weak moment. She had an attack of severe cabin fever and needed a change of scenery."

"And you just up and let her go?"

Ryan hitched his hip onto the porch railing. "Have you ever tried telling Thelma or any other woman what to do? But don't worry about Bonnie. Effie and I can watch her. I'm sure Effie knows about babies." He gazed at the doorway. "Hell, she knows everything else, just ask her."

Rory thrust the baby monitor at Ryan and trotted down the steps. "Bonnie's asleep right now. That gizmo in your hand will let you know if she wakes." He turned back. "But whatever you do, don't get it too close to your ear. Bonnie's crying can wake the dead. Emergency numbers are by the phone if you need anything. I'll be back in a few hours."

He rounded the house, and in less than a minute his Suburban pulled out of the driveway. Effie came back on the porch and pointed to the retreating car. "Is that Rory?"

"Needs to pick up a part for one of the tows. I told him we'd watch Bonnie."

Effie stood in front of him, eyes big. "We? Who's this we you're talking about?"

"You're a woman; you know babies, right?"

"All I know about babies is I was one. I'm an only child. My father's an accountant, my mother an attorney. We do professions at our house, not "Sesame Street." I don't actually remember even being a kid so much as a smaller adult who really liked Gummi Worms. Anyone under eighteen is a mystery to me. That was a long, nervous answer to your question. I do not know babies at all."

Ryan stood. "Somewhere in your life you didn't babysit? Don't all girls do that? Isn't it a rite of passage or something?"

"Like before we're awarded boobs?" Effie slapped her palm to her forehead. "What are we going to do? We're architects; we don't know about babies."

"First of all we need to stop yelling. The sound carries right up the stairway, and we sure as hell don't want to—" The monitor in his hand suddenly let out an ear-piercing sound, and Ryan dropped it as if it had bitten him. He exchanged looks with Effie. "Fuck."

Another yell split the late afternoon quiet, and they both took a quick step back. Ryan swallowed. "Look, we can do this. We build shopping malls that cover acres and acres, worth millions and millions. We can take care of one baby the size of a computer keyboard. Right?"

"No!"

Another cry emitted from the monitor, and Ryan grabbed her hand. "We'll have to try."

"I'm going to get you for this, Ryan O'Fallon," Effie

said as she ran behind him up the stairs. "This was not in my job description."

"Neither is wearing short-shorts and belly rings." It just kind of slipped out. Maybe she didn't hear. Maybe it was lost in the baby howling that was getting louder as they got closer to Bonnie's room.

He opened the door and peered into the crib. Bonnie belted out another cry, Ryan's jaw clenched and Effie said, "Pick her up, she's your sister. Do something."

"You're the woman. You're the one who gives birth to these things. What if I break her?"

Effie reached in and lifted Bonnie, one hand on each side, holding her out at arm's length as the baby flung back her head and yowled again. "I don't think she likes me," Effie managed over the uproar.

Effie looked frazzled, more frazzled than he'd ever seen her before. Usually Effie Wilson was . . . perfect. Perfect hair, suit, makeup. Even when they canvassed a sight with trucks and mud and earthmovers, Effie was perfect. But now . . . "Hold her close to you like you see in pictures."

"You want me to take advice from Hallmark cards?" But she did it anyway as Bonnie let out another cry. Effie walked around the room, bouncing Bonnie and making *shh* sounds. It wasn't working.

He came up beside Effie. Damn, she smelled good. And then things suddenly didn't smell good at all. "Check her diaper."

Effie looked as if she'd swallowed a lemon whole. "You check her diaper."

"We'll flip for it." He reached in his pocket and pulled out a quarter. "Heads," he called as he sent it into the air, catching it, holding it out in his palm.

Effie stuck her tongue out at him. "Bet it's a trick quarter." She laid Bonnie back in the crib, squinted her eyes and undid the diaper as if dismantling a bomb. "Ohmygod!"

"How can such a cute baby make such a mess?" Ryan asked as he pulled ten wipe things from a plastic container and handed them to Effie. He hunted up a clean diaper, and Effie dropped the dirty stuff into a plastic bag he held open. "I'll take this outside. Bet the raccoons won't get into the garbage tonight. Holy shit."

"I don't know about the holy part, but the other's true enough. On your way back get a bottle from the fridge. Warm it in the microwave. Don't make it too hot."

"See, told you that you knew about this baby stuff."

She glared. "Don't push your luck, O'Fallon!"

"Right." He ditched the diaper and got the bottle and hurried back to the room where Bonnie cried louder than ever. Effie tried feeding her, but she scrunched up her face and bellowed all the more.

"What should we do? Nothing's working. Do you think she's sick?"

"Dad warned me this could happen. I just didn't know what this was. I should have asked more questions. We can take her for a ride in the car. That makes babies sleep . . . at least in the movies."

Effie looked around. "No car seat. Probably in Rory's Suburban." She started toward the door. "The stroller. It's sort of like a car, a mini convertible. We'll make motor sounds and throw in swear words and creative hand gestures. It's the best we can do."

Ryan ran ahead of Effie and opened the front door. She gently laid Bonnie in the stroller, secured the strap, and together they lifted the stroller off the porch to the driveway. Ryan pushed, and Effie made unconvincing engine noises, but the yelling decreased. Effie grabbed his arm. "It's working. It's working."

"Make sounds. Don't talk." He pushed the stroller to

the end of the drive and headed for the dock, toward the low rumble of a passing barge. Not a car engine exactly, but close, and a hell of a lot better than Effie's feeble attempt. She gave him a thumbs-up sign and smiled.

Holy moly, it was that same smile she'd flashed Rory on the porch, the one Ryan wanted for himself. And now it was his turn. He was the recipient of it. His heartbeat kicked up a notch, and he smiled back. She paused for a second, her green eyes darkening, not enough that anyone would notice, but he sure did.

She put up the hood to protect Bonnie from the evening sun, and they walked down the deserted road. Their footfalls mixed with the hum of insects as they turned the bend facing the sun perched on the Arkansas levee. The river glittered as if someone had scattered a million diamonds across the surface.

His insides stirred. He felt closer to the earth than he had in a long time. The Mississippi like this—big, bold, beautiful—always had that effect on him. Bonnie quieted, and he stopped under a tupelo as the tow lumbered on, kicking up rollers of muddy river water and gradually leaving the Landing in peace. The earth paused, hanging in the balance between day and dusk. Peace.

Ryan set the brake on the stroller, and Effie whispered in his ear and pointed to Bonnie. "She's Rory's daughter all right. The river sounds put her right to sleep."

"G-good," he managed. Not because that surprised him, but the sensation of Effie's warm breath against his ear and neck and cheek instantly jolted his blood pressure into high gear. Did the earth just move? How could she have such an immediate effect on him?

Then he looked at the woman—vibrant, smart, sassy, totally sexy and delicious—and had his answer. Damn, he wanted to kiss her. He wanted to touch her face and feel her soft full lips against his fingertips. He wanted to have her body close to his. His gaze held hers as she seemed to lean toward him. Her eyes were now jade, their mutual attraction more intense than he ever imagined possible.

Slowly he slid his arm around her slender waist, his hand gliding over her smooth, damp skin where the blouse ended and the shorts began. Her eyes widened, then glazed, and the intimate contact made him hotter than the setting sun. Her mouth parted slightly on a silent gasp, her cheeks flushed to the color of the sunset. She smiled, looking at him in a way she never had before. Their nearness overwhelmed him, her reaction to him intoxicating.

"You're not the same man on the Landing as you are in San Diego."

"Neither are you."

The smile deepened, and her eyes shimmered like the river. She turned toward him, front to front, and she wrapped her bare arms around his neck, the heat from her skin seeping into him. "I'm not a man."

Hunger spiraled through him, settling in his gut. Desire settled lower, making him hard as stone. Some protective instinct kept his one hand on the stroller, but his other tightened around Effie, bringing their bodies tight. Her breasts swelled against his chest; her belly softened and nestled against his erection. She felt good, really good, better than any woman ever had before.

"Ah, sugar," he breathed on a sigh, the tone more Tennessee than California. Then he lowered his head and kissed her sweet mouth as her body slowly melted into his. It was if he'd waited his whole life to do this, to find Effie, to be here now with her, kissing him in this very place at this very moment.

Okay, Effie thought, kissing Ryan was not one of her better ideas. In fact, it was just plain stupid . . . great, but still stupid. Sure she'd wanted to kiss him since she laid eyes on the man, but where did they go from here?

His kiss deepened, her insides flipped and she suddenly didn't care what happened next. So handsome, so male, so energized. A sensual growl crawled up her throat. No woman in her right mind could say no to kissing Ryan O'Fallon in this dazzling sunset on the banks of a gorgeous river.

His lips felt seductive as silk sheets, chilled champagne and golden moonlight. His arm around her back felt protective, possessive but not demanding or overpowering as other men's with their cavemen approach.

She drew closer still, surprised by his big, hard erection pressing intimately against her middle. That she had this effect on him set her on fire. Of course the big, hard aspect of his anatomy against her had a lot to do with her reaction as well.

For a year and a half she'd thought about kissing Ryan, and here he was better than she'd ever imagined, and she'd imagined plenty.

His tongue touched hers for the briefest second, sending shivers across her shoulders in spite of the summer heat, leaving her weak and dizzy from the connection. She splayed her fingers across his strong neck, his hot, slick flesh drawing her in as his kisses deepened. His male scent, a mix of earth, sun and water, filled her head and drove away every thought other than Ryan.

She broke the kiss and looked into his wonderful ocean blue eyes, feeling completely lost in them . . . Then she suddenly didn't feel lost at all. This was where she wanted to be. "You are some kisser."

His hand slid below the waist band of her shorts, cupping her right cheek. He gave her a devilish smile and slight squeeze that said he wasn't about to let her go. "I think I need practice."

"Practice is good."

He brushed his lips seductively over hers. Her insides

fired, and passion flowed hot and wild through her veins as never before.

His mouth formed the words against hers. "And you're the perfect partner."

His fingers massaged her buttocks, and he took another kiss, his tongue tangling with hers, then mating with gentle thrusts. A warm ache lodged deep in her middle as she pressed into his erection, the juncture of her legs parting, moistening with anticipation.

"Ah, Effie, you taste of pecan pie and summer magic."

"You taste of hot, sweaty sex, and I want you so bad I could spit." Her eyes widened, and she stared straight into his. The whole world seemed to stand still.

"Ohmygod." She took a step away. Breathing hard, she slipped out of his embrace, and his hand reluctantly let her go. He looked as startled as she felt. "I . . . I can't believe I said that."

She exhaled a deep breath and held up her hands as if stopping something that needed stopping right now. "You caught me off guard. I wasn't ready for . . . this. Not that I didn't want to kiss you, I have for a long time and—"

Chapter 5

"You have?" Ryan's eyes widened.

She was not making things better. They were getting in deeper . . . and oh, how she wanted him deeper.

Good Lord, what was she thinking! Effie Wilson, architect bimbo. "I didn't know kissing you would be . . . so terrific. If we go beyond kissing, then what?"

He ran his hand over his hair, mussing it even more, as if they'd done exactly what she suggested. She wanted so much more than a suggestion.

He said, "That is the question, isn't it? I suck at relationships, Effie. You know that."

"Mine aren't any better. If we get involved, then get uninvolved, how will we ever work together? Look what happened between the mail boy and the VP on the sixth floor."

"Heard she didn't get her mail for six months."

"And we're on the same floor, the same projects. It would be a mess." She took another step away and pushed strands of hair from her face.

Ryan's breathing was as unsteady as hers as he said, "This is all my fault. I shouldn't have started something we couldn't finish."

"We were caught up in the moment; that's all there is to it. A sleeping baby, the setting sun, me in shorts, you with messy hair and San Diego a million miles away. None of this is who we are, least not usually. It's all work between us and trying to outdo each other, and we reacted because of . . ." Oh, dear God, why did they suddenly react this way after being together for all those months?

"Jet lag?"

"Yes!" She grabbed on to the word like a lifeline. "That's it, jet lag. You're absolutely right. It does strange things to people. Screws with their thinking patterns." Right now she didn't have thinking patterns because her brain was Swiss cheese. "We're different here. I don't know why, but we are. But soon we'll be back to work, back to real work."

"And we won't even remember this . . ."

"Jet lag," Effie supplied, knowing she was rambling but not knowing how to stop.

Ryan put both hands on the stroller. Much safer than putting them on her, but not nearly as much fun, Effie thought. And kissing Ryan was fun, electrifying, erotic. Could a kiss be all that? She considered his hand on her ass and his tongue seducing her mouth. Oh, yeah!

He engaged the wheels. "We should get Bonnie into her bed, and we need to . . ."

Their eyes locked for a moment, and Effie blushed. The result of we and bed mentioned together in the same sentence. "Work," she supplied.

"Work is good." He pushed the stroller up the hill.

"Maybe I should go back to San Diego just like you suggested." She touched his arm to stop him so they could talk, except touching him was a really stupid thing to do in the middle of a sexual meltdown. She yanked her hand back as he gave her several quick nods. "Good idea. San Diego."

"Tomorrow."

"Yes, tomorrow. Tonight we'll work on the plans and get as much done as we can." And they'd have something else on their minds besides each other.

She followed him up the path, her eyes zeroing in on his fine butt, perspiration slithering between her boobs. As long as Ryan O'Fallon was around he'd always be on her mind. The trouble was she wanted him between her legs and working on a shopping mall was a damn poor substitute.

The aroma of fresh morning coffee led Effie down the steps, and she sniffed her way to the kitchen done in sunny yellow and crisp white with accents of cornflower blue. Thelma hummed as she fed Bonnie a bottle. "Mornin'," she greeted Effie.

Effie waved, poured a cup of coffee, drank long and deep, letting the caffeine work its magic. She commanded herself to be coherent and smiled at Thelma.

The housekeeper grinned in return. "Not a morning person?"

"Ryan and I worked last night 'til Rory got home, but I couldn't sleep. New surroundings and all." Not to mention thinking about a certain kiss on the dock that never should have happened, but did, and not likely to be forgotten any time soon.

She sat at the table across from Thelma. "I love this kitchen. It's so bright and cheery."

"Painted it myself. Even mixed the colors and did the stenciling. You're all spruced up. Nice black pants. I need a pair like that. You heading off somewhere?"

"San Diego. There's too much"—temptation here, she thought, but instead said "—work to do at the office."

Thelma frowned. "Well, heck. I'll miss you, Effie Wilson. Thanks for the makeover for Conrad. I really appreciate it. Don't remember ever feeling so good in clothes and it didn't cost me an arm and a leg."

"How was the old boy? Did you have to deck him?"

Thelma looked at Bonnie, but there was a faraway expression on Thelma's face and a soft smile on her lips. Decking did not take place last night, but something did. Effie paused her coffee cup midair. She knew that look. It wasn't a you're-a-jerk look. It was an oh-my-goodness look.

"The date was okay."

"Okay's a lot better than I thought it would be." She waited for Thelma's reaction.

"Me, too. You know, I just went with him because I needed a night out and I'm a pushover for good cheese, wine and a nice car. But we actually sang old rock-and-roll tunes and drove along the river with the top down, and the stars were out and the moon and . . ."

She laughed. "We crooned with the Beach Boys. Do you believe it. Haven't done anything like that . . . ever. We both love the Beach Boys. Conrad says that outfit I wore last night made me his California girl." She blushed. "Thanks to you. I know he's so full of hot air and it's all so corny, but it was fun." She looked at Effie. "I really did have fun, incredible as that sounds. Conrad and me . . . together."

The phone rang, and Thelma put the bottle on the table and snagged the receiver from the counter. Her whole face suddenly lit up like a sunset over the Pacific.

Conrad! Effie knew it like she knew her own name. A man could do that to a woman. But this man? This was the wrong man for Thelma. Guilt ate at Effie. She'd been the one to encourage Thelma to go on this date and now look what happened. Thelma was . . . smitten!

Thelma laughed again at whatever was said on the

phone, and she handed Bonnie off to Effie as if her mind were somewhere else besides in the kitchen. Thelma headed for the hallway; actually she kind of floated into the hallway, her feet not touching the ground.

"That man is no good," Effie said to Bonnie. Her little pink face scrunched up into bellow mode, not interested one bit in Thelma's love life and far more concerned about the missing bottle. Yikes! Effie snagged the bottle and offered it to Bonnie. "I've got a killer headache, little girl. Don't cry! I'm operating on no sleep. Here. Eat. Yummy, yummy in the tummy. Good stuff."

Effie considered the white goo in the bottle. "Actually, this stuff looks gross. Can you say Godiva?"

"You're talking to a baby about chocolate?" Ryan asked from behind her in the doorway.

"It's never too early to talk chocolate."

He came in, poured coffee and leaned against the stove. He wore a navy T-shirt, jeans and gym shoes. "You look like hell. Didn't you sleep? You need breakfast."

He looked terrific, and she wanted him for breakfast. "You don't look any better," she lied. What was she supposed to say? Take off your clothes?

"I think it's the heat."

"Definitely the heat." Because she was damn near on fire. The T-shirt showed off more muscles than she ever expected he had. And the jeans. Holy mother-of-pearl! They were soft and worn and molded perfectly to a very nice parcel in front. She'd felt that parcel and wanted to feel it again, this time up close and very personal.

He took a long drink of coffee. "We aren't used to it."

"I'm sure not." Except they suddenly weren't talking about the same thing. She looked into his eyes—dark, mysterious, captivating, hungry and it had nothing to do with breakfast.

Yikes! Maybe they were. Now what? Now she'd take the chicken way out and change the subject. She held up the bottle. "Aren't you impressed, I can feed a baby?"

"You're a fast learner."

"Fear of going deaf can do that to a person." How was she supposed to carry on a conversation with Ryan when all she wanted to do was jump his bones right here in his own kitchen? "I have plane reservations. I leave at noon."

"Take the car. I'll borrow one of the company trucks from Dad. Where's Thelma?"

Effie nodded at the hallway. "Conrad called." Finally a safe topic.

"Isn't it kind of early?"

"They drove with the top down and sang Beach Boy songs. She's his little surfer girl."

Ryan nearly dropped his cup, coffee sloshing onto the floor. "Conrad! What the hell?"

"Something's going on." See, she could do this. She could think intelligently and carry on a conversation without getting all hot and bothered over Ryan. She just had to concentrate real hard on the conversation.

Ryan snagged a paper towel and wiped the coffee drops from the floor. "Maybe he really does like Thelma. There's no other reason for him to date her. Not like there's some ulterior motive. Thelma's just Thelma."

He shrugged as he threw the towel in the trash. "I guess he really has changed."

"When towboats fly." Bonnie finished the bottle, and Effie set her up. Now she had to burp the baby. That's what Thelma did.

"I know his kind," Effie continued as she gently patted Bonnie on the back. "Smooth operator, sophisticated, someone who's ignored you all your natural life. And suddenly, out of the blue, he starts hitting on you big time, giving you the big rush. You're mesmerized and happy and life is great, 'til you realize he's after information you have, like the bid your company made on a project so his company could underbid the company you work for."

When Ryan didn't reply, she looked at him.

His eyes studied her. "This happened?"

"Sorry. I got carried away, but yeah, it did happen. Parker Dearborn of Dearborn Designs. But that's ancient history."

"How ancient?"

"Last year. I don't want it to happen to Thelma. Getting used is no fun."

Ryan's voice lowered to a growl. "That no good son-of-a-bitch."

"Well, we don't know for absolutely sure if that's Conrad's agenda or not but—"

"I mean Dearborn."

"When most of our conversations dealt with construction costs instead of romance I finally realized what he was up to and fed him false information." She grinned. "We got the bid."

Bonnie suddenly burped, sending a spray of formula over Effie's black slacks. She stared wide-eyed at the white-on-black mess. "And I was doing so great. What went wrong?"

Ryan picked up a cloth from the table and held it up. He looked forlorn. "I think this is a burp towel?"

Effie kissed Bonnie on the head. "You should come with an instruction book, little peach."

"Or a warning label." Ryan took Bonnie and put her in her pumpkin seat that was on the table and strapped her in. Effie went to the sink and wet a towel. He took it from her. "Here, let me help, I can see it straight on." He hunkered down and brushed at one thigh, then the other. "I think I'm making it worse."

And he had no idea how much worse. His hand on her

legs, stroking, pressing—even with a towel and no intention other than cleaning up baby barf—was a complete turn-on. She wanted wild feral sex with Ryan O'Fallon right here and now. No more excuses. Just sex! "I better change," she blurted. "There's no fixing this." Other than a roll in the sheets, or anyplace else that was handy.

She headed for the hallway, saying as she went, "It takes a while to get to the airport and check in. They always pull me aside for one of those scans and I want to make sure I don't have a hole in my hose because I always have to take off my shoes and I'll see you in San Diego and I had a great time and watch Bonnie."

She glanced back, and for a moment the air between them seemed to sizzle in spite of her babbling. Ryan was so hot, and she was so horny. She was so out of here.

The next time she saw Ryan O'Fallon she wouldn't be a sex-crazed lunatic. They'd be in California, she'd be in a suit, he wouldn't be in jeans and they'd be back where they belonged, working, running around to get things done, taking great pleasure in one-upping each other with no time to think of each other in the sack.

He'd be his usual shallow, overabsorbed, bimbo-chasing self, and she'd be the urban professional searching for Mr. Right, with the right family and on the right corporate track, who would appeal to her parents, and all would be back to normal . . . right?

Ryan stood under the tall oaks and watched the white rental drive off down the road. Max pawed Ryan's leg for a pat, and he obliged, scratching behind the ears. Effie was gone. Amen to that. No more long blond hair and honey-smooth skin, big green eyes and sexy little ass to drive him nuts. He was here, she was there and that gave him time to forget the Effie he knew at the Landing. All he'd remember was uptight San Diego Effie.

Rory came up from the docks and asked, "Why are you standing here like a cement statue staring off down the road? Expecting someone? Going to head off Conrad and tell him to keep his mitts off our Thelma?"

"Effie's gone."

Rory raked his hand through his hair. "Why? How the hell did that happen? You two have a fight or something? And you just stood here and let her leave?"

"We have work to do, and she'll be more useful back in San Diego. She can field problems for a new project we're working on, and we can fax information back and forth."

"Christ in a sidecar, boy! I'm not talking about work. That woman's the best damn thing to come into your life. I can tell that by just looking at you, and you two finally realized it when you got here. Least that's my take on it."

He raked his graying hair and kicked a rock across the drive. "Hells bells. Love is damn well wasted on the young if you ask me. You got your girl right smack in front of you and you don't appreciate her diddly, and mine's off God knows where and in trouble and I'd give my eyeteeth to find her."

"Effie and I are not in love."

"Well, you should be."

"If there was anything of substance between us, why wouldn't it have happened in San Diego? Why would we have to wait 'til we got here to figure it out?"

"Because when you're in California all you do is work. The damn sun's done baked your brain to a brick." Rory walked toward the house. "Christ in a sidecar, I have a dipshit for a son."

"Dad!"

Rory turned and growled, "What?"

Ryan had to get his mind off Effie, and with his dad in this state all he'd hear would be Effie, Effie, Effie. Though that was better than dipshit son. "If you need a tow taken somewhere, I can do a run. It'll keep my captain's license up to speed."

Rory jammed his hands in his jean pockets. "Didn't know you cared a rat's patootie about that."

He didn't really, but it was a good excuse to get off the Landing and get his mind on something else besides Effie and that kiss and everything else about her that drove him nuts . . . which happened to be everything! Damn!

Rory stroked his chin. "*Annabelle Lee*'s run aground down by Rosedale on one of the damn sandbars. I was going to send the *Mississippi Miss* to help get them off. Just a short run and the *Annabelle*'s got a crew to help out so you can run alone. It'll give you some hours in the wheelhouse, and the *Annabelle* could use the help."

Ryan nodded and walked beside Rory. "I'll grab some food since there's no galley on that old lunch bucket and be on my way."

"Better mind the charts. There are some new markers, and Rosedale's getting mighty bony with the water dropping faster this year and sandbars popping up like warts on a frog."

Ryan headed for the kitchen. Running a tow was just what he needed to help clear his head. Being on the water didn't leave time to think about much besides the job. A five hundred horsepower diesel moving sixty feet of steel through the water demanded concentration. When he got back he'd be ready for work on the mall and to help his dad find Mimi, or whatever her name was.

He sweet-talked Thelma out of cold fried chicken, corn bread, cookies and lemonade, then scrounged around in the closet and located his boat shoes, work gloves and parka in case the weather went south. He headed for the docks, passing the spot where he'd kissed Effie and she'd kissed him back. He slowed for a second, his insides heaving a deep sigh of appreciation.

Damn good kiss. Good enough to put up a marker commemorating the moment. A plane soared overhead, and he imagined Effie on it . . . not that she was, because her plane didn't leave for another two hours . . . but she was headed back to San Diego all the same, just where she should be.

He helped fuel *Mississippi Miss* and climbed the two flights of steep grated metal stairs to the wheelhouse on top. He gazed around at the rolling river below, sandy shoreline, levee and blue sky that stretched over the earth. He fired the engine, triggering a deep rumble from the big diesel humming through the tow, vibrating into his feet clear into his bones, making him one with the boat.

The whole world looked different in a wheelhouse. Up here the captain was in charge; what he or she said happened. Hell of a lot different from the real world. Since yesterday and that kiss he'd had zip control over his life. Couldn't eat, couldn't sleep. All he could think about was Effie in his arms and wanting her in his bed.

But she was gone, his problems over . . . 'til he looked up and saw Effie Wilson running down the road in a soft white blouse, khaki shorts, gym shoes, golden hair flying. Waving a red parka she yelled, "Wait up!" Least that's what he thought she yelled because the diesel drowned out the words.

Holy crap! What now? She was supposed to be out of here, out of his life, least for a few weeks. She missed the plane? Forgot her luggage? That couldn't be it because he'd put her suitcase in the trunk himself. Maybe something happened to the mall project.

He leaned out the window as one of the dockhands helped Effie on board. Her eyes widened as she looked at the two sets of stairs. Maybe she'd reconsider, go back wherever she came from, giving them the space they needed. Except Effie Wilson was used to climbing around on girders and examining building infrastructures just like he did.

She grabbed the railings and started up. The deckhand gave Ryan a you-dog-you look and a two-thumbs-up sign. This wasn't a two-thumbs-up event. This was a disastrous event. He and Effie alone in the middle of the river! How could he keep his hands off her?

Whatever her reason for being here, they'd fix it; then he'd send her packing off to California tomorrow if he had to put her on that damn plane and strap her into the damn seat himself.

The deep growl of the engines echoed in Effie's ears and pulsated through her body like a mini earthquake as she studied the stairs. She tied the parka around her waist to use both hands and climb to the first landing. She looked down through the grating to the deck swaying below. She gripped tighter. It moved!

She wasn't afraid of heights. She climbed roofs and opensided buildings . . . except they stayed in one place and weren't over the water. She sucked in a deep breath and ran up the next set of stairs, yanked open the door to the wheelhouse and jumped inside, closing the door behind her. She forced the water issue from her brain and gave Ryan a big toothy grin. "Hi there. Long time no see."

Ryan's brow furrowed, his forehead wrinkling. "What the hell are you doing here?"

Not the greeting she'd hoped for. Getting swept into his arms would have been great because that's the real reason she was here and not on the plane back to San Diego. She hadn't even made it to the airport.

For eighteen long, tedious, frustrating months she'd had

the hots for this guy, and yesterday she'd realized he felt the same way, at least somewhat. Getting on a plane for San Diego without doing one darn thing about it—except for a heated kiss—was not the next step.

Well, it probably was the next logical step, but a horny woman was void of logic. And she was so void of logic she could barely function.

Ryan, however, didn't seem to share her intention. He just seemed pissed and grumpy. Didn't guys always think about sex? Maybe she could convince him, but for the moment she'd have to go with the other reason she'd come back. "I'm here because of Thelma."

"What about her?"

"I couldn't leave here knowing Conrad was up to no good." Effie spread her hands wide. "I don't trust the man as far as I can throw him. So, we—like in you and me—need a plan to figure him out. I don't want Thelma in a Dearborn or Emmerson situation."

His brow furrowed a little deeper. "Emmerson?"

"A guy who wanted to make partner in my dad's accounting firm and decided the fastest way was through me. I know an opportunist when I see one."

"You've dated some real assholes." He picked up a baseball cap and put it on backward looking casual, but his stance suggesting a man very much in charge. "What happened to me staying here on the Landing and you going?"

"Thelma helped raise you. You owe her. We can't let Conrad get away with whatever he's got planned. When it all falls apart Thelma could go loopy like I did. She's older than I was but not wiser at all."

"Meaning?"

"I put on twenty pounds. I don't want Thelma to have to deal with losing twenty pounds of ugly fat. I'd rather help her lose about a hundred and seventy pounds of it right now and ditch Conrad. We just have to figure out how to get her to do it. Any suggestions?"

He sighed. "Why couldn't you just get on that damn plane?"

"Haven't you been listening? Thelma!"

"I don't have time to argue. I have work to do. The *Annabelle Lee* needs help getting barges off a sandbar." He pointed to a tall chair that offered a great view out the windows on all sides. "Sit there."

Yes, she was in! Off to a good start.

He thrust a long book open to a map of some kind at her. "Charts." He pointed to a spot. "We're here. Keep an eye out for sandbars as we go; not all are marked. We've got radar and depth sounders, but there's nothing like your eyes on the road. We have about a five-hour run down to Rosedale."

He looked at her. "Did you ever consider that Conrad has changed? That you're in a panic and missed your plane for no reason?"

She took in Ryan's good looks and great build. This was the really good reason!

"Conrad Hastings is way too slick, too cool with his songs of the Beach Boys. He's into the Blues, told me so himself. Surfer Girl? Give me a break. He's a lying, no-good blob of pond scum."

"But there's no motive for him being pond scum with Thelma. She's just who she is."

"That's what we have to think about." Among other things. Though obviously she was the only one with other things on her mind. "Did you bring food? I'm starved."

He ran his hand over his face. "I got a feeling this is going to be the trip from hell."

Her spine stiffened. "Excuse me. I'm trying to do the

right thing here. A little cooperation and some suggestions would be appreciated."

A horn blasted loud over their heads, and she jumped from the chair, dumping the book to the floor, and grabbed Ryan's arm. "Are we going to drown? Did we hit something? Do we have lifeboats? Where are the personal flotation devices? Should we abandon ship? Women and children first? That's me. Should I jump for it? Do you need help?" She gripped tighter and clenched her teeth.

Ryan gave her a long, steady look. "We haven't left the dock. One long blast from the horn is the signal for leaving port so everyone knows to stand clear. Ever been on a large boat before?"

"Once and it wasn't pretty. Wilsons are land people, members of the if God wanted man, or woman, in the water we'd have gills club." She gave him another toothy grin. "I like planes."

"Then why the hell aren't you on one? And what are you doing on this boat if you hate water?"

Trying to get laid!

Chapter 6

Not only does a horny woman have no logic, she has no shame, Effie thought to herself as she gazed at Ryan. One by one he peeled her fingers from his arm; then his strong hands snagged her around the waist.

This was more like it. She could forget about water and concentrate on Ryan. Instead of thinking about charts she'd think about being in his arms, in his pants, him in her pants. This was her one chance to have him. Once they got back to San Diego it was all over. She looked into his eyes, searching for signs of passion or romance or something. He lifted her back onto the chair. "Don't move."

"All right," she purred.

"We have lower temperatures today, and the river isn't a sauna like it usually is in July. Try and relax. You jumping around the wheelhouse or anyplace on this tow isn't what we need, especially when we get near the *Annabelle Lee* and the grounded barges. Things could get a little hairy, a lot of bumping boats together and shoving. You can't be in the way."

In the way! Barges? What happened to a little romance? Sex! She narrowed her eyes in pure frustration. "You're awfully damn irritable."

"You shouldn't be out here. This isn't a pleasure boat. But if I threw you off, Dad would go ballistic, and getting called a dipshit son once today was enough."

Effie bit her lip to keep from laughing.

"Glad you think it's funny."

"My parents never called me dipshit, but proletarian and blue collar crept into a conversation or two when I talked about being a park ranger."

"Park ranger? You?"

"It was one of those fleeting ideas kids get." He hadn't tossed her overboard; that was a good start. They'd be together all day, and that was a good middle. It gave her plenty of time to come up with a plan that could make a great ending.

She watched him at the controls. "Where's the wheel? The guy on the dock said this was the wheelhouse."

The big—actually it was huge—boat pulled away from the dock and out into the muddy water. She gripped the sides of the chair, her heart pounding, her eyes blurring, and this time it had nothing to do with Ryan.

"Wheels went out with Mark Twain." He nodded to the console. "This chrome handle in the middle controls the engines. These handles on either side are called sticks and work the rudders, left side and right side."

"What's that black button for?"

"Starts the engines. Screens are for the radar that shows other boats and for depth readings. If they start making squealing noises, something's too close or too shallow or too something, and we have a problem."

"Problems? Oh, God!"

"You can talk to Him later. Since you got yourself on this tow you'll have to pull your own weight and work like everyone else around here."

"There isn't anyone else around here."

"That's the point. Go down on the deck and see if you can calculate how much line we have coiled on the bow. We need it for pulling the barges off."

"Down there?" She pointed outside and swallowed. "I'm watching for sandbars up here. Very important job, remember?"

"Do both. It's just you and me, and stuff needs to be done."

"What would you do if I wasn't here?"

"Well, you are, so get busy." He reached to the floor and retrieved an orange work vest. "Put this on so I can see you if you fall overboard. It has flotation so you won't drown, least not right away."

Did her eyes just bulge out of her head?

He took his hat off and slapped it on her head. "Keeps the sun out of your eyes. If you fall in the water, throw the hat back onboard; it's my favorite."

She folded her arms and looked defiant. "What if I don't want to do any of this stuff?"

He let out a long sigh. "You're right. It's asking a lot of a woman. I'll drop you off in Memphis. You can get your nails done and have a pedicure and get back on the plane to San Diego."

She slammed the chart book against his chest.

"Ouch." He grabbed it with his free hand.

She slid from the chair. "Look, Buster, I crawl over roofs and girders and through pipes and ductwork and over muddy fields and everyplace else architects go, and I never play the I'm-the-little-woman card. I can do this, too, even if you are behaving like a dictator."

She jammed her arms into the vest. She didn't know what pissed her off more, his attitude about her not being up to the challenge, the manicure crack—she could really use a manicure—or going back to San Diego without winding up in the sack with him. Though he was such a prick right now the sack part had lost some appeal, not all, of course, because he still looked damn good.

He handed her a walkie-talkie. "Green button is on."

"Drop dead, O'Fallon."

He gave her a smarmy smile. "Then who would steer the boat?"

"I'd figure it out. And I could use your corpse as fish bait and maybe catch something to eat. That looks like the only way I'm going to get fed around here. I'm starved."

He snagged a bag from the console. "Food. Work first, eat later."

She took the bag and stomped out of the wheelhouse and slammed the door closed behind her, rattling the windows.

"Zip up your jacket, Wilson," barked the walkie-talkie in her hand, making her jump. As if she wasn't jumpy enough. It was like that blasted baby monitor. She spun around and glared at Captain Bligh through the window. She considered mutiny but instead gave him the third-finger salute and turned for the stairs.

She stuffed the walkie-talkie in a mesh pocket on the vest, the food down the middle vee. She grabbed the railing and backed her way down, taking one step at a time, her stomach rolling with the sway of the tow. She felt sick, her head throbbed and she was dizzy. But she'd deal. If she didn't, Ryan would needle her for the rest of her natural life. Well, screw Ryan O'Fallon and the horse he rode in on. She bit back a laugh. Isn't that what had gotten her into this mess . . . minus the horse.

She reached the deck and let her body feel the rhythm of the boat, getting her balance and losing some of the dizziness. This was all right. She could handle it. She put the bag by the stairs and shuffled her way to the coil of rope that was as thick as her arm. She considered the number of coils, the size of the reel, did some math and hit the green button.

"Yo, Bligh. You have about a hundred and ten or so feet of rope down here. Make a hell of a noose. Want me to show you? I could bring it up to the wheelhouse and demonstrate."

"It's called line," the walkie-talkie garbled back. "Now do the same with the cable on the stern—that's the back of the tug—and then if you're not too afraid, sweep off all the decks so the deckhands don't slip on loose gravel or whatever if they have to come aboard when we move the barges around. And then find all the work vests down there. The coast guard will want to check them out when they come aboard. And watch for leaks on the port and starboard side. The *Miss* is a really old tug. Think you can handle all that?"

Leaks! Her hair stood straight up on end, she was sure of it. What kind of boat was this? Not that she could do anything about it in the middle of the river. She'd gotten herself into this, and now she'd have to deal with it.

The sun sank toward the horizon as Ryan steered the tow, pushing the last barge into the twelve-barge tier that formed a cut of three across and four down. The *Annabelle Lee* was good to go. The crew quickly lashed the barge to the others, Effie watching, standing portside, hair flowing in a gentle breeze. She'd come a long way in eight hours. She'd gone from basic fear to fascination with the river and the work on it.

That had been his plan from the beginning, when he'd goaded her into doing a bunch of busy stuff that didn't need to be done at all. Course, if she ever found out he'd manipulated her like that, she'd probably use that noose she mentioned earlier and hang him from the top deck.

He signed off to the *Annabelle* and brought the *Miss*

hard to port. Effie waved to the deckhands, and they did the same. California girl meets Mississippi men. She turned away and crossed the deck. He heard the clatter of the steps, much faster than when she first went down those same steps. She opened the door and jumped inside. She gave him a salute, or was that the bird? "Okay, now what?"

"Now we go home."

She held her hands out. "That's it? We're done?"

"Wasn't that enough? It took us four hours to get those barges off and retied."

"What if we go on down to New Orleans? I've never been to New Orleans. I hear it's great."

"We don't have enough fuel on board, and the *Miss* isn't really set up for that kind of run." He gave her a sideways glance as he headed up river. "Why don't you want to go back to the Landing? Haven't we been out here working long enough to suit you?" He tapped the console. "A cable came loose on the depth sounder. I have to reconnect it. Can you just steer for a minute?"

"Me?"

He pointed out the front window to the green triangle on shore hanging from a pole. He put her hand on the brass stick that controlled the rudder. "Aim for that triangle there and just hold the tug steady in this direction. Don't move the rudder or we'll lose the channel and be trimming the bushes."

"What bushes?"

"River talk for we'll be too close to the shoreline and run aground, especially this time of year during the dry season. I've had my fill of sandbars and grounding for the day. Time to go home."

She bit her bottom lip. "Uh, sure."

There was a little glint in her eyes. What the hell was that? He didn't care; he was too tired to care. Tedious work pushing barges around shallow water, men hopping on and off, making sure everyone was safe. "All I need is a minute here. I don't want to run the river without the depth sounder working."

He bent down and rooted around on the floor. "I got the cable; the plug's worn. We need new wire. Actually we should get a new system. This one is outdated and—" Suddenly the tug slowed, slowed more, then came to a gravel-sliding stop, the tow listing slightly to starboard. "What the hell?"

He jumped up and cracked his head on the console as he tried to stand upright. He looked around, rubbing the sore spot. "We're aground!"

He spun around, facing Effie. "What happened?" He pointed to the setting sun. "The green triangle's over there. Why are we over here pointing east, heading in the opposite direction? Hope I can get us off." He turned for the controls, but she blocked his way.

"I don't want us to get off." Her eyes were liquid green, her lips parted.

"Why the hell not? Are you out of your mind?"

Her eyebrows pinched together in determination, and she looked a little crazed. She poked him in the chest with her index finger. "I got on this boat and I hate water. I swept it clean, got it ready for the coast guard, who never showed up, fixed life vests for deckhands who never came aboard, and I watched for leaks. I broke four nails, got blisters and took all kinds of grief from you because I was hell-bent on staying here."

"Because of Thelma."

"Thelma's reason number two, and now I'm going to tell you reason number one." She got closer still, the scent of fresh air and sun and the river mixing with her own special scent and driving him nuts.

"It was the kiss. I want more."

"More?" He swallowed.

She took a step closer, her body touching his, her gym shoes touching his boat shoes. "I've wanted more for eighteen long, frustrating, maddening months, Ryan O'Fallon. Since the day I walked into your office and laid eyes on you."

"Eighteen months?"

"I tried everything to not want more. Rivalry, smart-aleck cracks, taking bets on your love life. And then we kissed, you grabbed my ass and all my great plans fell apart."

She brought her face to his, their noses nearly touching. "I'm not going to leave here and be frustrated for another eighteen months."

"You want—"

"The cure." Her lips touched his. "I want sex."

Chapter 7

Conrad put down the living room phone as Arthur strolled in. "Well, how's operation Gold Digger coming along?"

"Hell of a lot of work, I can tell you that." Conrad nodded to the back of the house. "We better watch what we're saying. I sure don't need anyone knowing about our plan."

"Not a problem. Denise isn't here. I saw her leaving as I drove in."

"Hell, I forgot I cut her back to half days. Told her I wanted to start taking care of the place myself."

Arthur chuckled. "And she bought it?"

"She's not the brightest bulb on the tree, and I couldn't very well tell her I was butt-ugly broke, now could I? Especially with me courting a soon-to-be heiress." Conrad went to the sideboard and poured two tumblers of whiskey. He handed one to Arthur as he sat down.

"Well, spill it. Tell me what's going on," Arthur said.

"I went to the grocery store and asked around about Thelma without trying to act too conspicuous. Me having any interest in her at all is cause for some suspicion. Seems the woman loves the Beach Boys. I borrowed a CD from one of the clerks who also happens to appreciate their warbling, and I memorized the songs, thank God for simple lyrics, then took Thelma on a picnic. We drove around singing things about having good vibrations. Guess that's better than bad vibration. Christ almighty, the woman has no taste."

"So, what's the next step?"

"Just made reservations for dinner. The country club. Going to take Thelma there tonight. Impress the hell out of her. Bet she's never been to any place better than Slim's. I told Lemond to seat us toward the back. God knows what she'll wear. Last night the style of her clothes wasn't too bad, but the quality was right out of Wal-Mart."

He brushed a crease from his Perry Ellis slacks. "She had a good time, and that's all that matters."

Arthur tossed back his drink and stood. "Bring her flowers. Women are suckers for that shit."

"I'll make a stop at the grocery. Need to return that CD to the clerk. I drove into Memphis and picked up a few Beach Boy CDs of my own. Got to get with the program if I'm going to make this work."

Arthur nodded. "Get the flowers at the grocery. Sure as hell don't need florist quality for Thelma McAllister."

Conrad checked his watch. "I better get moving. Don't want to be late." He let out a sigh. "Why couldn't a sexy babe with big tits and a nice ass and taste for decent music and clothes inherit two million bucks?"

"All you have to do is tough it out for a year, get your finances totally mixed together, and you're an instant millionaire." Arthur pointed to the window. "When are you going to sell the Ferrari?"

Conrad raked his hair. "I'm working on it, okay. Selling a car like this and getting a Ford or another piece of crap takes some getting used to."

"So do hunger pains."

"The Ferrari impresses Thelma."

"Who are you kidding; it impresses you. If you want Thelma to think you've changed, you need to do something different or she'll smell a rat, and if she doesn't, the O'Fallons sure as hell will, and you know how they feel about Thelma. If they suspect you're conning her, you're dead meat."

Arthur put his glass on the sideboard. "Sell the car, simplify, do things you don't normally do. That's the only way she's going to believe that the old Conrad no longer exists and the new improved version is in love with her. Sell the damn car."

He left, and Conrad watched the Audi disappear down the driveway. An Audi for Christ's sake, how could Arthur appreciate a Ferrari?

Conrad considered switching clothes to something stylish before he picked up Thelma. What a waste. She'd dress in some old rag and look perfectly pitiful as always. He didn't need to impress her. He just had to convince her he was madly in love with her and do it damn quick before those handwriting experts finished up.

He closed the door behind him and slid into the Ferrari, cranked over the engine and listened to the rich hum of the perfect motor. He revved it just a bit in idle while running his hand over the Italian leather seats. Sell it? He felt ill at the thought. Maybe he could get a loan, use it as collateral. He couldn't imagine selling.

He selected BB King on the CD player and put the car in gear. A few minutes to enjoy some decent Blues between his house and the O'Fallons'. He drove slowly, appreciating the moment before picking up Thelma. Then the assault of Beach Boys and all things tacky would commence and last the whole damn evening.

He stopped at the grocery and five minutes later reluctantly pulled into the O'Fallons' driveway. He slapped a fake smile on his face that he hoped didn't look too contrived and went to the front door. With a little luck that Effie woman wouldn't be around. She was a little too smart, a little too skeptical, a little too urban.

Thelma opened the door before he hit the bell. "Conrad!" She beamed, her eyes a bit wistful, a blush in her cheeks. Well, hot damn, she was falling for him. He knew it would happen just like he knew what tie went with what pants, what wine to serve with what cheese and what music set the scene for a successful seduction. All of these would come in handy in the very near future. He was one damn good con artist.

"Hello, my dear." He handed her the flowers wrapped in cellophane. It was the first bunch on the rack. He'd grabbed them, paid and run without even looking. He eyed her dress that resembled second-rate sofa upholstery. Cheap flowers for a cheap broad, he thought, but said, "Pretty flowers for a pretty lady. I thought of you when I saw them." Hell, that much was true enough.

She took the flowers, a smile nearly covering her face now. Well, she didn't have bad teeth, least that was in her favor.

She stood aside so he could enter, and she self-consciously brushed at her dress. "I intended to go into Memphis to get something new for tonight, but Bonnie was fussy and Ryan and Effie aren't that comfortable with her yet and Rory was helping fix an engine that was busted. He's got Bonnie down at the docks now. I think the racket from those tugs puts her right to sleep. She's an O'Fallon sure enough."

Like he cared about some sniveling baby. But he smiled and nodded all the same and followed Thelma into the kitchen, where he leaned against the doorjamb. "Rory should bring the tug over to the dry dock and let my boys take a look-see. I have some great guys working for me."

She bit at her lip, her smile slipping a notch. "Ah, sure." She pulled a vase from the cabinet and filled it with water. "That's . . . that's a great idea. I'll remind Rory. It probably just slipped his mind."

That was odd. "We've been doing business together for years."

"Of course you have." She smiled sweetly, but it didn't look sincere. Not Thelma at all. She took the flowers from the cellophane and one-by-one put them in the vase, the scraggly bouquet of lilies and daisies and carnations with some green stuff suddenly not looking as forlorn as before. She stood back, admiring the bouquet. "Thank you, Conrad. They're so beautiful. I've never had flowers from a man before."

Her voice was low, eyes misty. He couldn't remember a woman ever taking that much time with flowers he'd bought before or so thoroughly appreciating them, even the hellaciously expensive flowers he got from the florists in Memphis. Thelma was one easy dame to get around. He mentally salivated. A little slick talk, some other romantic crap, a few more bunches of cheap flowers and the million was as good as his.

"Shall we go?" He assumed a gallant, sophisticated pose and held out his arm for her to take. Glowing, she slid her arm through his, and they headed down the hall toward the front door. "I thought we could stop by my place for a drink before we have dinner." He made himself gaze lovingly at her. "If that suits you, of course."

She seemed slightly bewildered and stopped in the middle of the hallway. "You want to take me to Hastings House?"

The evening shadows trailed long across the wood floor; the old clock clicked off the seconds. Good God, how many more did he have to endure before this night was over?

"I'd be honored, Conrad. Your home is one of the finest examples of antebellum architecture in the Memphis area. Designed by *the* Robert Mills, the same man who designed the Washington Monument."

If she'd smacked him upside the head with a dead skunk, he couldn't have been more surprised. "How'd you know that?" He opened the door, and they walked down the steps to his car.

"Once when I was nine I got lost in the woods and wound up at your place. I thought it was a castle out of a fairy tale. I was crying, and your dad dried my tears and brought me into the kitchen and gave me a cookie. Chocolate chip."

Conrad laughed, a real laugh this time as he thought of his father. "Dad loved his chocolate chip cookies. He didn't share with just anyone, you know." Conrad slid in the driver's side and fired the engine.

"Then he took me home in his car. It was blue and big and smelled of leather and cigars. Your dad was a wonderful man, and I think I fell in love with your house right then and there. When I got older I did a little research about it."

"Well, it's no castle, but I sure like it well enough. I like it a lot as a matter of fact." He turned down the road, and BB King sang "The Thrill Is Gone." Amen to that, Conrad thought as he caught another glimpse of Thelma and her dress.

But she liked his house, and that was a real stroke of luck. He had the feeling she'd jump at the chance to live in it, and he needed all the luck he could get with only nine days to convince Thelma to marry him. An added bonus was that the house wouldn't be part of the divorce since it was in his name before marriage, unlike her inheritance that would come along after they were married. Joint property! But nine days . . .

He squirmed, considering the amount of time he had.

"Are you okay?"

"Terrific." He hit the CD player and changed the music. "BB's great but not as good as the Beach Boys." He touched her hand. A little forward, but he didn't have time to take it nice and slow. "We need our Beach Boys, right?" He squeezed her hand just a tad.

She looked at their hands together, her surprise giving way to delight. Go, Conrad!

"You didn't need to change the music for me."

"Hey, the Boys are great." His insides cringed as he joined in the song about some dumb girl who had too much fun and then her daddy took her T-Bird away. It's a Ford for God's sake, get over it. What a stupid song, hardly a match for BB.

They pulled into the circular drive of Hastings House, and Thelma gazed around, a little breathless, a lot in awe. He knew the feeling, had it damn near every time he came up the drive. The stately white columns, wood shutters, big front door and the deep red bricks made right here on the property always captured his attention.

"I've never seen such a beautiful home." She got out of the car.

"It's been on the National Register of Historic Places since 1970 and was featured in *Southern Living* two years ago." He skipped up the stairs. "Come on. I'll give you the five-cent tour. You can see if anything's changed in the kitchen since you were here last." He opened the front door for her, but she didn't move.

"Do you mind if I see the grounds first? Grant's army was quartered here, wasn't it?"

"A fact most Southerners would like to forget," he said on a laugh until she started around the house to the back.

Oh, damn! The backyard looked like a freaking jungle. He couldn't afford to have the gardeners do more than cut the grass there. He caught up with Thelma and stuffed his hands in his pockets, trying for a nonchalant air. "I'm having the back redone, but the landscaper hasn't gotten to it yet."

She stood in the middle of the grass area, and he pointed beyond the overgrowth. "It drops off to the creek. In the spring you can hear it flowing."

"I remember crossing it when I was lost. There used to be a footbridge." She went over to where weed and trees took over. "What's this?" She pointed to a rusted half barrel perched on a garbage can caddy hidden in the brush.

Great, the place was looking more derelict by the minute. "Just some old piece of junk that got shoved back here by the workmen."

She pushed aside the weeds and grinned. "I knew it. It's a grill."

She tugged on the handle, working it free, then strong-armed it out into the grass, getting a smudge on her dress. Dear Lord, he was dating Martha Stewart. "I think it was my dad's."

"It's a little rusty here and there, but it's a real beauty." She studied it as if it were some long-lost artifact just unearthed.

"I don't know if I'd jump right to beauty." He eyed the steel drum cut in half and welded onto the cart. "My mother nearly fainted when Dad brought this thing home." He nodded toward the house. "I just bought a really fine stainless steel outdoor grill from Williams Sonoma that I bet you'd like, and sometime we—"

"Don't know any William Sonoma on the Landing. This here is a real Memphis grill. Holes and grating across the bottom to hold the coals and let the ash drop through and the air circulate. This is a classic beauty. Bet your dad had Ben Slides make it for him. Ben was the best."

She stood back and admired the piece of shit. "The

O'Fallons have one, but it's not this nice." She chuckled. "Don't tell them I said that."

Other women he'd dated thought the Ferrari or a particular tie he'd picked out in New York or something like that was great, not a damn rusted grill. What kind of woman got excited over a grill?" He gave her a quick look. Thelma obviously liked to eat. Way too plump for his taste, but maybe he could use this whole mess to his advantage. Impress the little woman . . . who wasn't all that little.

Now was as good a time as any to make another move. "You know, I was thinking about building a big brick patio out here in a month or so." After I get my hands on your money and can hire a contractor. "This grill would be the perfect addition, a remembrance of my dad and the barbecues we used to have out here."

She faced Conrad, her eyes bright. Ta-da, score one for the old Gold Digger.

"That's a terrific idea, Conrad. And add a picnic table. Barbecue and picnic tables just seem to go together, don't you agree?"

He hated picnic tables. Hiking his leg up was so . . . dog-like. He faked an astounded look. "Well, that's just what I was thinking. And maybe put in a horseshoe court." The guys at the country club would get a big hoot out of that. Horseshoes? Him? What a joke!

She pointed into the overgrowth. "And you can clear out this brush that blocks the creek and get those torches that keep the bugs away. It'll be lovely."

"I can build a stone path through the trees, maybe add a gazebo."

She spread her arms wide. She looked as if she'd just discovered gold. He was so good at this con shit he scared himself. In nine days she'd be his, no problem.

"Why don't we do it now? We can build it ourselves. I

hate to see you lose half the summer because your land-scaper is too busy."

Breath left his lungs in one long whoosh. He coughed. "E-excuse me?"

"I'll help you build the patio. Your father would love that you're building something onto the house, making it yours. We can start tonight by drawing up some plans to scale. We don't have to go to the country club, I don't mind. We'll work here. I love working on projects."

"Tonight?" Work? Projects? He hated both.

"We'll take some measurements of the house and decide how big the patio should be. A curved outline would be nice to follow the flow of the house around the kitchen and library and garden room and soften the angles."

"What happened to dinner? Aren't you hungry?" He gave her a warm smile and hoped his eyes twinkled.

"Do you have something in your freezer? We can cook on your daddy's grill as we work."

So much for twinkling eyes. Was he losing his touch? What the hell just happened? Work! He hated all forms of work. Grill? He had no idea how to grill.

She continued, "It'll be a little celebration for finding it." She studied the ground. "I bet there's some hickory around here. Can't have a proper grilling without hickory. Tomorrow we can drive into Memphis and go to Lowes and—"

"Who's this Lowes person?"

"Home improvement store and . . ." She laughed and nudged him. "You're so funny. You're just putting me on, Conrad. What a tease. Everyone knows Lowes."

Wanna bet!

"They have a selection of how-to books that can tell us exactly what to do."

A thrill a minute.

"Then we can go to the brick yard tomorrow and order the sand and pavers we need. The color should complement the colors of the house. I know we can't match, so we should go with something that blends but is different and—"

"Hold on a minute. Do you know how much work it is to build a brick patio? You have to dig out the dirt, put down polyurethane, then rock and sand and pack it down, then lay out the bricks. We won't be done 'til Christmas. I'm an engineer. I know what's involved."

She gave him a strange look. "You're an engineer? Conrad, I'm so impressed. You know exactly how to do this. It's going to be a wonderful patio."

Christ Almighty! What the hell had he done? Conrad Hastings didn't build things. He golfed at the club, dined at fine restaurants, went to the theater, screwed lovely women. But one look at Thelma told him she was really, really into this project, and pleasing her and impressing the hell out of her, even with his engineering degree and his hard work, was all that mattered at the moment.

Back-tracking was out of the question; she could get suspicious. Shit-fire! This was not part of his plan. Dinner at the club was his plan, not grilling out on a piece of rust. But, like Arthur said, he had to change.

Okay, he could do this. He forced a grin. Damn, he was doing a lot of that lately. "I have steaks in the freezer, and we can defrost them in the microwave. We can throw potatoes wrapped in foil into the hot coals. A salad and a bottle of wine would be nice." Lots and lots of wine.

Her eyes danced. "That sounds wonderful."

He pulled in a deep breath because he couldn't believe he was going to say the next words. "Building the patio ourselves is a great idea, Thelma. Something we can work on together." He gave her a little wink to seal the deal while his words made him light-headed and dizzy. This was how he reacted in anticipation of great sex, not back-breaking work.

She took his hands and held them tight as his eyes gazed into hers. They were sort of washed-out blue, like the sky on a cloudy day, but they were kind and vulnerable. Vulnerable was damn good. She said, "I'm so glad you like the idea. It's the real you, Conrad. I can tell. You have fantastic ideas."

He held her hands tighter. "There's nothing better than building something yourself to get a feeling of accomplishment. We both know that." Like hell! "And what I like most is we're doing it together."

Thelma looked at Conrad's fingers intertwined with hers. How had this sudden attraction happened between them? Yesterday she'd gone on a picnic with him to get out of the house for a while, and today he was bringing her flowers and they were holding hands and she was helping him build a patio onto Hastings House. He'd said he was a changed man, wanted to prove it to her, and he wanted to be with her.

And right now she wanted nothing more than to be with Conrad. She'd never met anyone like him . . . ever.

But this mutual fascination was so sudden. And crazy. Twenty-four hours ago she didn't even like Conrad Hastings and was far from convinced that he liked her. But now . . .

His eyes were deep brown, sincere, gazing at her as if she were the last woman on earth. But she wasn't the last woman on earth; heck, she wasn't even the last woman on the Landing. For sure she wasn't the prettiest or the youngest or richest, all the attributes that attracted Conrad.

What had happened to make him feel this way about her? To make him change?

"Let's take a walk down to the creek," she said, trying to break the spell that surrounded her, needing time to figure things out.

"It's weedy and buggy, and we're hungry." His eyes darkened to cocoa. He took his one hand from her and gently tucked a strand of hair behind her left ear, making her shiver, her breathing stop. "Very hungry," he said, his voice low and sensual and needy.

She might not be the most experienced woman on the Landing, but she knew the difference between hungry and hungry.

She laughed, but it was a nervous laugh, not one of those ha-ha kind but the holy-moly now-what-have-I-gotten-myself-into kind. She said, "The creek's not all that far. We can pace it off, figure out how long the path should be. Maybe we'll be able to see it from the new patio and . . ."

He looked her dead in the eyes, and she had no idea what she wanted to say next.

"We?"

She blushed. She could feel the heat crawling up her neck and settling in her cheeks. "I mean you. The we is you and me putting it in . . . the bricks, I mean . . . for the patio." Time to shut up, Thelma!

His fingers touched her cheek, then trailed down to her throat. His other hand held hers a little tighter. Her heart fluttered. She hadn't known her heart could still do such a thing. For sure it was out of practice. But flutter over Conrad Hastings? This was all so strange. And then he looked into her eyes, and it didn't feel strange at all. It just felt really good.

He leaned toward her, their bodies almost touching now. He lowered his head and whispered, "You are so beautiful. I don't know why it took me so long to see just how attractive and interesting and irresistible you are."

The whole world tilted. Was she ready for this? Where was this all coming from, and most important, where the heck was it going? She yanked her hands free of his, took a step back, then walked quickly off into the undergrowth, following some weedy path that she figured led to the creek. "We need to see the creek before we can draw up plans," she called over her shoulder. "We're not sure exactly how far away it is, and we need to check."

How pathetic of an excuse was that? The brush and weeds whipped against her ankles, but she kept going faster and faster. Amazing what apprehension and inexperience could make a woman do.

"Wait up." She heard Conrad's voice behind her. She had no idea where she was going or what the heck she was doing. Should she kiss Conrad or not kiss him? Fall for him or not?

Was she falling? This fast? Too fast? Twenty-four hours was fast by anyone's standards. How had life suddenly gotten so complicated? She followed the path around a tree and nearly slid into the creek, pulling herself up short at the last moment, her back against Conrad's firm chest, his arms winding around her, holding onto her.

He turned her around to face him. His hot breath falling across her lips made her feel hot, too, and it had nothing to do with the July temperature.

Birds darted here and there; the hum of the insects mixed with the trickling creek. Her heart hammered against her ribs. "Your hair's mussed."

He smiled. "Want me to comb it?"

"No, I like it this way." He looked unkempt, less than perfect and a little vulnerable. She understood vulnerable. Suddenly Conrad wasn't this rich playboy; he was here with her in the woods, holding her and looking imperfect.

She rested her forehead against his chin, trying to calm

her nerves. "What are we doing here, Conrad?" Catching her breath seemed impossible.

"We're enjoying each other, least I hope so. Don't fight it, Thelma. What we have is so rare, so wonderful. You make me so happy."

"I do?" She brought her gaze to his.

"Yes, you do. More than you can imagine. I like us together."

She touched his hair, and there didn't seem to be enough oxygen in the atmosphere.

"I want to kiss you, Thelma. I've wanted to for so very long. I kept thinking I'd get over you, and I never did. I felt more and more attracted to you each day, and now you're with me. Don't run away from me. I can't bear it." Then he captured her lips with his, and she thought the world would never stop spinning.

How could this be? How could kissing Conrad be so incredible? She didn't have a clue, but all she wanted was for the kiss, his kiss, to never end.

Chapter 8

"A cure? Sex!" Ryan looked down at Effie. Green eyes, blond hair, great shape, the woman he'd wanted to bed for the last year and a half.

She said, "I know, that's usually the guy's line. You're the ones who think sex is the cure for everything. But this time, I'm doing the suggesting."

Even with AC running full blast, heat swirled around them in the wheelhouse. "We already had this discussion, and nothing's changed. What happens when our relationship falls apart? How are we going to work together then? I don't want to quit my job, and neither do you."

She held up her hands. "Did I say anything about a relationship? I'm talking plain sex here. Fast and furious, a one-time deal to quell the beast inside."

He felt his eyes widen by half. "You have a beast?"

She gave him a sultry look and growled deep in her throat. Question answered.

"Then I leave tomorrow and go back to San Diego. All the mystique of sex between us is over, and we can get on with our lives and not be constantly wondering what if." She swept her hair from her face, looking hotter and more enticing by the minute. "We'll have all the answers to what if. Great idea, huh?"

He wasn't really sure what a growl meant but was willing to find out. "What if we like the sex?"

Her eyes kind of crossed. "I think that's a given, Ryan. It's all I've thought about for a really long time. The salvation is we don't really like each other; we just want each other. We get the sex out of the way, the tension is over and we go back to working together with none of the complications. You have Mr. San Diego, in your future, and I have a Chanel blouse in mine." She kicked off her shoes.

"You think what's going on between us is curiosity?"

"Or we're in heat. Right now it's darn hard to tell. Are you one of those guys who talks sex to death before you actually do something about it?"

"What if having sex makes things worse between us."

"You are one of those talky guys, and how can you think having sex can be worse than not having it. Look at me. I'm ready to rip my clothes off every time I see you."

He arched his left brow. "No kidding."

She unbuttoned her blouse. Both eyebrows arched. She wasn't kidding!

"Am I the only one who realizes there's enough pent-up frustration between us right now to light up the whole city of Memphis."

He brushed her hand from her blouse, and she said, "You don't want to do this? I think you're making a huge mistake by not taking me up on this offer. Think about the future. When we get back to San Diego things will be worse than ever between us. We'll never get any work done because all we'll be thinking about is sex and what if we'd done it and what it would have been like!"

He looked into her eyes of darkest jade. "I want to do the unbuttoning. I've fantasized about your rack since the first day you walked into my office. Now I finally get to unwrap the package."

Every muscle in his body went rigid with anticipation. Logic and sex didn't come together very often in his life; in fact, they never had until now. Usually his brain said something like "Ryan, this is a really bad idea" while his body said, "Go for it!" He intended to enjoy the hell out of all this sexual logic. Then Effie would go back to California and—

"*Mississippi Miss*," came a voice over the VHF radio. "This is *Dodger Dog* off your port bow. Everything okay? You needing some help there? Over."

Ryan's fingers froze on the blouse buttons, and Effie jumped and looked around. "Who the heck's that? Where are they?"

He snapped up the mike on the console and turned his attention to the passing line hauler pushing twenty barges some four hundred feet away. Ryan stepped in front of Effie in case the tow captain had his binoculars out. Ryan replied into the mike, "*Mississippi Miss* here. Everything's fine *Dodger Dog*. Breaking in a cub pilot and lost the channel. I can get her off. Over."

Effie tickled him in the ribs and giggled. "Get her off . . . Is that a promise?"

Ryan nearly dropped the mike, and the captain on *Dodger Dog* said, "Rodger that, *Mississippi Miss*. Have a good one."

"Damn, it better be good." Ryan puffed out a deep breath, waited 'til the line hauler passed, then turned to Effie. "We got ourselves a problem. Every tow that passes is going to ask if we need help. This is never going to work. We should wait 'til we get back to the Landing and—"

The rest of the words died as Effie slid her arms around

his neck and kissed him, her tongue halfway down his throat. Speech was impossible. Neither his mouth nor brain worked. Okay, forget waiting.

"You're right," he panted as he reclaimed his tongue. "But all we got time for is basic no-frills sex."

"Basic works. I'm not asking for frills." Her voice was ragged, her eyes dilated, looking more black than green.

"We're perched up here for all the world to see like goldfish in a bowl." He glanced at the radar screen. "Another tow's about ten minutes away."

Her eyes rolled around in her head, not focusing all that well. "Ten minutes. We can do ten minutes. Right now all I need is about five."

"Oh, flipping hell. Protection." He reached for his back pocket and his wallet. "I don't know if I have anything with me. I wasn't exactly—"

She grabbed his hand and slapped a condom into his palm. His gaze fused with hers. "You really did have this planned."

"Desperation does strange things to a woman. I can't do eighteen more months of nothing." Her fingers fumbled with the snap of his jeans. "Ten minutes and counting. I hate zippers . . . should be outlawed . . . only Velcro."

He finished with the buttons on her blouse and pushed back the sides, his eyes feasting on the little gold ring at her navel that he never would have suspected in a million years and then traveling up to her hard pink nipples straining against a white lacy bra. His heart slammed against his ribs like a crack of lightning over the Mississippi, and he suddenly felt weak. "Ohmygod."

He'd deal with the ring in a minute. Right now he needed to taste her sweet breasts, material and all, a fantasy come true. He opened his mouth, nearly drooling with anticipation until he felt Effie's fingers gently close around his dick.

He gasped, taking her nipple deep, nearly suffocating. What a way to go!

She moaned. He did the same, but no sound escaped with his mouth full. His erection throbbed, his gut clenched, climax threatened as her hand stroked him in a seductive rhythm. With her nipple against his tongue he couldn't tell her to slow down or this would be over in way less than ten minutes.

Out of sheer necessity he took his mouth from her breast and looked up at her as she asked in an uneven breath, "How much time do we have left?"

Hard to think with Effie's breasts right in front of him and his for the taking and her massaging him.

He looked at the monitor. Blinked a few times to clear his vision. "Six minutes or so. And you're still in clothes."

"So are you."

He slid her blouse from her shoulders and spread it out on the captain's chair. "This should be the right height for what we have in mind."

"A chair?"

"We're a little desperate here, sugar. A chair will do fine." She blushed as he unbuttoned her shorts, then unzipped them, peeling the material over her silky hips, then letting the shorts drop to the floor in a soft whoosh. "Never imagined you as a girl in pink."

"What did you imagine me in?"

He gave her a devilish grin. "Nothing."

She huffed out a breath and blushed. "You've imagined me naked for eighteen months?"

He kissed her deep. "I intend to make up for lost time." His slid his fingers into the waistband of her panties.

"Here, let me. We don't have time for the slow stripping routine. And I don't just mean because of the barges." She brought her full open lips to his, kissed him, then bent over, sliding her panties over her hips and thighs and down her legs.

Her back was smooth and bare, except for the bra strap that marred the picture. He unsnapped it, and in an instant she righted, her head connecting with his chin and knocking him backward into the controls.

"Ohmygosh!" She cupped his face between her hands and massaged his chin. "Are you okay?"

"Wh-what happened?"

"You undid my bra and it kind of surprised me."

"Kind of?"

She looked at him close. "I think you chipped a tooth."

He gazed at her, taking in her nakedness. He growled. "It was worth it."

Her breathing kicked up a notch. "Hurry?"

He fumbled with the condom until she snatched it from his fingers, but didn't have any better luck than he did until she tore it open with her teeth. She spit out a piece of foil. "Ta-da."

Then she unrolled it over the head of his erection. He gritted his teeth, fighting for control. "Hurry." This time he said it.

"You're kind of big here, not that I'm complaining, but it's like trying to put ten pounds of sugar into a five-pound sack."

Her eyes met his, and he laughed in spite of the heat eating at his insides.

"Something my grandma used to say. Though knowing grandma, I don't think this is exactly what she had in mind."

He snagged her around the middle and set her on the chair, his face level with hers. "I really want to kiss you again."

"We don't have time." She spread her legs until they connected with the armrests of the chair. "That'll be good enough, right?"

"If this is meant to drive all thoughts of sex from our brains, it's got to be better than good, sugar." He took her left foot and placed it on one side of the console, the right foot on the other side, opening her wide, caging himself between her legs. What a great place to be.

Her eyes covered half her face, and she turned red as the parka she'd brought on board. "This is a little embarrassing. I'm spread wide open like a Christmas turkey, and you still have on your clothes."

He yanked off his shirt, his fingers trembling. He dropped the shirt to the floor. "That's all the concession to my nakedness. You'll have to deal."

His gaze never left her delectable body. The feel of her thighs on his now bare sides made blood rush like liquid fire in his veins. He touched the tiny ring at her navel, making her muscles quiver, his also. Her eyes darkened even more with arousal as he trailed his index finger from her navel to damp curls. He lingered a moment there, savoring the silky strands, then slipped beyond, separating her damp folds and grazing her swollen clit. She gasped and gripped his shoulder.

"Ryan?" she rasped. "What are you doing? Just sex. No frills."

But he wanted more than just sex. He wanted to explore every inch of her, give her mind-boggling pleasure. Feel her wet and hot and delicious just for him. His fingers slid into her as she bit her bottom lip. "Do you like that?"

"Oh, God, Ryan," she whimpered in a breathy rush. "We don't have . . ." The rest of her words were lost as he pulled his finger out, then added another as he entered her again. Deeper this time, a bit faster, his hand pressing against her lush mound as he stroked her inside, making her tremble. The euphoric expression on her face nearly sent him over the edge.

"Please," she gasped, her tone pleading, her eyes glassy.

He wanted nothing more than to make this last all night, take her slowly, make her whimper again and again with pleasure. No woman had ever responded so completely to his touch, and he didn't want it to end so—

"Ryan! The time?"

"Fuck."

"Yes, I agree."

He took his fingers away and slid his erection into her, expanding her tight passage and realizing he'd never wanted a woman so desperately as he wanted Effie right at this moment. The scent of sex drenched the air. Harsh rays of sunset pierced through the cabin from one window to the other, and the astounding sensation of her tight body surrounding his drove him wild.

He claimed her mouth as he slid partially out, then pushed farther into her with the next stroke. She moaned, then gasped, her mouth opening, knees bending back, giving herself completely to him, making every fiber of his body scream for release.

He slid his hands under her buttocks, taking one smooth round cheek in each palm, lifting her slightly and bringing her firmly into him. He took her faster and deeper with each hard thrust, building their desire into a wild fury until he climaxed in a mind-numbing haze of passion as the world swirled around him like the Mississippi on a rampage.

Effie couldn't breathe, her body rigid with release as passion pounded through her hot and furious. Having sex with Ryan wasn't supposed to be so intense. What happened to basic? Fast? God knew the furious part was there.

Her head sagged onto his shoulder. Speaking was impossible and not necessary . . . 'til she opened her eyes, focused and spied a tow rounding the bend. "Ohmygod."

"I know, sugar." His voice was thick and deep. "Me, too. You are incred—"

"Boat!" She felt him tense as his head snapped up.

"Boat?" He looked at her, then turned his head and stared out the window. "Oh, shit!"

Slowly he eased himself from her, her body missing the profound intimacy more than she thought possible. Course, getting caught with her pants down—actually they were completely off, as was every other piece of her clothing—took precedence over intimacy, no matter how profound.

He snagged a paper towel from the console and disposed of the condom while she dove for the floor, below the window line, to keep out of sight.

"You okay down there?" he asked.

"Better than up there with you. Can you imagine the gossip? You're supposed to be the father of one woman's baby, and here you are poking another for all the world to see. Rory doesn't need to deal with talk like that. He's got more than enough on his mind."

She handed Ryan his shirt, and he slid it on as she yanked on her bra and panties, shorts and blouse.

The radio came to life with, "*Mississippi Miss* this is *Tennessee Tootsie*. You needing some help getting off that there towhead? Over."

"*Tennessee Tootsie*, this is *Mississippi Miss*. No problems here. We'll be getting under way shortly. Over."

"Rodger that, *Miss*. You take care now, you hear."

Ryan gave a little salute as the big diesels rumbled on by. He looked down at Effie. "We have to get out of here."

"This gives a whole new meaning to the word quickie."

She stood and dusted off her backside. "Guess we should have gone below to the work quarters. We wouldn't have had the threat of an audience."

Ryan cupped her chin in his palm and looked deep into her eyes. A slow smile spread over his face, and he smoothed her hair from her cheek, his fingers lingering seductively at her temple, turning her insides to mush. "Any river man worth his salt who didn't get an answer on the radio call would have come on over to investigate. We could have had a face-to-face audience and been the talk of every barge on the Mississippi. That could make getting over each other more difficult because of all the comments flying around."

She swallowed, mesmerized by his touch, his look. "It wouldn't matter because it didn't work. I . . . I'm not over anything, Ryan. I want more."

His eyes darkened. "More as in . . . ?"

"Sex," she whispered, then let out a deep breath and waved her hand around the wheelhouse. "This made everything worse." She grabbed the front of his T-shirt in her fists and brought her body tight to his. "Much worse," she ground out as desire pumped through her again. How'd that happen so fast, so intense?

He swallowed and loosened her fists from his shirt. "You're just suffering from . . . afterglow deprivation. No time to let the feeling of good sex sink in. Like eating fast and still feeling hungry. Your brain doesn't have time to compute that you're satisfied. That's the problem of quickies—no afterglow. No satisfaction."

"So, you feel the same way I do? Now what are we going to do? Things are worse instead of better between us. Neither of us is satisfied about anything."

He stood tall. "Guys don't do afterglow. We operate in the moment. I'm satisfied, curiosity gone." He held out his hands. "When I meet up with you back in San Diego we'll be like . . . pals."

"Pals." She nodded, trying to convince herself. Then she looked him over. No pal she ever had was built like or looked like or had sex with her like Ryan O'Fallon. "I'm going down on the deck. Pack away all those work vests. The deckhands on the *Annabelle Lee* didn't use a one, and the coast guard didn't stop by either. Wonder why?"

"Happens sometimes." He handed over the work vest. "I'll get us off this towhead, and we'll aim for home. Hold on when I rev the engines in reverse. It could get bumpy."

She remembered her back bumping against the high captain's chair as he took her again and—

Effie tore open the door and stepped outside. She inhaled a deep breath, filling her head and lungs with river air instead of Ryan's enticing male scent. She descended the stairs, the heat from the setting sun scorching her skin . . . like Ryan's touch.

Why couldn't she let it go? Forget his scent and his touch. Think afterglow! Think about something else! Just be satisfied! She was not satisfied!

The tug steamed up river, and she stood at the bow as the wind blew through her hair and the setting sun streaked the sky. Okay, she could concentrate on those things . . . until she looked up at the wheelhouse. Thank the Lord she was leaving tomorrow because here on the Mississippi, Ryan O'Fallon, hunky riverboat captain and astonishing sex partner, was totally and completely irresistible, and no afterglow in the world could change that.

What she had to do was figure out how to live with it.

The tug chugged on, rounded another bend. The sun was dipping below the horizon as she spotted O'Fallon's

Landing. Back to the real world of work and family and responsibilities.

Was that Rory and Max on shore with the stroller? She returned Rory's wave as the tug neared the dock, then kissed the pilings as the engine died. She tossed Rory the ropes, or lines as they said on the river, and he slipped the loops over some big metal knob-looking things used to keep the tug in place.

Rory helped her off the boat, and she said, "Are you the official welcoming committee?"

"It's how I get Bonnie to sleep. I bring her down to the river, we listen to the tugs—I think she knows the difference between a line hauler and a lunch bucket now—and she's out like a light. How'd you and the river get along?"

She thought about how she'd felt when she got on the tug and how she felt now. More colors swept the sky in the last throes of sunset. "It's really beautiful out there." And she meant it, every single word.

"The river's not always like that," Rory offered. "Can kick up one hell of a storm."

She bent down and scratched Max behind the ears and took a peak at Bonnie, her little blue eyes half closed.

Rory turned to Ryan as he came onto the dock. "What happened to you today? I must have had ten captains telling me you were aground around Rosedale. Thought I sent you there to help the *Annabelle* off, not get stuck yourself."

Ryan raked his fingers through his hair. "It's been a while since I worked a tow, Dad."

"Hogwash. You got river flowing through you just like the rest of the O'Fallons. What did you do, fall asleep at the switch?"

Ryan's eyes hardened a fraction. Not that anyone else would notice, but Effie did. She'd worked with him long enough, seen him handle difficult situations and be calm on the outside and know he was steaming inside. For some reason he was in steam mode. He said, "That's you more than me, Dad. The Landing is your place, not mine."

"Actually," Effie cut in, suddenly feeling bad about running the barge onto the bank and causing words between Ryan and Rory. "It was all my fault we wound up on that sandbar. Ryan asked me to take the stick while he reconnected a plug, and I was watching the shore and not paying attention, and before I knew it, bam. We were stuck."

The bam might have been a little over the top, but Rory looked as if he bought it. She slipped off her work vest. The evening heat wasn't much better than the afternoon heat.

"Seems to me . . ." Rory countered. Then his voice trailed off as he looked from Effie to Ryan and back again. A slow grin split his face, and he stroked his chin and chuckled softly. "Well, I'll be. Forget I said anything. My apologies. You two just keep doing whatever you need to be doing. I'll see you up at the house. Come on, Max."

He turned the stroller toward the road, and Ryan called, "What the hell's that supposed to mean?"

"It means I want Max to come along just like I said." Rory chuckled again.

Effie whispered to Ryan, "He knows! I don't know how, but he does. We were careful, timed it right. No tows around to see anything. How?"

Ryan looked at Effie, and his eyes widened a fraction. "Your blouse is on inside out."

"So is your shirt." Their eyes met, and her insides suddenly felt heavy and warm as she thought of the afternoon.

"Thank heavens you'll be gone tomorrow."

"For sure!" Going to San Diego was her only hope of getting over Ryan. "So now what?"

"We eat. I'm starved. Sharing one bag lunch didn't do much for either of us. And then you pack."

"I didn't unpack." She watched as he swiped his brow dotted with sweat that hadn't been there a moment ago, and she added, "I'll get an early flight."

Effie lay on the bed, staring at the ceiling, watching shadows and wishing for sleep. She'd worked on the shopping mall project for a few hours to get her mind off Ryan. When that hadn't worked she tried reading *Huck Finn*. After today she could relate to a raft on the Mississippi, but smoking cigars was a new one. She'd have to try that.

Still not sleepy she counted the ticks of the grandfather clock echoing up the staircase, recited the alphabet backward and thought about her "special place" that she'd learned about in pilates.

Yeah, well, that might work at the gym, but it sure didn't work with Ryan sleeping ten feet away. The only special place she could conjure up was the wheelhouse of the *Mississippi Miss* and having wild, hot, earth-shattering sex with Ryan.

She remembered his hands on her, his fingers in her, then him in her, every inch of him stretching her, filling her with himself and . . .

She threw off the sheet and jumped out of bed, her sweaty body suddenly cool in the air-conditioning. She had to get out of here or go loopy. She pulled her gym shoes from her bag. Her nightshirt was good enough covering for two A.M. Besides, she'd packed everything but her traveling clothes.

She crept down the steps and slid out the front door. Humid air fell like a damp blanket around her, the only relief a slight breeze off the river. Crickets and frogs set up a summer chorus as she made for the flowers by the side. She could think about them instead of Ryan; least that was her plan until Conrad's Ferrari zoomed into the drive, taking her thoughts there.

What was Thelma doing out so late with Conrad-the-snake? This was a good time to see how far he'd slithered into Thelma's life. Effie hunched behind a big concrete urn of impatiens, Max suddenly at her side, the two of them watching as Conrad helped Thelma from the car.

Chapter 9

Bodies close and talking the way lovers do, Thelma and Conrad walked toward the porch 'til Conrad snagged Thelma behind a big oak and kissed her senseless.

Effie whispered to Max, "I'd say the guy's a first-class prick for kissing Thelma like that, except she's enjoying it so much."

Max growled.

"I agree. Thelma in lip-lock with Conrad is not good." Effie waited 'til Thelma went inside and the Ferrari zoomed off. Effie patted Max as the engine sound faded away. "Keep watch out here. I'll see what's going on inside. If Conrad comes back, bite him."

Quietly she let herself in, saw that the kitchen light was on, kicked off her shoes and headed down the hall. With any luck she'd find Thelma and not Rory raiding the fridge and get the lowdown on Conrad.

"Effie?" Thelma spun around. "What are you doing up?" She held up a glass of juice. "Want some?"

"Couldn't sleep. Thought I'd come down and get some of those cookies you baked this afternoon." She sat at the table.

"How did you enjoy your first encounter with the Mississippi?"

"Fun, exciting." Making love to Ryan O'Fallon incredible. "How was your date with Conrad? Did you enjoy your dinner at the country club?"

Thelma poured juice for Effie, then snagged the cookie jar off the counter. "Didn't make it to the club." She sat at the table and pulled out a macaroon. "You won't believe this, but instead of eating there we stayed at his house and designed a brick patio." She laughed and bit into her cookie. "We're going to do it ourselves. If we wait for the contractors to get around to the job, the summer will be over."

Effie stopped her glass halfway to her mouth. "Wait a minute. Conrad Hastings is going to put in . . ." She took a sip and swallowed, giving herself time to consider this latest development. "Conrad's going to dig in the dirt with a shovel? Put down bricks in neat little rows? Get sweaty and hot and messy?"

Thelma let out another quiet laugh that brightened her whole face, making her look young and in love. Young was fine; the in-love part sucked monkey butts. "I sort of talked him into the patio idea. Tonight we grilled steaks on his daddy's old grill and had foil-covered baked potatoes. We even toasted marshmallows on sticks for dessert like kids. Do you believe Conrad's never had s'mores?"

"Conrad grilled something as in not ordering it off an expensive menu from some restaurant?" Alarm bells jarred Effie's brain. Guys like Conrad didn't change, and they didn't fall in love, except with themselves or somebody who had something they wanted.

Thelma beamed. "I know." She clapped her palms to her cheeks. "He truly is a changed man, Effie. For as long as I can remember I thought of Conrad Hastings as an insufferable snob." She tipped her head as if considering her words. "No, not a snob, closer to an insufferable ass." She laughed outright and took a bite of cookie. "But he's so different now. I think he's matured, not shallow and not so impressed with himself. He's fun to be with and will do anything to please me."

What the hell!

Thelma looked back to Effie as if suddenly remembering she was there. "I don't understand how or why this is all happening to me, but Conrad makes me so very happy. He's sweet and charming and kind and . . ." She stifled a yawn. "And he tires me out, and I'm sure you're tired of me rambling on and on about Conrad Hastings."

Thelma popped the rest of the macaroon into her mouth. "I better get to bed. Bonnie will be up at the crack of dawn. Are you still leaving for San Diego tomorrow? You said you had last minute mall plans you forgot about to finish up today."

"Sure, tomorrow."

"It's great having you around here." Thelma put her juice glass in the sink, then came back to Effie and took her hand, holding it between hers. "Girl talk is wonderful. My parents never paid me much mind, mostly wondering where their next drink was coming from. The O'Fallons gave me a live-in nanny job when I graduated high school. Mary, God rest her soul, was busy with the kids, and I was shy, so we didn't talk all that much. Then she died, and Rory and I raised Ryan, Keefe and Quaid. I'd forgotten what a conversation without work and boats and cars was like. The O'Fallons are manly men through and through." She winked. "Not that I have to tell you that. See you to-morrow, at least tomorrow morning."

Thelma headed for the stairs. Effie froze, the cookie like paste in her mouth. *Today I had great sex with Ryan O'Fallon* must be tattooed on her forehead. How'd every-body know? The curse of the inside-out blouse, no doubt.

Except Thelma hadn't even been there to witness the blouse incident or been around Rory to have him fill her in on what had happened.

Effie downed the last of her juice. She was paranoid, that was it. Not everyone on the Landing knew or even cared about her and Ryan's sex life. Well, not exactly sex life so much as a sex encounter. She had to get over it, and the best place to do that was in San Diego, far, far away from here.

But what about the Thelma-Conrad issue? It had gone from curiosity to swept off her feet. Not good with someone like Conrad. Thelma was a grown woman and, like Ryan said, very capable of making her own decisions.

But was she really? Especially when it came to this man. He was snowing her like a blizzard in the Rockies, and Thelma didn't have a Dearborn and Emmerson in her past to make her the wiser. "Damn. Now what?"

Effie headed for Ryan's room. She'd have to tell him what was going on with Thelma and Conrad and bequeath the Save Thelma Campaign to him.

Quietly she turned the doorknob of his bedroom and tip-toed to the side of his bed. A sheet covered him from the waist down, his naked back bathed in creamy white moonlight. She hadn't counted on this. Don't look!

"Ryan," she whispered, her eyes shut. "Wake up. I need to talk, just talk, so don't get any ideas."

He didn't move. "It's the middle of the night. The only idea I have is sleep. You should try it."

One eye cheated, and she studied his broad bare shoulders, firm smooth back that tapered to his waist, a hint of ass showing above the sheet. She swallowed. That man had such a fine ass, and here it was inches away just waiting for her touch. Her fingers itched. No looking and no touching. "This is important. Screw sleep."

"I'd rather screw you."

Both her eyes flew open as he snagged her around the thighs, and she swallowed a yelp as he toppled her onto his chest. She was nose to nose with him, his eyes dark as midnight, his lips a breath away. "What are you doing?"

"I want you."

"No, you don't. You said you were over me. That you were cured. That men don't need afterglow. And I'm leaving tomorrow. All's well. You said your only idea was sleep."

"I don't know about you, Effie Wilson, but I'm not cured of anything. If we're going to put one fling behind us, we can put two." He flipped them over, her under him now, the sheet wrapped around him.

She'd wanted him for months, and their time together in the wheelhouse hadn't done a blasted thing to squelch it. Obviously it hadn't squelched anything of his either because his erection was pressing full and firm and ready between her legs. "This isn't why I came here."

"I don't care why you're here." He kissed her, his lips firm and delicious. "I'm just damn glad you are. You look sensational in moonlight, by the way. Hell, you look sensational in any light."

She was in Ryan's bed, under his incredible body, ready for action, and he thought she was beautiful. Lust pooled between her legs, making her hot and wet for him. Saying no to having sex with Ryan required one heck of a lot more willpower than she possessed right now. "Are you naked under that sheet?"

He grinned, his teeth white against the darkness. "Why don't we find out together?"

He slid his tongue to hers, and her hips arched hard against him, the thin barrier of material between them driving her crazy.

"Ryan," she breathed heavily, looking into his eyes. "What are we doing?"

"You can figure it out in California, and I can figure it out here." He levered himself up on his elbows and snagged her nightshirt into his fist, bunching it at her waist. "I want to see you again, Effie. Every luscious inch of you. I've been lying here thinking about you naked, the way I saw you on the tug."

"What happened to your only thought being sleep?"

"I lied."

Oh, hell. Truth be told, she'd probably lied, too, saying she just came in here to talk. No woman went into a man's bedroom at night just to talk!

She pushed against his shoulders and using her foot for leverage rolled them over, teetered on the edge of the bed for a second before sliding. She grabbed to keep from dropping off the edge, Ryan did the same but all they managed to do was drag the sheets with them as they tumbled onto the floor in a soft thud.

She smothered a laugh against his shoulder. "I'm not too good at bedroom bingo."

He whispered in her ear. "Neither am I." He rubbed the back of his head where it had thumped against the floor. "You are one dangerous female. I think you're trying to kill me."

"Are you okay?"

"My tooth is still chipped." He smoothed her mussed hair from her cheeks, his eyes sultry as the Mississippi heat. "But I'm fine right now," his voice a husky rumble.

He brought her mouth hungrily to his, kissing her, taking little love bites from her sensitive lips. Her toes curled, her stomach somersaulted and any thoughts about discussing Thelma and Conrad right then crumbled like a shanty in a California earthquake.

Panting, she sat up, her bare legs straddling his narrow hips, his erection throbbing through the sheet right into her, open and ready and wet for him. Sweat collected on her upper lip, and she yanked off her nightshirt and tossed it on the bed, leaving her in yellow panties and a deep blush. Sitting over a man like this was a new experience. So was his hard cock burning beneath her. "I still don't know what's under that sheet."

He arched his left eyebrow and smirked. "Oh, I think you know."

She felt his erection growing harder as he cupped her breasts, driving the air right out of her lungs and making her skin tingle. "They're perfect," he said. "Just made for my hands and my mouth."

He stroked the pad of his thumb over her sensitive nipples, making her suck in a quick breath. She bit her bottom lip to keep from crying out and waking the whole house. They'd had enough problems with audiences for one day. His blue eyes turned as dark as the shadows around them. Her need increased with every look, every touch, every tease.

"You had your way before."

"Are you registering a complaint?"

"I am. I get naked and you don't. No more." She slid off of him, taking the sheet, breathless with anticipation to see his—"Boxers? You're wearing boxer shorts to bed? What happened to sleeping in the buff? Isn't that what all studly guys do? You have a reputation to live up to, you know. Boxers aren't part of it."

She plucked at the material and looked closer. "They have little lips all over them. You bought these? Paid good money for these? Is this like some . . . fetish I should know about?"

"No fetish, least for boxers with lips. Though I do have a thing for the inside of a woman's thigh." He laid his hot hand possessively on her leg. "Here, where your skin is so soft and smooth and vulnerable and made for a man to kiss."

Her gaze melded with his. The air around them nearly sizzled.

"The boxers," he continued, his eyes not leaving hers, "were a Valentine's Day present I got in college from some girlfriend. I found them in my bottom drawer, and sleeping in the buff with all that's going on in this house didn't seem like a great idea. Too many surprises."

"Hope you're in the mood for one more." She snagged the waistband and pulled it below his hips. "Now that's more what I had in mind. Better. Much better." She looked again. "And bigger?"

"You tell me."

She leaned over him and kissed his lips, her fingers massaging his hard length. His hands skimmed down her bare back, stopping at her panties. "These have got to go. You want to take them off or should I?"

She gave him a siren's smile, knelt and stripped her panties over her hips to her knees. She sat, then slid them all the way off, twirled the bit of yellow on her index finger, then flipped it off into the air.

"You're incredible."

"I'm glad you think so." She leaned over, but instead of his lips, this time she kissed the tip of his engorged penis.

"Effie," he hissed.

The rest of his words faded away as she coddled his testicles and licked one side of his erection, then the other, taking her time, savoring the length and heat of him.

"You're a devil."

"What happened to incredible?" Then she took him slow and deep into her mouth, loving the smooth, sleek, firm texture and savoring the intimate connection.

Ryan felt every muscle in his body go hard for wanting

Effie. He gripped the sheet tight, keeping control as her mouth stroked and fondled him. The experience probably singed his eyebrows, her desire to give him pleasure, something he never expected, catching him completely off guard. But pleasure went both ways, and if he didn't stop her right now, he was done for. He wanted Effie, and this time he wanted it to last more than ten minutes. It had to because this was the last time they'd have sex. No more. Then they'd move on, right?

He sat up, snagged her left arm and tugged her up, her face only inches from his. "Enough."

Her eyes shone smoky green, lips wet, and she purred, "I wasn't finished."

He opened the top drawer on the oak nightstand behind them and pulled out a condom. Her eyes cleared a little, and she studied it. "You knew I'd come here?"

"I'm here, you're across the hall and we had incredible sex not all that long ago." He tore open the package. "If you didn't come to me, I sure as hell was coming to you."

She grinned, and he knelt over her this time, took her hands in his and kissed the palms. "Sex with you is amazing. I want you to know that."

Then he took her hands and brought them together over her head and wedged his body slippery with perspiration between her silky legs. The heat from her sex enveloped his erection, and he could feel her moist and ready against him. "Do you know how much I want to just push into you and take you right here and now?"

"Okay."

Her hard nipples rubbed against his chest. "But then I'd miss all the delicious parts of you just waiting for me to enjoy. I want to taste you, Effie, have you in my mouth, your sweet skin against my tongue, and kiss you in places you'll never forget."

She tried to free her hands, but he held tight, wanting to give her pleasure. She said, "This is cheating. You had your turn on the tug. That was all you. This was my turn."

"Sugar, we had ten minutes on that boat. That wasn't a turn; it was a preview." He kissed her. "And now I'll show you the rest."

He kissed her once more, lingering this time, her lush lips on his, fueling the flames searing his insides. "You're kind of sneaky, and I don't trust you to let me have my fill of you." He sucked her bottom lip slowly into his mouth, then released it. "And I intend to have my fill."

"You think you can have your way because you're stronger than me?"

"You won't mind, I promise." He set a line of kisses across her cheek to her ear, his tongue dipping into the delicate folds there, then the tender space behind. She gasped as he laid out more slow, sensual kisses to her other ear, nuzzled her neck, then suckled her lobe.

She squirmed. "You're getting more than your turn." Her words were uneven and breathy.

"I know." Keeping her hands in his, he brought them down by her sides and trailed kisses from her slim throat to her sternum, pausing at the apex of her lovely round cleavage, inhaling her womanly scent of sex and unrepentant need. He licked one taut dusky nipple, then breathed against it, cooling her flesh, watching it bead harder still.

She moaned, "Oh, Ryan, no more."

"Oh, yes. You started this when you sent your panties flying."

"That was just a tease."

"I can tease." He grazed his teeth across her stiff peak, watching her quiver. She whimpered, squirmed, her back rising off the floor as he ran his tongue over the areola, then gently took the nub between his lips, tugging ever so gently.

"I can't do this anymore, Ryan. You're killing me."

"You're not dead, I guarantee it." Then his mouth fondled her other breast.

Her hands fought against his.

"Just a few minutes more to enjoy all of you."

"This is it. You've seen it all."

He lapped at the indention of her navel and planted a kiss next to the little ring that tantalized him. He released her hands and put his flat palms against her silky thighs, one on each side, and pressed her apart. "Not all."

"But . . ." Her words trailed off as he nuzzled the velvety soft curls between her legs. He pushed her legs farther apart still, and his tongue anointed, then caressed, her wet waiting sex.

She whimpered, her hips arching as he said, "You are so sweet, so hot and ready for me, Effie."

His tongue tasted her again, then again as he spread her more, taking in every inch, building her passion and his own as he made himself a special part of her.

Her legs quivered. "I want you inside me. I want you with me," she pleaded.

He released her legs and kissed his way over her delectable mound, across her navel and chest to her face. He framed her flushed cheeks with his palms and kissed her damp red lips that so welcomed his. He slid himself hard and deep and swiftly into her, filling her with his thrust, her legs opening to take him in.

She gasped, and he swallowed her desperate whimpers as he drove into her again and again 'til she climaxed, bringing him to his own climax, more powerful than he ever imagined.

His breaths came in uneven gulps he couldn't control, his mind numb, his heart beating wildly in his throat.

"Oh, God, Effie," his voice rang hoarse with emotion and awe. His head sagged next to hers, tangles of her hair teasing his cheek. He lay there for a few moments, wondering what the hell just happened. No sex had ever been like this. Finally, he pushed up on his elbows and gazed into her watery eyes. He kissed the tip of her nose. "That . . . You are sensational."

Her breasts rose and fell in short pants against his chest. "You are an incredible lover."

He froze, their eyes holding, the term lover hanging between them. Her gaze cleared. "Not that this has anything to do with making love."

"Mutual pleasure and mind-blowing sex is what this relationship—"

"Or lack of relationship is all about," she added, trying to clarify what just happened.

A cocky smile fell across his mouth. "Guess this was kind of a bon voyage party."

"Right. But then I need you to do something for me."

"Sugar, I don't know if I'm up to it right now, but give me a few minutes—"

"Not that," she whispered and gave his arm a playful swat. "I need you to take over my Save Thelma Campaign. I ran into her downstairs. She'd just gotten home from a date with Conrad. That's why I came in here, to tell you we have a problem. There won't be time tomorrow. I have a ten o'clock flight, and this is important."

He rolled off of her and sat on the floor. Not that he wanted to, but the moment was clearly shot to hell and back by Ms. Buttinski. "Do you ever mind your own business?"

"Well, not really, but this is different than the lunchroom pool. This is watching out for someone. If you saw a blind person walking toward a cliff, wouldn't you try and stop them from taking the plunge?"

"What Conrad and Thelma do isn't any of your business or my business. Leave it up to them to figure out." He took her chin between his thumb and forefinger and turned her face to his. "We have all we can do to figure out our own situation here. Thelma's a mature woman with—"

"Who has no experience with shyster men." Effie pulled her head away. "I don't think she has all that much experience with men period, and guys like Conrad are way out of her league. She is so heading for that cliff, Ryan."

Effie snagged her nightshirt dangling from the edge of the bed. He liked it a hell of a lot more when she was in the mood for tossing it there.

"You're overreacting," he whispered. He stood, took a tissue from the nightstand and disposed of the condom, then snagged his boxers from the floor. He sat on the bed. "Think about this. Conrad can only like Thelma for Thelma. There's no motive for him to like her for any other reason. She has nothing anyone wants, especially Conrad. A few thousand dollars in the bank and a Pontiac Sunfire are not shyster material. Conrad's got family money, the family business . . . though from what I hear it's not doing that well. There's no reason for him to go after Thelma other than he truly cares for her."

"He's building a patio."

"Gee, that sounds like a shyster to me." Ryan helped Effie up, and she sat beside him.

"He and Thelma are building it together. She talked him into it, which means Conrad's agreed to work. Work? Conrad? Doesn't something about that picture bother you, like he's trying real hard to impress Thelma? But why is the big question."

Moonlight tangled in Effie's hair and kissed her cheek. He wanted to do both, but the Save Thelma Campaign raged full force. "Conrad said he was changing, and he is. I don't see the problem."

"It's Dearborn and Emmerson all over again. They're

cut from the same cloth. The kind that has dollar signs on one side and a broken heart on the other."

"Consider this. What if you stick your nose in and mess things up for Thelma? You ruin the best chance she's ever had at happiness? She's from a rotten family, had a crappy childhood, had no self-confidence and never dated. But now this great guy, least she seems to think so, shows an interest in her and is even willing to change his ways for her."

"The bottom line is Conrad's going to ruin Thelma for some reason we don't know about. It's up to you to find out what it is and put a stop to it since I won't be here. You think she had no self-esteem before; wait 'til Conrad makes a fool out of her. The whole town will know."

He held up his hands in surrender. "I am not getting into this. I don't see the problem. It's strange, but since we just had sex in a wheelhouse and on my bedroom floor we're in no position to call someone else's relationship strange."

"You won't take over the Save Thelma campaign?"

"Hell no. There's nothing to save her from. Conrad likes Thelma, end of story."

Effie's eyes lit with the fire of fight. "Fine. Then I'm staying. I'm not letting Thelma jump off a cliff."

Ryan took in the determined tilt of Effie's chin and cringed. "What you mean is you're going to snoop."

"Snoop is such a distasteful term. I prefer to think of it as investigate, and if that's what it takes, I'll do it."

"You're a damn architect. What do you know about investigating anything but a building? Leave it alone, Effie. I know Conrad. He's a harmless SOB. Maybe he's realizing he's not happy and wants something stable in his life. Thelma's not a glamour queen, but she is kind and sincere and loyal."

"Has Conrad Hastings ever in his whole entire selfish

life shown any interest for someone of those qualities? I've been used like Conrad's using Thelma, Ryan. It sucks. If you don't want to help figure this out, fine. I can do it myself."

"Butt out, Effie."

"Go to hell, Ryan."

She stood and turned for the door.

"Effie," he stage whispered. She turned, and he tossed her panties to her. She tossed them back. "Keep them as a souvenir because you sure won't be getting into them again anytime soon. This time I think we found the real cure to our problem, and I don't have to go to San Diego to make it work."

The grandfather clock in the hall chimed six P.M. as Effie frowned at the blueprints for the Sundance Mall spread out over the dining room table. She said to Ryan, "These plans are a piece of crap."

"They're not that bad. We've been working at them all day, and you're just tired."

"What I'm tired of is you and your know-it-all attitude and insisting you're right. The parking garage should be on the north side, and a fountain in the center of the mall." She jabbed her finger at a rectangle on the paper. "Your parking garage is too high, has too big a footprint and is ugly as a buffalo's butt. How can you not see that?"

"That's a garage. It's not going to look like the Louvre. Anything other than a concrete box is going to take the project over budget."

"It's a gray slab of ugly concrete polluting the landscape, and you can kiss any awards for environmental excellence good-bye and—"

"And," Rory added as he came into the dining room, "I don't know why you two have been arguing for the last nine hours over everything from grass to garages to the color of the sidewalk." He looked from one to the other. "Jimminy Christmas. What the hell's going on?" He waved his hand in the air. "Yesterday you're swapping spit and clothes and chipping teeth, and today you're fighting like two snakes in a barrel."

Ryan stood and tossed down his pencil. "We're getting nowhere. I'm going into town for a while. I'll ask around about Mimi, see if anyone knows anything or heard any gossip."

Rory shrugged. "The PI I hired already did that. Came up with nothing."

"Locals open up to locals more than strangers, especially if I'm buying a round or two." Without looking at Effie he headed for the hallway, his heavy steps tromping across the hardwood floors, followed by the front door closing with a solid thud.

Rory wagged his head. "All this over a mall? Can't imagine there's all that much to argue over."

Effie stood. "Just a big difference of opinion." Resulting from basic lust, sexual frustration, and the Save Thelma Campaign. "Where's Bonnie? I think I need to be around someone who doesn't talk back for a little while."

"You better enjoy it now because in a few years she'll be like the rest of the O'Fallons, opinionated as hell, determined to get their own way and raising Cain when they don't. Thelma's heating her bottle and feeding her some goop that looks a lot like wallpaper paste but is supposed to be cereal. You can feed her a bottle if you like. We'll share. Thelma's on her way out; she's got another date. Lord have mercy, don't know what she sees in that man."

Effie dropped her own pencil on the pile of blueprints and asked in a lower voice, "Guess we don't have to guess who that man is?"

"Christ Almighty, she's been with Conrad the whole damn day. She came home filthy. Said they were working on a project together." Rory raised his eyebrows. "Conrad working? Now that's a new one. Said she wanted to grab a shower, see how things were getting along here, and then she's heading back over to his place this evening. She and Conrad are putting in some kind of patio thing. What the hell's that all about?"

He stroked his chin. "I can't remember that man doing one lick of anything physical. I suppose he really has changed. Something sure has."

"My bet's on the something."

"Except there's no dang reason for Conrad to take a fancy to Thelma other than he cottons to her."

Effie followed Rory into the kitchen. She scooped Bonnie out of her pumpkin seat, remembering to support her head. The little warm bundle in her arms felt incredibly comforting after a stressful day with the architect from hell. "Come here, sweet thing."

Rory sat down at the kitchen table across from Effie. "I suppose we should be telling Bonnie stories and reciting nursery rhymes. I got one of those baby books, and that's what they said to do. Makes 'em good at reading."

Effie smiled. "Hey, I can do stories. I've got great stories. Once upon a time there were three little tailors, Prada, Escada and Verchai, and they each had a fabulous collection of incredible clothes that they made just for Princess Bonnie."

Thelma let out a hardy laugh as she handed Effie the bottle. "Lordy, you're going to be giving this little girl some high-and-mighty ideas and have her spoiled rotten in no time at all."

Effie winked at Rory. "I think her daddy's the one who'll be doing the spoiling." She offered Bonnie the bottle and cooed, "And then he'll take you for rides on his big towboats and show you how to keep an eye out for leaks so the tug doesn't sink right out from under you and how to line the work vests for the coast guard and measure cable and line and . . . "

The kitchen got unusually quiet, and Effie glanced up. Thelma and Rory stared at her as if she'd sprouted another nose. "What? You don't want Bonnie on a towboat? I just assumed that you'd—"

Rory said, "She'll be steering a tow and running barges before she's driving a car." He arched his left eyebrow. "But what's all this malarkey about checking for leaks and lining up the vests? Where the devil did that come from? What kind of books have you been reading?"

"And I suppose the coast guard doesn't mind if the deck is spotless or not?"

Rory shrugged. "It's a work boat. It gets hosed down from time to time, painted as need be, but that's about it." He scratched his head. "You been reading some kind of books or . . . or . . ."

His eyes met hers, widened, and he let out a whistle. "Oh, boy."

"Yeah, and I'm going to string oh boy up by his—" Balls, she thought, but instead said, "Toenails." There was a baby present. "The boy had me running all over that tug, checking out stuff and doing whatever else came into his little pea brain." She eyed Rory. "You have two other sons. You won't even miss this one."

Rory chuckled. "I don't know what's going on, but I sure can't picture you letting Ryan order you around, telling you to do this and that. You don't seem the sort who'd stand still for such a thing."

"I'm not," Effie growled, feeling as if she had a sign with *I'm a gullible stupid-ass* hanging around her neck. She set Bonnie on her lap, snagged the burp towel from the top of the pumpkin seat and gently patted the baby's back. "I fell for the oldest male trick in the book. Ryan said I wasn't up to working on the tow because I was a woman.

Said he'd drop me off in Memphis to get my nails done instead."

Rory laughed, joined by Thelma. Tears trickled down her face. "Have mercy. I sure wish I'd been a fly on the wall when that conversation happened."

Rory swiped his own tears. "Then Ryan proceeded to order you about?"

"Ryan and I are always trying to outdo each other. I couldn't very well not do what he said or I'd look like a big female wuss. Bet he's off somewhere laughing his butt off right now."

"Or running for his life if he knows what's good for him," Thelma added on another chuckle.

Effie handed Bonnie to Rory. "Where'd that slimy piece of donkey dung you call a son go tonight?"

Thelma nodded to the door. "I'm guessing he's gone over to Slim's. It's the local watering hole around here where everyone gets together, especially at night. The place has the best cold beer and barbecue on earth, even beats mine. I sure do love Slim's."

Rory gently rocked Bonnie in his big strong arms and fed her the rest of the bottle. He winked up at Effie. "I'm bettin' there's going to be a hot time in town tonight. Some first-class hell-raising for sure. If it wasn't for Bonnie here, I'd be going with you just to get myself a front row seat for the action."

Effie stood. "I'll bring you an order of ribs and be tickled pink to give you a rundown on the evening's events."

Chapter 10

Damn the fucking heat and mosquitoes and black flies and gnats! Conrad grabbed his shirttail and swiped sweat from his forehead. The early evening sat sweltering and still. Fuck! Was there any other way on the fucking Mississippi in fucking July? Except this day in July he was digging up his own fucking backyard instead of downing cool martinis—extra dry with two olives—at the fucking country club and trying to decide between the fucking poached salmon or the fucking breaded veal for dinner. Fuck!

He dropped the shovel and yanked off his work gloves. Blisters across his palms! Three with ragged broken skin, watery and hurting like hell, the rest just waiting for the opportunity to pop and get gross and ugly. He glanced down at his favorite old tennis shoes he usually wore when lounging around the house. Covered in red Tennessee dirt. And what the fuck was that godawful smell that followed him everywhere. Did something die out here?

He looked at his cobalt blue Ralph Lauren shirt now stained with circles of sweat. He sniffed the material. Oh, God, that odor was him! He smelled like a fucking sewer! He kicked at the shovel on the ground, putting another smear on his shoes. How much did he have to endure for a million bucks? Why did a Martha Stewart clone have to get this inheritance? Why not a Jennifer Lopez clone?

"Conrad," Thelma called in a cheery voice as she rounded the house from the front, carrying a basket. She waved and smiled. "There you . . ." Her words faded as she came up beside him. She looked from him to the two-foot-deep patch of ground that covered about five hundred square feet. "What . . . What did you do?"

Damn near killed myself to impress you, he thought but said, "What's wrong?" Good grief, what did he have to do to please her? Turn back flips across the damn lawn while spitting fire? Probably be easier than this!

"I can't believe you did this."

"I dug a hole."

"You dug up all the rest of the area where the patio is going to be and . . . and you even laid out some of the bricks."

She looked him dead in the eyes. "You worked much too hard in this heat. You should have waited 'til tomorrow for me to come back and help you. But . . . but . . ."

She put down the basket and wagged her head and pointed to the space he'd dug, deep enough for the gravel and then sand and bricks on top. She said, "You curved the edges. It softens the appearance, and it looks so elegant. The design's perfect for the house."

She pointed to the bricks he'd laid out to get a feel for the design. "A basket-weave pattern? It's formal but graceful."

Big fucking deal! But he said, "Well, I have to take the bricks up and put down more sand and tamp for a solid foundation. This was a sample of what's to come." What was to come was more fucking work. He was a damn laborer.

"How'd you do this?"

Sweated my ass off. He slapped a smile on his face. "A

brick patio isn't exactly a bridge or dam or an expressway, but I know how to do it."

"It's really going to be beautiful, Conrad. Your dad would love it." She beamed at him as if he were some kind of god. First time anyone had ever looked at him that way.

"You're wonderful." She put the basket down on the grass, then kissed him on the cheek. She didn't seem to care he was hot and sweaty and dirty. He thought of all the jewelry he'd given to women and vacations he'd taken them on and fancy dinners he'd bought, and he couldn't honestly remember any woman ever saying anything more than the obligatory thanks. Then he dug this hole in the ground, and Thelma went all ape-shit. Dumb broad. Over a stupid hole in the ground and some bricks. Amazing.

No, what was amazing was that Thelma McAllister was such an easy mark that it scared him.

"Is something wrong, Conrad?"

"Not a thing." Actually everything was perfect. He should astound her a little more. "I plan on adding a matching walkway down to the creek, to that gazebo we talked about."

"A lovely place in the spring when the creek's flowing fast and in the fall when the leaves are turning."

Simpleton! He looked deep into her eyes. "I'm glad you like it, Thelma. I thought of you when I made the plans." He wasn't lying about that!

She stared back, her eyes not leaving his. She blushed and looked away. "I . . . I brought you dinner."

Stammering was a good sign. Meant she wasn't in control. Something was happening to her. He chuckled to himself. Conrad Hastings was what was happening to her.

She continued, "I have fried chicken and fresh green beans from my garden and pecan pie." She gave a nervous little laugh. "Can't have a picnic without my pecan pie."

"That wasn't necessary. I'll get cleaned up, and we can

go to the country club for dinner." Though she was dressed in cheap slacks and cotton T-shirt. He frowned at that, then realized she was frowning, too, least her eyes were. Her lips seemed frozen in a smile. Oh, God, what now?

Shit. He'd just insulted her stupid fried chicken. Nice going, Hastings! Great way to snare a two-million-dollar sucker. His gaze met hers. "Not that your chicken doesn't sound wonderful, my dear," he recanted. "I just meant that you deserve a night out because you helped me with the patio this afternoon. My way of saying thank you."

His stomach rolled as he thought of greasy chicken instead of poached salmon. "But since you fried the chicken and did all this work, we'll go to the club some other time."

"You need to eat something right now, Conrad. You're looking worn as an old kitchen towel."

Tennesseeisms, just what he wanted from his future wife. "You set the dining room table inside, and I'll grab a quick shower and then—"

"You should eat first, just a few bites. I bet you haven't eaten all day. You didn't eat anything when we worked earlier." She pulled a plaid blanket from the basket, fluffed it into the air and it settled onto the grass under the oak that he intended to shade a corner of the patio against the brutal western summer sun. That's why he designed the patio to curve at the end, to wrap around the oak.

"Sit down," she said. "Then you can shower." She peered at him hard. "You're starting to look peaked."

"I'm filthy. I'll get your blanket dirty, and I can't eat with such grimy hands." Though he suddenly did feel a bit weak. Working all day in this heat wasn't his strong suit, or any suit since he'd never done it before.

"The blanket will wash." She gently took his hands and tugged him down beside her. It seemed easier to just do what she wanted than not. Besides, he suddenly felt tired to the bone, a little shaky. She didn't let go of his hands when he parked across from her. She touched his palm. "Oh, Conrad."

"My hands are a mess."

"What terrible blisters." She pulled an insulated bowl from the basket, peeled off the lid, scooped a glob onto a plate and set it in his lap. She handed him a fork. "You eat a few bites, and I'll go inside and get some ointment and a washcloth." She stood.

"But—"

"I'll find it on my own, you just relax," she called as she made for the house.

"There's a first aid kit in the kitchen pantry," he called after her.

He looked at the mayo-covered potatoes and celery and eggs and bacon bits. Botulism in a bowl. He made a face. Maybe he could just fling a blob somewhere and she'd think he'd eaten it. Then he looked up and saw her coming out of the house carrying a tray.

Damn! Too late for flinging. He forked up a little dab, prayed his antibodies were up to the challenge, then smiled at Thelma as he held up the offering. He put it in his mouth.

It tasted cold and fresh and totally . . . incredible. Not too tart, not sweet, perfect. Thelma might dress for shit, but the woman could cook. A novel diversion from the glitzy women he usually dated. Their idea of cooking was dumping water into the coffeemaker. Homemade meant spooning carryout onto plates.

She put the tray with soap, towel, pan of water and the first aid kit on the blanket and knelt down beside him. "Now let me see your hands. I want to wash the blisters and put on ointment and a Band-Aid."

"In a minute." Maybe he'd just overreacted to how good the salad tasted because he was so hungry. He scooped up another forkful and ate it. Nope, same incredible taste. "This is really good, Thelma," he said around a mouthful. And he meant it. Probably the first thing he'd said to her that he did mean without some hidden agenda attached.

"Why, thank you, Conrad." She smiled and took his left hand and gently washed it. Her touch was soft and caring as she washed the blisters and applied ointment and gauze. "This will last 'til after we eat. Then you can shower, and we'll do a better job of getting you fixed up."

We. Whoa, baby! He was making great inroads, and it was nice to have a woman dote on him for a change. Usually he did the damn doting . . . frequently to get into some woman's pants. But this time he didn't give a flying-fuck about screwing.

"I have fresh-squeezed lemonade."

His parched mouth watered at the suggestion. "This is a great picnic." Least he'd eat well for the next year and have someone around who truly seemed to . . . care about his well-being. Hell, that had never come up before.

He studied Thelma for a moment. She was easy enough to get along with. Not that it mattered, he reminded himself. What did matter was the money she brought to the table and the share he'd walk away with.

Since things were going so well tonight it gave him a perfect opportunity to step things up to the next level. He only had about a week to get her to marry him; that didn't leave much time, even for someone as smooth as Conrad Hastings. He watched as she loaded his plate with fried chicken, more potato salad, biscuits and green beans. She had a twinkle in her eyes. And she hummed?

He laughed to himself. Holy shit, she was crazy about him. All the blisters, bugs and sweat were worth it. She was in awe of him. He had her right where he wanted her.

He picked up a drumstick and bit into it. Damn! Good as the potato salad.

She took a bite of green beans and said to him, "The way you're going at that chicken leg, I don't think you've eaten in a month."

He laughed and wagged the drumstick at her. He needed to keep things folksy between them, down-home and cozy, nothing highfalutin. "It's your cooking. I haven't tasted food like this since . . . since my mom."

Oh, that was good. Very down-home, very Tennessee. And, wonder-of-wonders, true. "Boy, she could cook. You're so much like her." He studied Thelma for a second. Damn, another truism.

"I didn't know your mama, but I'll take that as a compliment."

He wolfed down the potato salad and helped himself to more.

"Why are you doing this, Conrad?"

He nearly dropped his plate. Alarm snaked up his spine. What had he done wrong to tip his hand? "Ah, what do you mean, my dear?"

She waved her fork over the yard. "All this work? You could have paid to have it done, but you didn't. Why do it yourself?"

"For you, of course. Yesterday we had fun together. We grilled out and planned the patio and decided what we needed to order from that Lowes place. You like doing things yourself and so do I. I never knew that about you, Thelma."

He nearly choked on his own words. "I wanted to do this for you." He put down his plate and then put hers down, too. He took her hands in his and assumed his most sincere look. "I like being together, Thelma. I like spending time with you . . . It's the highlight of my life. I can't wait to see you each day and talk to you on the phone and make plans with you."

He nodded to the shallow hole that had nearly killed

him to dig and said in a low voice, "I did this because you enjoy it. And it's something we did together. I did it for us."

Her eyes rounded to the size of softballs. "Us?"

Gotcha! He kissed her, his lips caressing hers, lingering. Then he eased his tongue inside her mouth. She gasped, taking his tongue in deep. Her body tensed at the sensation; then she relaxed. She didn't pull away but leaned toward him, her lips widening but not with the ease of someone used to French kissing. She held his shoulders, her fingers shaky. Then her hands went to the back of his neck, stroking him in short, clumsy gestures. Her tongue finally connected with his, and he felt her body shudder and a little whine sound deep in her throat.

He ran his hands around her back, holding her tighter, coaxing her from a sitting position to slide toward him so her torso connected with his and her legs curled against his. He could feel her breasts growing firm against his chest, her nipples hardening through her blouse and his shirt. She was a little chunky and not much to look at, but at least she had a decent set of knockers.

"Oh, Conrad." She breathed his name into his mouth. She looked at him, her eyes clouded with passion. "I don't understand what you do to me. I've never felt this way before."

"Neither have I," he said in return, faking breathiness of his own. And he really hadn't ever felt this way because he'd never seduced a woman for money before. What a piece of cake.

He licked her bottom lip, her eyes widening. "You're so sweet," he said after he released her. "So sexy."

"Sexy?"

To convince her, his mouth covered hers again, careful not to move fast. He didn't want to scare her, just tantalize, suggest what she could have. Thelma was not an experienced lover, that was obvious. Luring her into his little trap just kept getting easier and easier. His tongue teased hers, darting then flirting. At first she didn't seem to know what to do, how to play. Then her tongue and lips imitated his.

Least she was a quick study and her kisses weren't sloppy. He hated a sloppy kisser. And she didn't smell bad, some floral scent, not too disgusting, but no designer fragrance. His fingers inched down her back and slid under her cheap T-shirt. Good. Another indication of a low-maintenance wife. That left more money for him. His fingers touched her bare skin at her waist, and she seemed to freeze in place.

Uh oh, too fast. He didn't need to alarm her. He needed to give her motivation as to why he felt as he did and get her to cooperate.

He took his mouth from hers, faking more short pants. "Thelma, we're going too fast. We need to slow down. You . . . excite me more than I thought possible." That sounded pretty good.

He pulled his hands away from her back and sat upright, taking his chest from hers and separating them. He ran his hand over his face, studying her from between his fingers to judge her reaction to this sudden change of pace. She didn't look thrilled that he'd pulled away.

Great! "I want us to take our time. Enjoy each other." He looked back at her. "I want us to get to know each other little by little."

He stood. "I think you should go." He studied her reaction from the corner of his eyes. She looked confused, as if she didn't understand and, most important, she looked turned on.

He continued, "We both should get our bearings and figure out what we're doing and what we want. This is all happening so fast for me." He glanced at the uneaten potato salad and chicken. His insides wept. Flipping hell! What fantastic food and now he had to leave it. He should have eaten more chicken when he had the chance.

"But Conrad . . ." She sounded as if his leaving her defied all reason. He wanted the next move to come from her, the ideal disguise for throwing her off track in case she suspected ulterior motives. And even if she didn't, those interfering O'Fallons might and get antsy over this big rush act. She could tell them that spending time together was her idea as much as his.

"Thelma." He reached down and framed her face in his hands, his expression sorrowful. "What will people think? That I'm rushing you?"

"You're not rushing me. I'm an adult. I do know what I'm doing." A hint of desperation laced her words. He gave her his best fake sad grin, the one he usually saved for women when he told them he wasn't good enough for them and they could do better. Course, that led to a few more dates and some really good sex, and when the end came they both felt satisfied.

He knelt down on one knee and put the covering back on the potato salad and placed it in the basket. "We can picnic some other time."

He reached for the chicken, wondering if he could take a couple of bites without blowing his cover. Damn, not really. No chicken. He wouldn't look too sincere and forlorn with a chicken leg in his mouth.

"I don't care what anyone says. This is between you and me."

"I'm not good enough for you, Thelma." He cupped her chin in his palm. "I know that now. Everyone around here knows that." Self-condemnation always evoked sympathy. He stood. "I'll call you . . . later, maybe next week."

"You don't want to see me anymore?" She sounded so upset. Yes!

He stood and held his hands out to her in a hopeless gesture. "Of course I do, but you . . ." He trailed the words off, looking devastated.

She stood. "But what?"

He took her in a reckless embrace and pulled her hard against him. "You turn me on," he ground out, then captured her mouth in a wild fevered kiss, enticing her with long thrusts of his tongue, as if unable to restrain himself or resist her. He let her go and stepped away, making his steps unsteady and gasping for breath. "I can't be around you right now. I want you too badly, and we need time."

He trudged off toward the house, remembering to keep his head low, giving the impression of a depressed man caught in the throes of unfulfilled sexual desire and willing to sacrifice himself for the good of his woman. She'd think about him all night, get horny as a toad and come back tomorrow wanting sex. Her idea, not his! A much better approach.

In two days he'd propose, feign rapture and absolute need to make her his, and then they'd elope. He'd sell the Ferrari to buy a ring and have lots left over for the mutual investment thing Arthur insisted on. A guy in Memphis created paste mock-ups that looked like real diamonds enough to fool Thelma McAllister, least 'til the divorce. Then who gave a shit.

Four days, five tops, and the little pigeon was all his . . . along with a million bucks. He could feel her watching him as he went into the house. He rounded the corner of the hallway, then peeked back out through the panes of the door so he could see her outside with little chance of her seeing him.

He laughed out loud, the sound echoing through the empty house. She looked confused and hungry and not for food. She wanted him bad. He jammed his hands in his pockets and headed for the stairs, whistling "Happy Days

Are Here Again." He needed a shower. The clock on the living room mantel chimed seven. If he hurried, he could make dinner at the club. Poached salmon tonight. He waited for his taste buds to salivate at the thought . . . and they did, except not over poached salmon but the best fried chicken he'd ever put in his mouth.

Thelma watched Conrad go into the house. Well, heck! What had made him leave her at the exact moment she wanted more!

She scraped the remains of their uneaten food in a bag and put everything back in the basket, thinking about his explanation. He'd left because she turned him on? Well, guess what, he turned her on, too. But why'd he leave just when things were getting very interesting!

She headed for her car and sat in the driver's side, gazing at the big brick house. She didn't want Conrad to take things slower for her sake. She didn't need time for them to get used to each other. She wanted Conrad, the new and improved version, with her here now.

Romance had passed her by on more than one occasion, more like two occasions and at break-neck speed and neither all that terrific once they found out she couldn't be used as an easy roll in the hay. Damn humiliating to be used by a guy for sex or any other reason.

But this time terrific seemed very possible. The only thing missing was Conrad, and he wasn't after anything. Since he left her, she'd have to go to him . . . or did she? She nibbled her bottom lip. Could she really do that, be so forward? Then again, could she not?

She summoned every ounce of courage she possessed and climbed out of the Sunfire, went to the front door, picked up the heavy brass knocker and felt her courage vanish like the fog over the river. She turned and headed back to the car.

What a chicken! Except being on the fading side of forty

didn't give her time for chicken. She needed to grab romance now or lose out again, maybe forever. She ran back up the steps, yanked open the door—because if she knocked, she'd lose her nerve again—and went inside. Her heart raced as she reminded herself to breathe so as not to pass out right in the middle of Conrad's hallway. The quiet of the house surrounded her. She got herself this far, now what?

She searched the front room for Conrad, then the kitchen. Nothing. She went back to the hallway. What would she do with Conrad when she found him? She considered the question, and a warm, excited feeling swept through her, leaving her dizzy, a little off balance and a lot horny. Oh, she'd had sex before, just not the warm, exciting, dizzy, off-balance kind. More like the wham-bam-slam thank-you-ma'am kind.

Was that water running from upstairs? The shower Conrad had talked about. She gritted her teeth and ran up the steps, basic lust spurring her on. Whistling trailed down the hall toward her, and she followed the tune of "Happy Days Are Here Again." Was that a good omen or what!

Conrad's bedroom? She entered and eyed the open bathroom door as the whistling continued. She'd never been in a man's bedroom before, except the O'Fallons' for cleaning and redecorating. Conrad didn't need to redecorate anything. What great taste. Very expensive taste. So why did he choose to go out with her? Why was Thelma McAllister here now in his bedroom and not some other woman?

She spied his dirty shirt on the floor. Because Conrad had changed just like he said, and if he could change, so could she. She'd waited all her life for something to happen, for someone special to come her way. And now he had, and she needed to make the next move. No more waiting.

More "Happy Days" floated from the bathroom. Did that mean Conrad wanted her as much as she wanted him? What else could it mean? And he didn't act on his feeling because he wanted her to be sure? Well, right now she felt plenty sure enough for both of them.

She whipped off her T-shirt, kicked off her sandals, yanked off her slacks and bra and panties. She squared her shoulders, pushed up her boobs, encouraging them to perk up. She summoned all her courage as she padded her way across the Oriental rug and pushed the bathroom door wide open. Rolls of steam billowed out, a small Jacuzzi sat in one corner, the fogged glass-enclosed shower stall stood in the other.

She opened it, and Conrad stopped mid whistle and stared wide-eyed, his mouth slightly open. Suds trailed down his middle, bisecting his firm chest, navel, then over his nonexistent arousal. Well, she'd change that quick enough. "Move over, Conrad. You have company. Your happy day's about to get even happier."

Did she really say that? Hell, yes! She stepped into the massive shower and closed the door behind her. Droplets fell around them in a steady rhythm, her heart beating like the drums in a Beach Boys song. "I've come to wash your back . . . and front." Then she kissed his open mouth. "And every other part of you so you better hold on to your butt, or better yet, hold on to mine."

She winked and kissed him again, this time her tongue insinuating what she wanted to do while here. But what did he want? Up 'til now she'd called the shots. What if he didn't want her here at all?

He grinned, slowly at first; then it covered his face. "What a surprise."

"Me, too."

This time he kissed her, his hot wet lips moving hungrily over her, his tongue possessing hers as his arms took her in an enthusiastic embrace. "Damn, you never cease to surprise me, woman." He chuckled.

"Yeah, well, this time I pretty much surprised the hell out of me, too." She bit her bottom lip, water trickling over her face and off the end of her chin. "Uh, is this a good surprise or a bad one?"

His gaze and his palms slid around the curves of her breasts, making them feel full and heavy and incredibly perky. Her heartbeat kicked up another notch, and a slow grin curved his lips. His eyes connected with hers. "This is good, very good, my dear. Better than you can ever imagine."

Chapter 11

Thelma smiled at Conrad, some of the tension eating at her fading away. "Your hair looks good even in the shower. In fact, all of you looks good in the shower." She glanced around. "I've never been in a shower with so many jets and even a bench. And we don't have to worry about getting pregnant. Menopause does have its advantages."

He laughed, the rich sound echoing against the tiled walls. "You do think of everything."

"I . . . I like you, Conrad. I really like you." Heat rushed to her cheeks. "I know this is awfully forward of me, but I don't want to wait for . . . anything. We aren't kids anymore; we know what we're doing."

Ha! She hadn't a clue. This was purely a hormone-driven decision.

"I'm glad you're here, Thelma." He bent his head to hers. "I can tell you're nervous, so I'm going to kiss you and you'll know everything's okay." He brushed his wet lips against hers, then gave her a reassuring kiss. "Now I'll show you that this is more than okay." His mouth covered hers, completely taking her breath away. Holy Lord!

Droplets and steam swirled around them. "I feel like we're the only two people on earth," she panted against his enticing lips.

"Me, too," he said in an emotional voice. Then his tongue stroked hers, and his body molded to hers. His knee slid between her legs, parting them, then inched up between her thighs and connected with her hot wet mound. She held onto his shoulders for support as her legs parted more, and his thigh pressed a bit harder, slid deeper between her legs, 'til his leg perched on the bench behind her.

His hands skimmed down her back and cupped her derriere, and he pulled her hips firmly to his own. She seemed to be perched on his knee, one thigh on each side, the pressure against her sex making her desperate to have him. She glanced down at his erection. She'd never seen one in daylight before, except in books or magazines, but not in the flesh. This was definitely the flesh.

"I want to wash your hair, Thelma. You have such wonderful hair, all thick and rich and brown with strands of pure gold when lit by the sun."

He caught droplets on his tongue, then slid them into her mouth. Her insides flamed, her legs opened wider. "Conrad." She could barely get out his name. "I can think of other things besides washing my hair right now."

He kissed her again, his tongue now sliding in and out of her mouth in smooth, silky steady strokes that set her on fire. "I want to see bubbles slide off the tips of your lovely nipples and across your belly and tangle in the silky patch of dark curls below."

He took the shampoo bottle from the rack and squeezed a creamy dollop into his palm. He massaged it into her hair, gentle strokes as his leg moved, mimicking the stroking motion between her legs, the coarse hairs of his thigh against her sensitive lips making her heart palpitate with the same rhythm and her insides quiver in anticipation.

Suds trickled down her head. "Close your eyes, Thelma. You'll get soap in them."

She did as he said, making his touches and strokes all the more tantalizing and seductive. "What are you doing to me, Conrad?"

"I want to pleasure every inch of you, Thelma. I want to make love to you in a way you'll never forget."

"Forget? There's no danger of that happening." She felt his finger sear a path from the tip of her chin, down her throat that shuddered from his touch, over her left breast that swelled with expectation, stopping at the peak of her stiff nipple. She gasped as he rolled her beaded nub between his thumb and finger. She couldn't open her eyes or she'd get soap in them. All she could do was revel in the unbelievable sensation of Conrad's lovemaking. "You're cheating. I can't even watch you."

"You don't need to watch. Just feel me, Thelma. Feel me do things to you, make you as happy as you make me." His arousal moved against her; his lips met hers, his fingers still tugging gently at her beaded nubs driving her wild. "And there's so much to come."

Then his clever fingers trailed a path across the underside of her breasts, across her middle, lingering at her belly button, finally stopping where he'd wedged his thigh between hers. Her eyes flew open; her heartbeat thudded out of control as his finger tangled into the wet curls, teasing the tender flesh underneath before sliding into the slick softness between.

"Oh, Conrad," she whimpered, her head falling back, letting the gentle rain of the shower fall on her face.

"I'm right here, Thelma," he whispered in her ear. His leg dropped away, and his fingers gently fondled her clit. She gasped, not expecting the incredible sensation roaring through her now. "Open your legs for me wider, sweetheart. Let me touch you more."

Then his fingers fondled her again, giving her more pleasure than any man ever had. Her body trembled with every invasion of his finger, then two fingers, and she wasn't prepared for the swift climax that suddenly overtook her as his fingers plunged deeper, again and again with each thrust.

"Conrad!" She called as she held onto him. The world around her was suddenly white-hot, her body rigid with a new sensation that set her on fire in an explosive climax that surely rocked the world.

Well, hot damn! Happy days were here faster than he'd planned, Conrad thought as he held Thelma close, her body tight to his, shuddering in climax. She responded so easily to his touch, so completely. Who would have thought?

He kissed her hard, her full, swollen lips melting against his. He turned them around and sat on the bench. "Make love to me, Thelma."

She stared at him, her eyes wide. "I've never—"

He cupped her ample hips with his hands and pulled her close. It was good to feel real woman, some flesh, and not skin and bones like others he'd taken to bed. "Let me help you." He wedged his knees between her legs as he brought her to him. He parted her legs with his. "You're beautiful like this, Thelma. A woman ready for making love is irresistible to a man."

"You find me irresistible?"

"You have no idea." And, he meant it, because . . . because of the money, that was it. "Put your hands on my shoulders and just ease onto me, sweetheart. Take your time, let yourself get the feel of me inside you."

She looked from his engorged penis to his face and swallowed. "You're so big."

He grinned. "And you're a flatterer."

She gave him a tentative smile. "I'm serious. What if I hurt you? What if I'm not big enough for you? There seems to be pretty much there, Conrad."

"This won't hurt, Thelma. I promise."

She bit her lip and spread her legs wider and lowered

herself 'til her heat touched his tip. Her gaze fused to his as she sucked in a quick breath. "That's it, sweetheart," he encouraged. "Let me have you, every sweet inch of you."

He tugged on her hips; her skin was like velvet. He brought her down, her body opening for his, letting him gradually slide into her heat.

"You're so ready for me. We were made to make love like this."

Her face flushed, her breaths becoming shallow as she lowered herself more, his erection suddenly throbbing with anticipation. Not that self-control was a problem. He knew how to keep himself in check, waiting for the woman to climax before achieving his own release. He prided himself on women coming before he did. He was a terrific lover, and he intended for Thelma to climax at least once more before he did. He wanted her to find him irresistible.

Her body relaxed more, letting him fill her deeper. She gasped, and her mouth suddenly found his in a kiss. He hadn't expected that. Usually women were intent on the sex part, the actual intercourse, and nothing so emotional as a kiss. And this kiss was emotional, filled with sweetness and caring and the need to have him close.

Then she suddenly let herself all the way down, taking him fully inside her body. He gasped. Hell, he never gasped, and she kissed him harder, her mouth suddenly devouring his as she slid him in and out of her body in a frantic rhythm. He hadn't expected this or her ability to arouse him so quickly, bringing him to the brink. "Slow down, sweetheart."

"I can't," she gasped, her movements faster, her heat stroking his. "You are an incredible lover, Conrad."

Her sweetness, her freshness, her complete giving of her body and her heart to him overwhelmed him. His hips arched up, his thrusts in rhythm with hers, filling her harder and deeper each time, his excitement and desire to have her out of control spilled over to himself as he climaxed in her with a raw, unrestrained release that shocked him. He felt Thelma's climax as she trembled in his arms, her sex tightening around his dick, her face buried in his neck as the spasms rocked her head to foot.

Her body continued to shudder, or was that his, as the warm water rained over them. The steam was coming from their bodies more than the water, he was sure.

"Conrad," she whispered in a ragged breath in his ear. "That was incredible."

And it was. He couldn't remember the last time he'd climaxed like that. Usually it was a mutual form of . . . recreation more than anything else. But this . . . This recreated the hell out of him.

"Where did you learn so much about sex?"

She looked up at him, her eyes bright, and she smiled sweetly. "From you." Then she kissed him and placed his hands on her breasts. "Let's do it again."

And he realized that's exactly what he wanted to do as his tongue mated with hers. How could this happen? How could he want to take her again so quickly? Her breasts swelled at his touch. Her hips arched against him. His muscles hardened, and he gazed into her beautiful brown eyes.

It was the lure of the money, that was it. That's why he couldn't get enough of her. The money!

Ryan walked toward town, needing to get away from the mall plans and Effie. Perspiration pasted his T-shirt to his body like a second skin as the late afternoon sun baked the Landing. A few insects darted here and there, but even bugs had enough sense to stay out of the boiling sun at this time of day. Too bad he didn't. He passed the bank already closed for the day, then Burgers-n-Bait. The town did need a facelift, bad. He waved to Betty Lindel ringing up a customer at the market, passed Doc Shelton's, then crossed the street and headed for Slim's.

Smoke from the outdoor grills behind the bar swirled into the air, the scent of Memphis barbecue making his mouth water. No one did barbecue like Slim. If he could bottle the scent, he'd make a damn fortune.

Ryan pushed open the door. The sudden chill of air-conditioning set just above blizzard made him suck in a quick breath. The rhythm of B.B. Boogie vibrated through the old frame structure bedecked with photos of Slim and B.B. King, Carla Thomas, Ruby Wilson, Howlin' Wolf and Ryan's personal favorite, Aretha Franklin. Now, there was a voice.

Ryan sat at the bar, and Sally wandered over, her dark eyes and hair in perfect harmony with her dark skin. Ryan was sure all the boys in their class had had a crush on her at one time or another over the years, him included. She flashed him a wide grin. "Well, I'll be. Look what the cat finally dragged in."

She popped the top from a cold beer, put it on the bar, leaned across it and kissed Ryan full on the lips. "'Bout damn time you got your sorry white ass back home to see your own baby." She winked. "But I know you, Ryan O'Fallon. I'm guessing there's more going on there than meets the eye."

Ryan took a long, cool swig. "Just because you got an MBA from Harvard you think you know everything."

She laughed and quirked an eyebrow. "Keep it down, okay. Give the place a bad name with talk like that."

He laughed in return. "Too late, everybody already knows all about you."

"Yeah, but you don't have to keep reminding 'em." Sally took a sip of his beer. "Where's Bonnie? Your dad hasn't brought her in today. We're going to introduce her to the sounds of Rosco Gordon. Get her used to the good stuff."

"He's feeding her right now."

Sally tipped her head with suspicion. "Not you?"

"It's a granddaddy thing."

"Sure it is." She gave him a look that said she wasn't buying any of the bullshit story he was selling. He bent across the bar, leaning on his elbows and keeping his voice low enough to get drowned out except for Sally. "How well did you know Mimi DuPont while she was here?"

Sally pursed her lips. "Do I get to know why you're asking?"

"This is just between us, and you can probably figure it out."

She considered that for a moment, and her eyes sparked. "Mimi and Rory? Well, that sure makes more sense than the talk that's going around about you and Bonnie." Sally wagged her head. "Wish I could help, but I don't know anything about Mimi really. Nice gal. Liked Rory, made him real happy." She chuckled. "Obviously happier than I thought, but I'll keep that bit of information to myself since I'm guessing that's the way you all want it to be for some reason."

"Anyone ever come asking about her?"

"A guy nosing around last week, but before that nothing. I don't know anyone around here who she got friendly with. Not even Thelma. Mimi just kept to herself."

"Any strangers poking around since?"

"Always new crew and captains for the tows, so it's hard to tell who's poking and who's just getting acquainted." She shrugged. "But I'll keep an eye out."

Ryan nodded his thanks, then sat back. "You getting bored around here yet and ready to head on back to New York City and play the business game with the big boys again?"

"Hell, no!" She let out a hardy laugh that drew a few looks. "Not in this lifetime. Three years on Wall Street

about did me in. I don't need to be on ulcer pills and looking at triple bypass before I'm forty."

And Slim needed her to help run the place after her
mama died. Sally continued, "I'm right where I want to be
and tickled pink. Besides"—she winked—"I got myself a
new beau, and he's a real pretty one."

Ryan slowly shook his head. "You didn't wait for me?"

"Last time I checked hell hadn't frozen over. I'm afraid
you and I passed that stage a long time ago. I've been seeing a guy for about two months now. He's a real estate in-
vestor from Nashville. Going up and down the Mississippi
scooping out a place to build retirement homes for the
empty-nester set. Asking a million questions about the
Landing, the people here, wanting to know if they accept
outsiders and the like. I think he's really interested in the
place. Could be good for the local economy, and the town
could use some sprucing up."

She took another sip of Ryan's beer. "With Conrad's dry
dock not doing too good people need more jobs to fill in.
That man sure can spend money. Too bad he doesn't know
as much about making it."

"I think he knows. I don't think he cares." Ryan looked
around. "Is your man here now? I got some stories about
you that could curl his hair."

"His hair's straight, and let's keep it that way. Besides, if
we're sharing stories, the ones about you way outshine
mine." They laughed over old times; then his gaze suddenly
met hers, and he remembered a particular time in a fishing
boat. One starry spring night on the banks of the
Mississippi when angling for catfish turned into angling
for a whole lot more and they lost their virginity to each
other. He smiled at Sally, and she smiled in return, a slow
smile that turned her face soft and warm and totally beautiful as if remembering exactly the same thing. They never
made love again, their attraction more deep friendship
than intimate. But no one ever forgot their first time.

"His name's Demar," she said, interrupting both their thoughts and bringing them back to the present. "And he's back in Nashville 'til tomorrow. You'll like him."

Ryan took Sally's hand and kissed the back. He kept her hands for a moment and said, "What matters to me is that you like him and he treats you good."

Her eyes danced, and she gave him a slow, easy grin. "He treats me just fine. And I do like him. So does Dad." She hitched her chin toward the back door. "He's out back grilling. You can ask him when he comes in."

"Smelled the barbecue all the way here, drove me crazy. Didn't realize how much I missed it 'til now."

"That's the way the Landing is. When you come home you realize just how good it is. If you play a little something for the customers, I bet Slim could be persuaded to give you dinner on the house. Bubba keeps his sax in the back, and you know he has extra reeds in the case. Bet he wouldn't mind."

"I should help Rory. Thelma's out tonight, and he could use an extra hand."

"What about that cute blonde you brought with you?"

"Effie?"

Sally winked. "How many did you bring?"

Heat crawled up his neck, and he nearly knocked over his beer. "We work together is all."

Sally rested her elbow on the bar and parked her chin in her hand. "You can save that line of crap for someone else. That look in your eye means this Effie's more than a work partner; she's got you all twisted up inside."

"There are extenuating circumstances."

"Honey, this Effie's got you. About damn time somebody did."

"Like hell."

Sally grinned. "Play some music, city boy."

Ryan stroked his chin. "Been a while for me."

Sally gave him a wicked grin. "I so doubt that."

He wagged his head. "Damn, I missed you."

"Yeah, me, too. Now you just got to figure out a way to keep yourself and that cute little blonde here."

"It's San Diego for me, and Effie has no interest in the Landing."

Sally set another beer in front of him. "Stupid, stupid man."

Effie pushed open the door to Slim's, the chill taking her breath away for a second. Some bluesy-jazzy song flowed through the room as her eyes adjusted to the dim interior and hovering cigarette smoke. She coughed and tried not to choke. What happened to the smoking and nonsmoking section? She sat at the back table and looked for Ryan.

"What'll it be?" asked a huge man in a barbecue-smeared apron with a gold ring in his left ear. She was cool with that; heck, she had one in her belly button.

"I don't have all day here."

She hadn't considered the eating aspect until she got out of the car and inhaled heaven-on-earth. With an aroma like that permeating the atmosphere, even Richard Simmons didn't stand a chance at not eating at Slim's. "Could I see a menu, please?"

He gave her a what's-a-menu look.

"Can you just bring me whatever you have cooking that smells so good?"

"Ribs, chicken, sausage."

Slim didn't seem the sort of man interested in answering a lot of questions about this being one item on the nonexistent menu of this establishment or three separate items. Discussing side dishes and beverages was definitely out. She went with, "Okay."

This time he gave her a dumb-tourist look and trudged off.

So much for blending in with the locals. More soul music filled the room as she looked for Ryan. That's why she came, to beat him about the neck and shoulders for tricking her into working like a deckhand. She'd bet her Italian shoes he'd done it as payback for the lunchroom betting pool. Whatever, she didn't appreciate it, and she intended to tell the big fat handsome, terrific-in-bed louse just that. She shook her head. She had to forget that last part, and he definitely wasn't fat. More lean and trim and muscled. Aw drat!

She checked the packed bar and tables but no Ryan, until she studied the lovely woman with the incredible voice and the man playing sax beside her. Effie blinked. Ryan on sax? And he was really good! He never played so much as the spoons back in California, and there it was, Ryan on sax!

The music captivated her. Who was she kidding. Ryan captivated her. He seemed part of the instrument, an extension of some part of him that she'd never seen before, and considering the last twenty-four hours she'd seen pretty darn much!

Her body swayed with the rhythm as did everyone else's. Her soul soared with the high notes and crashed with the low ones as the woman sang about no joy when he's gone. When the piece ended everyone clapped and whistled and Effie joined in, thanks to her granddad teaching her how to put her two little fingers in her mouth and whistle big-time. Course, her parents didn't appreciate this particular talent.

Ryan was incredible, least that's what she thought 'til he swooped the beautiful singer in his arms and kissed her full on the mouth.

More clapping and wolf whistles, this time without Effie because her breath lodged in her throat, her jaw dropped and her eyes popped. How could Ryan do that? How could he have frantic sex with her last night and less than twenty-four hours later be kissing another woman like that!

She'd kill him dead. The no-good, lying, two-timing son-of-a-bitch deserved it. She was more pissed off than before. She watched Ryan pack up the sax, put the case against the wall, then head for the door, stopping to talk to friends as he went. His woman headed for the bar and served up beers. Effie stood and followed Ryan as more misty music, from a recording this time, filled the place.

The door to Slim's closed behind her, and she followed Ryan down the step onto the sidewalk. She grabbed his arm, bringing him to a halt and turning him around to face her. "You dirty rotten pig."

He stared, his eyes round. "Effie? What are you doing here?"

"Ha! Didn't expect to see me, did you!" The heat outside matched the heat boiling in her gut. "I've come to beat you to a pulp."

"Why?"

"I have a list, and it's getting longer."

"Hey there, Ryan," a guy in jeans and a T-shirt called out. "How're you doing?" He nodded at Effie. "See you got yourself another pretty gal. You do have the knack, always did."

The man walked into Slim's, and Effie felt smoke curl from her ears. She pointed toward the man. "That's why. How can you do it? How can you be fooling around—"

"Wait." Ryan took her hand and dragged her off the sidewalk and toward the side of the building. "I don't think I want this little confrontation broadcasted all over the Landing. This place is ground-zero for gossip, and right now because of Bonnie I'm already in everyone's crosshairs."

He peered down at her. "What's got you so fired up?"

"You tricked me on that damn boat. You got me to do all kinds of stuff that didn't need doing just to show me who's boss." She half closed her eyes. "That was really, really, low, Ryan. Just because of my extracurricular lunch-room activities, and since when did you start saying fired up?"

"Always . . . except in California, and I didn't make you run all over the tow for the reason you think. I did it to get you used to the boat. You were a basket case sitting in the captain's chair."

She squared her shoulders. "Okay, so I was a little nervous. Big deal."

"You were heading for the lifeboats because I blew a horn. If you didn't get over it, you would have had a stroke when we started pulling and pushing those barges around in the river when we got to the *Annabelle Lee*. I should have dumped your sorry butt back on the dock, but I didn't have time for a fight, and you were in no mood to cooperate."

She waved her hands in the air. "Why didn't you just tell me all this in the first place?"

"Yeah, something like 'Oh, Effie, I think you should stroll around the tug and acquaint yourself with the aspects of a working barge,' was sure to get you off your ass and moving instead of having a death grip on that chair."

She folded her arms and tried to look pissed. "It could have worked."

"The only way you were going to move was if I told you that you weren't up to it because you were a woman. You hate that. You go ballistic when guys tell you that you can't do something because you're a woman."

"I do not go ballistic. I get . . . miffed. And what about the singer in there." Effie pointed to the building.

"What the hell does Sally have to do with you and me and the tug?"

She growled, "How can you be messing around with me one night and kissing her the next?"

"That wasn't a kiss."

"Well, you sure fooled the hell out of me, Mr. Sax . . . or should I say Sex!"

He raked his hair. "What I mean is it wasn't a kiss kind of kiss. Sally is a friend. We've known each other since birth. We're . . . friendly." He folded his arms and rocked back on his heels. A little smile slowly tipped the corners of his mouth, and he looked smug as hell. "Why, Effie Wilson, I do believe you're jealous."

Chapter 12

"Jealous?" Effie repeated the word. If the top of her head popped off, she wouldn't be surprised. "All that's between you and me are raging hormones and a big dose of curiosity, and that's been taken care of . . . twice!"

"So why the hell do you give a hoot who or how I kiss someone?"

That was a darn good question, wasn't it! She pulled in a deep breath and assumed a controlled look, though she was anything but. "I don't care, not really. More of a knee-jerk reaction triggered by my Dearborn-Emmerson experiences. I was feeling used, that's all. A member of the bedroom bingo club. One night me, one night that girl."

"Sally."

"Fact is, I don't really care if you screw every woman in Memphis and surrounding areas and tattoo every one of their names on your butt to keep track. Though it didn't seem to me your butt was big enough for all those names."

She turned and made for the sidewalk. "I have chicken, sausage, ribs waiting for me inside, and I intend to eat it or them or whatever turns up. I'm starved."

She rounded the corner, stomped onto the porch, yanked open the door and went inside. This time the air against her hot skin felt good as she made her way back to her table where the biggest platter of food she'd ever seen sat square in front of her chair. She didn't eat that much meat in a month. And there were potatoes and an ear of corn, and was that a pitcher of beer and a glass? If the food angels suddenly appeared and sang the theme song from *Cooking With Emeril*, she wouldn't have been surprised.

She sat down, fluffed a paper napkin onto her lap, tore off a piece of rib and did Effie Wilson's rendition of lion on the Serengeti. She polished it off down to the bone, then picked up the pitcher of beer and guzzled from the side like the frat boys did in college.

"Hi," came a voice beside her, talking over the music. Effie looked up at the pretty singer. "Mind if I join you?"

Effie nodded, her mouth too full of beer and food to form words. The woman sat and leaned forward to be heard. "Most of the time when women are mad at Ryan they come in here and cry, literally, into their beer. I like your reaction a lot better."

Effie swallowed, reminding herself to take smaller bites and gulps. "Yeah, I yell back."

"I know. Could hear you clear through the wall." She nodded behind the bar. "And you eat when you're mad, a woman after my own heart." She waved her hand over the feast.

"There is that." Effie's gaze met the woman's, her eyes bright, trusting and sincere. They shared a smile, and Effie said, "Once I got so hacked off at a guy I ate four boxes of those cupcakes with the pink marshmallow and coconut coating." She shivered at the memory. "Haven't been able to look at one since." She bit into a chicken leg, then held it up. "Much better than cupcakes."

"I did the same thing with six bags of Fritos. Haven't touched another in five years. Just the thought of them makes me cringe. I want you to know Ryan and I really are just friends. I wouldn't want you to be mad at him over me." She held out her hand to Effie. "I'm Sally Donaldson. My dad owns this place, and I've known Ryan forever."

"Ryan and I are just friends, too. We've known each other eighteen months, it just seems like forever and that's not necessarily a good thing."

"He's a great guy."

"Oh, the man's flipping terrific." Effie wiped her fingers on a napkin, then another, with barbecue nearly up to her elbows. She took Sally's hand and smiled. Out of the corner of her eyes she saw Thelma and Conrad enter and make their way to a table near the front.

"Now, there's a guy who's not so flipping terrific." Sally pursed her lips as she studied the couple. "Don't know what's going on with him and Thelma, but those two have been spending a whole lot of time together the last few days, and I can't imagine why. They're nothing at all alike. Why would Thelma have anything to do with Conrad Hastings?"

Sally turned back to Effie. "Has Thelma said anything to you in explanation, or do you think she's just plain lost her ever-loving mind?"

"She says he makes her happy."

"So does rocky-road ice cream and that makes a lot more sense."

"She sort of floats around the house and looks like she's in a trance." Effie gulped some beer, picked up a sausage and bit, grease trickling off her fingers. She licked her thumb. "I've been trying to convince Ryan something's up with Conrad, but all Ryan sees is a changed man who now realizes what a wonderful woman Thelma is, just like the rest of us do, and wants her in his life. Ryan says there's no reason to think otherwise."

"That's too simple an explanation for my taste, but it's pretty much the way everyone else sees it. I have to agree there's really no other reason for Conrad to date Thelma other than he likes her. And, giving the devil his due, Conrad has been acting kind of nice to people these last few days. But this is all so sudden, too sudden, like he woke up one day, had some kind of epiphany and turned his whole life around. I like Thelma, I don't want her hurt and I have a bad feeling this has hurt written all over it."

"Amen." Effie felt a little light-headed, the result of guzzling beer straight from the pitcher. She waved a rib bone at Sally. "I dated guys like Conrad."

Sally nodded as she snagged a chunk of sausage from Effie's plate. "Yeah, sooner or later we all date a Conrad. But with Thelma it's looking kind of serious, like they skipped the dating stage and went right to enamored."

"She convinced him to build a patio, as in doing all the work himself."

Sally's eyes rounded huge. "Oh, shit. He's making his move, trying to impress Thelma." She snagged a grilled potato. "I dated a sleaze like that in grad school. All he wanted was me to get him through microeconomics. He acted sweet and cooked for me until he got his 'A' in the class. Then it was sayonara, baby." She ate the potato and said around a mouthful, "I've known Thelma a long time; she's a good person. I have to find out what's going on with Conrad."

"Count me in." Effie pushed back the beer, hiccupped and belched and blushed. She slammed her hand over her mouth to smother a laugh. Mother would have a coronary. "Provided I sober up."

Sally bit back a laugh. "You're pretty much fun plastered, Effie Wilson. Got any ideas on how to get Conrad to fess up to what's bubbling in his brain?"

Effie eyed the beer. To drink or not to drink, that was the question. "Too bad we didn't know he and Thelma would be here socializing tonight. We could have paid a little visit to Conrad's house while he was out and seen what's happening in the old boy's life."

"Except we didn't know each other 'til five minutes ago to even get this plan together." Sally looked back to Conrad and Thelma. "Besides, Conrad never comes here. He's slumming, probably to please the little woman, just like building the patio. This gets curiouser and curiouser." She studied Effie for a moment and leaned close. "Would you really break into Conrad's house?"

"Let's call it drop in uninvited. And I'm sort of zonked so, yeah, I probably would pay Hastings House a visit." Effie took another swig of beer, and the whole room swayed with the song about a man leaving his woman and feeling bad about it. "If we could figure out a way to get the lovebirds back here tomorrow night, we could go for it then. What about you're our ten-thousandth customer and get a free dinner tomorrow night at Slim's? That would get 'em back."

Sally drummed her fingers on the table, deep in thought. "That's not exactly in sync with the ambiance around here, but I guess I could give it a try. I'm a business major; folks will chalk it up to my big-city ideas. But Conrad willing to grace us with his presence two nights in a row seems a bit over the top. Doubt if he'll go for it."

Effie quirked her left brow and grinned. "Except we got the impress-the-little-woman thing in our favor. Thelma loves this place; she'll want to come. But how do we get into Conrad's since we're uninvited? I could break a window or something, but he probably has an alarm."

Sally giggled. "Oh, girl, I do so know the answer to this little problem. Denise! Conrad's housekeeper. He cut her back to half days, and we hired her on yesterday. Bet she can get us into Hastings House. She loves Thelma. Helped her take care of her sick husband last year. Bet she doesn't like Conrad and Thelma together any more than we do."

Effie held up a chicken wing in triumph. "Sally, we have a plan."

Sally popped another sausage into her mouth and said

around a mouthful, "You're good at devious. What do you do in San Diego, work undercover CIA or something?"

"Build stuff. Stay out of trouble. Fret over my 401K, be really boring." Drool over Ryan. Where'd that come from? Effie felt her head swim and let out another belch that would do a truck driver proud. "Amazing what a pitcher of beer does to my brain."

"I'm thinking we should leave Ryan out of this great plan of ours since he thinks all's well in paradise. He would not approve."

Effie grinned. "If he knew we were breaking and entering, he'd go nuts." She focused hard on Sally, trying to see only one of her.

"All of a sudden you're not looking too good, girl."

"All of a sudden I'm not feeling too good." She stood and wobbled.

"Want me to have one of the guys walk you home? I'd do it, but I've got a bar to run."

Effie shook her head. Not a good thing to do when sloshed and full of greasy food. "Call me tomorrow night when Conrad and Thelma get here. I'll swing by and pick you up. Though right now swing's the last thing I want to do."

Sally nodded. "You sure you're all right?"

"I'm okey-dokey." She headed for the door and stepped outside, the muggy night air making her feel worse. She eyed the car. In her present condition driving was out of the question. She'd walk.

A few cars rumbled by, but mostly she had moonlight in the trees and critters scurrying in the bushes for company, and as long as they stayed there she'd be fine. Oh, please, no furry things with tails and beady eyes to deal with right now!

A tow horn sounded alone and forlorn, and she spied the silhouette pushing barges upriver, the moonlight glistening off the rolling wake left behind, turning it into a ribbon of silver. Peace hung in the air along with the humidity. No traffic, no noise, a million miles from San Diego. Life was different here; she was different here.

In San Diego she always followed the rules; here there weren't any. Not only had she talked Ryan into having sex with her, but she intended to break into Conrad's house. She made a quick sign of the cross. For sure she was going straight to hell, but at least it was for a good cause.

She took the curved driveway leading to the O'Fallon house, Max at her side, her stomach churning like a tow diesel needing a mechanic. "You are one great dog. No one gets by you, do they, boy?" He rubbed against her leg as if understanding every word, and she petted his sleek head. "Good dog. Good Max."

She entered the house, found a treat for Max, then headed to her room to die in peace. How could she still be alive and feel so bad?

She gingerly lay down, closed her eyes, wished the room would hold still while praying for her demise. Beer and barbecue now officially joined the ranks of pink coconut cupcakes.

"Effie?" Ryan whispered through her door. "Are you in there?"

"Effie died. Go away."

He opened the door, his boat shoes making soft sounds on the wood floor. "Sally just called and wanted to know if you made it here."

"Tell her not to worry, I'll be fine by tomorrow night for our excursion . . . oh, damn!" Her eyes flew open.

"I didn't know you knew each other. What's going on tomorrow night, and what's wrong with you now? I've never seen you like this."

"That's a lot of questions for a woman with too much beer on her brain. Tell Sally I'll call her tomorrow."

"She already hung up. I said I'd call her if there's a problem." He sat on the end of the bed, the mattress sagging under him and her, rolling their bodies together. "Is there a problem, and what excursion? Since when did you two get so chummy?"

"Since Sally heard us arguing and wanted to reassure me there's nothing between you two but friendship. You're rocking the bed, and I'm a little hungover here. We shared food and got acquainted. Now you know everything. Go away. But do it slowly and quietly."

"You left out the part about tomorrow night. What's up with that?"

Blast her inability to keep her big mouth shut while under the influence of booze. She needed a lie, something good and believable, except her brain wasn't fully operational right now. "We want you to play tomorrow night, the sax, romantic music, for Thelma and Conrad. They won the ten-thousandth customer contest at Slim's." She held her breath and waited to see if he bought it.

"Conrad was at Slim's?"

"You know how Thelma loves that place. They won the contest. Sally and I thought you playing sax would be a nice touch"—and keep you the hell out of the way— "since you've known her for so long and all."

Effie cranked open one eye and flashed Ryan a big, toothy grin that she hoped would be testimony to the innocence and sincerity of her words.

"You are the worst liar on the planet."

She opened both eyes and gripped the sheets to hold the bed steady. Soft moonlight kissing his square jaw made her want to do the very same thing, no matter how bad she felt. "Hey, it's the truth, I swear." Just not all the truth.

His eyes turned velvet soft. He twisted a strand of her hair in his fingers. "Slim would never do something like the ten-thousandth customer routine, and Conrad is not exactly a big-time patron. Why would he come back? Once is his quota for the year. And what the hell are you hiding?"

"I think Conrad's doing dinner again for Thelma, just like he's building the patio. He's up to something. I know you don't believe it, but Sally and I do."

She tried to think of something besides Ryan's fingers stroking her hair and now touching her cheek. "Sally thought the ten-thousandth customer idea would be good for business."

"Business at Slim's is fine. Why do I feel like I'm missing something?"

She was the one missing something. She missed him! She missed the intimate feel of his body hard against hers. She missed talking together, laughing. She missed the sex! She took his hand and kissed his palm, his heat against her lips setting her on fire. Their eyes locked, and she felt the pulse in his wrist accelerate, matching hers.

He said, "Thought you were angry at me?" He took his hand away and let out a breath. "You're hammered, and that's no way to have sex. You'd get up tomorrow and hate me and yourself."

He kissed her on the forehead. "Good night, Effie Wilson." His breath seared her skin. "I'm going to work for a while on the mall plans, and you can add your thoughts tomorrow."

He walked out of the room, closing the door quietly behind him.

Oh, God, how she wanted that man! Every time they wound up together she wanted him more and more. What to do? Think about something else! Like tomorrow night. What should she and Sally be looking for at Hastings House? What kind of information would they get?

She wasn't sure, but the one thing she hoped they wouldn't get there was caught!

Late afternoon sun drenched the earth as Thelma slowly drove her Sunfire down the rutted road to Hastings Drydock. She headed for Conrad's Ferrari, the Mississippi rolling lazily on by. It promised to be another beautiful night, and she hoped it would be half as wonderful as the last.

Dinner at Slim's with Conrad. Making love with him again and again in his big four-poster bed that needed a little step to climb into. Windows wide open, night air and moonlight surrounding them. She'd felt like a princess . . . a floozy . . . a vixen . . . a woman desired.

How could something like this happen to her? How could she be so lucky to have a man like Conrad Hastings interested in her, a nobody from the backwater? He was handsome; she had average looks, and that was on a good day and twenty pounds lighter. Conrad had class and impeccable manners; she had to think when to use the salad fork, and the only class she knew was the kind she'd taken at the community college.

And Conrad Hastings was the best lover God put on earth while she barely knew what went in where. Whatever was responsible for Conrad taking a shine to her she'd be grateful for the rest of her life.

When she pulled to a stop, the Ferrari and an old truck were the only other vehicles in sight. She killed the engine and headed for the weathered sign hanging still and tired with *Office* stenciled in faded letters. She went inside. No one around and more dust on the desks than business. Looking for Conrad, she went out the back door that led to the huge dry-docks where tugs parked when needing repairs. Except the docks were vacant, no repairs anywhere. From the looks of things there hadn't been any in some time.

"Thelma?" Conrad said as he came her way. "What are you doing here? Thought we were meeting at Slim's at seven for dinner?"

He smiled down at her, but the happiness didn't reach his eyes. He kissed her forehead. "Didn't you get enough of me today after we spread out all that gravel and sand? Thought you'd be home soaking in a hot tub."

She felt a blush creep into her cheeks. "We already did that, remember. In your tub."

"And"—he grinned—"I remember we did a lot more than soak."

She winked and smiled back. "Why, Mr. Hastings, so we did." She smiled more. "It was fun, that's why I came looking for you. Seven o'clock seemed so far off, and I missed you."

"It's already six-thirty."

She blushed. "I saw Denise at the market. She said you were here taking care of dry dock business. That Billy Joe quit and he was your best welder."

Conrad shook his head. "Don't know what I'm going to do without him. Though the way business has been lately . . ."

"Where's your office manager? Did he or she have any idea why Billy quit?"

"I have three managers, but they're in Vegas probably wineing and dining clients."

Thelma shrugged. "Sounds expensive." She looked around at the decaying building and empty berths. "What clients? And why three managers, Conrad?"

"My managers are friends, Thelma. I'll take care of my business."

"Of course you will. Your father and his father made a wonderful success out of this place, and you will, too. Your friends probably have big plans for repairing the rusting roof and docks and cleaning up the storage areas and buying new equipment and advertising and—"

His lips thinned. "Now you're a business magnet?"

"No, but I've been around enough business with the O'Fallons over the years. It doesn't take a PhD in economics to realize this place needs help and that three office managers are excessive because you have no business, least that's the talk around town."

He grinned at her, though it didn't look real at all. "You

are absolutely right, my dear. Smart as always. But my friends are changing all that. That's why they're in Vegas with clients. Courting the big money for contracts. Everything's going to be fine. Trust me."

He kissed Thelma, his lips warm and persuasive, his arms around her pure heaven, making her forget all about docks and no business. Of course she trusted him. He was the one with the big fancy education.

"Now," he said as he slid his arm through hers, "let's go to dinner."

For a moment she didn't move, but gazed up at him. Would she ever tire of looking at him? Never! "You sure you want to dine at Slim's again? I don't mind if we go somewhere else. You can choose the place this time. Country club, a place in Memphis, anywhere you like."

"Nonsense." They walked through the empty office, their footsteps the only sound in the deserted building. "You like Slim's, and I like being with you. All that matters is we're together and have a wonderful evening. Then again, we always have wonderful evenings together."

"I know I do."

He opened the other door, and they went outside. The sky was a million colors at once. She turned and kissed Conrad again. A perfect moment.

"The Mississippi is so beautiful. I love it like this. I love being with you, Conrad, more than you can imagine."

He smoothed back her hair and looked deep into her eyes. "And I love you, my dear."

Her heart lodged in her throat, pounding a million miles a minute. "You . . . you . . ."

He kissed her again. "I love you, Thelma McAllister. I can't imagine my life without you. A future without you in it is no future at all for me. I've never met anyone like you. You're smart and beautiful and make me do things I would never do before. You make me a different person. A better man. I know this is sudden and we haven't been together long, but I've had my eye on you, and now that I got you I don't want to give you up ever."

Tears stung her eyes, and she could barely get the words out. "Oh, Conrad." She threw her arms around him and embraced him for all she was worth, and right now she felt worth a lot. Her heart soared, her knees wobbled and her stomach did flips. "I'm so happy, happier than I've ever been in my life. You're incredible. You're my whole life, Conrad."

He took her arms from around his neck and smiled down at her. "We need to celebrate. We'll dine at Slim's but leave early, if you don't mind. I want you all to myself tonight. I don't want to share you with anyone. Just the two of us alone. We need to make plans."

"What plans?"

He smiled sweetly and kissed her lightly. "That can wait 'til tonight."

The pearl gray of dusk settled like a warm damp blanket over the Landing as Effie got out of her car, the gravel in Slim's parking lot crunching under her shoes. Conrad's sweet-humming Ferrari pulled up next to her, Thelma waving like mad. "Fancy meeting you here," she said to Effie as Conrad helped her from the car.

"Here for your prize? It's great you guys won."

Thelma grinned and walked close to Conrad, her arms hooked possessively through his. "I never win anything. It's because of Conrad. He's the lucky one."

Conrad patted Thelma's hand. "I'm the lucky one because I have you, my dear."

Oh, boy! Effie's stomach rolled as Thelma giggled and held tighter.

"It's going to be a truly wonderful night," Thelma proclaimed.

She looked radiant, completely happy. Mesmerized. Okay, Effie thought. What line of crap did slime-ball

Conrad feed her now to put that look on her face? For sure he'd done something. Only a man special to a woman's heart could make her glow like that.

Conrad opened the door, and they all went inside. Memphis Blues pulsed through the room as Thelma asked Effie, "Why not join Conrad and me."

"Absolutely." Conrad beamed, though the enthusiasm didn't reach his beady little eyes. He definitely wanted Thelma alone, and he was definitely up to something. Effie could feel it in her bones. And tonight, as Conrad gorged on barbecued ribs and listened to Ryan on sax and fed Thelma more lies, the visiting female architect and the local business guru would go snooping and find out what the hell Conrad Hastings was up to.

Effie said, "You two have a wonderful evening. I just stopped by Slim's for a moment, and then I have to get back. I have a ton of work to do."

Thelma patted Effie's hand. "You need to get out more. Have some fun." She winked at Effie. "I think Ryan's going to play the sax tonight."

Effie smiled back. "I'm sure he is." Effie watched Thelma and Conrad head for a table, then made her way to the far corner of the bar. Sally served up three beers to patrons, then hustled over. Effie gripped her hand and whispered. "Got the key?"

Sally pressed it into her palm, her eyes not leaving Effie's. "Here. But there's a glitch, Sherlock. I can't go."

Chapter 13

Effie's eyes widened as she stared at Sally, her partner in crime, not believing what she heard. She whispered, "What do you mean you can't come with me?"

"Dad twisted his ankle about an hour ago and is sitting in front of the TV with it propped up and iced. I think he did it on purpose so he could watch the Braves play the Yankees, but there's not much we can do about it. The place is packed, and I can't get anyone in here last minute. Maybe we can go tomorrow?"

"Then we'd need another excuse to get Conrad and Thelma out, and that won't be easy." Effie shook her head and nodded over her shoulder at Thelma. "Look at her. She's gaga over Conrad. Whatever he's up to he's putting on the rush big time. We've got to figure out what's going on now before she gets in any deeper. I'll go alone."

Sally's eyes narrowed. "Not a good idea. Think of something else."

"Actually it is a good idea. You can make sure Conrad and Thelma stay here. Ply them with free desserts or beers or things barbecued, whatever it takes. It'll give me more time to look around."

"You don't know the area. You'll get lost."

"If I can read a blueprint and that hen scratch contractors and engineers throw my way, I can follow your directions. Tell me where to go."

Sally closed her eyes and put her hand over her face. "I hate doing this, but you're right. It's now or never. Conrad's on the move. He's got a slicker than usual look about him, and that's going some."

She took Effie's hand. "Park on the dirt road beyond Conrad's house, pull the car into the bushes and go in through the woods. There's an overgrown path that leads that way marked by broken rock steps here and there. There's a creek and an old footbridge over it. The start of the path has a crumbling hitching post where soldiers kept their horses during the war."

Effie's eyes rounded. "You had a war here?"

"Civil, honey, the only one that counts in these parts. With a little luck Grant won't be moseying about."

"Grant the dog?"

"Grant the general. Kept his troop here and likes to come visit from time to time." Sally held up her hand before Effie could protest. "It's the Landing, Tennessee, and not the big city, California. Things are different, and it's best just to go with it. If you hear someone barking orders, just yell out yes, sir and keep on walking."

"That's crazy."

"Probably. Wish you had a blue hat. Grant sure likes the blue hats. Go three miles south on the two-lane. Hastings House is the big Georgian on the right that overlooks the Mississippi, and the dirt road's directly beyond."

"Got it, general and all. I'll be fine."

A misty tune came on about some guy not happy about being in jail, and Sally's gaze glued to Effie's. She nodded at the jukebox in the corner. "You don't need this to be your theme song, girl. If you get caught, Ryan will skin us alive. One brown hide and a white one, side by side, right over his bed."

"He'd do it, too."

Sally grinned. "Damn straight. Got any idea what you're looking for?"

"Some reason for Conrad's great transformation. There's a reason he's doing what he is, and we both know it because we've been there. We've just got to find out what he's after and why Thelma." Effie gripped the key and nodded. "Don't worry. I'll be fine."

"Come back here when you're done. I got to know what happened. I'll worry myself gray if you don't."

"You keep the lovebirds busy."

Effie left, the earth more dark than dusk as she got into her car, fired the engine, flipped on the lights and headed out of town. She went the three miles and found the big antebellum on the bluff, then slowed 'til she came to the dirt road. Hanging a right, she pulled into the brush beside the creek, the crumbling stone hitching post exactly where Sally said.

Effie paused and listened, no military orders shouted her way. Guess Grant was off haunting Vicksburg. She killed the headlights, the car suddenly drenched in darkness. Oh, hell! A flashlight would be good here. Why didn't she think of that back at Slim's and get one from Sally?

She grabbed her purse and rooted around, everything but a flashlight. Her cell phone the only thing close. She flipped up the top and clicked it on. Half-charged battery. Not great, but it gave off light . . . least for a little while. Faint moonlight peeked through the trees, lighting her way to the post. She peered into the woods, black as India ink.

Holding the phone close to the ground, she followed what looked like a path and came to a slab of broken rocks once a step. Yippee, Skippy. A game of connect the steps and she'd get to the house. San Diego girl does Indiana Jones.

Quiet surrounded her. She'd never heard so much quiet. Dead quiet. Bad choice of words considering the Grant warning.

The woods closed in around her. She walked faster 'til her foot caught a root, and she tripped to the ground.

"Halt," came a whispered voice from behind. A stick broke somewhere in the distance. Footsteps? Her hair stood straight up on end and went white, she was sure of it. She scrambled to her feet and ran, her eyes adjusting to the darkness, seeing parts of the path.

"Effie. Stop," came from somewhere behind her.

"Like hell!" Too scared to look behind she looked forward and spotted the big house dark against a charcoal gray sky.

"Effie."

"I'm from California. It wasn't in the war. Leave me alone." Sweat slithered between her boobs, her heart raced and adrenaline gave her energy she didn't know she had. She pushed into the clearing, tore across grass, then sand, at NASCAR speed, her feet not touching the ground. Panting, she shoved the key in the lock, punched in the numbers to disengage the alarm, ran inside, poked in nine, then one, but stopped before pressing the last one. Who'd she ask for? Ghost busters? And cell phones didn't work in these parts anyway.

"Effie," came the voice behind her, and she turned and threw the phone at . . . "Ryan." She'd know that silhouette anywhere. The cell bounced off his forehead with a solid thud, then clattered onto the floor.

"Dang, woman!"

"You broke my phone, O'Fallon." She put her hand to her chest to hold her heart inside, afraid it would jump right out from beating so hard.

He focused his flashlight at her, making her wince as she continued, "You scared the hell out of me. What are you doing here?"

He dropped the beam, and they stared at each other through the darkness. "Getting out of here with you unless you want me to forward your severance pay to the Tennessee State Pen. You must have lost your mind to be doing something so totally stupid as breaking and entering."

She put her hands to her hips. "The only thing broken around here is my phone, and that's your fault. I'm fine unless someone followed you here, and if I don't do something, Thelma could deal with a lifetime of heartache. Go away and leave me alone. Besides, I'm not talking to you. What you did to me on the *Mississippi Miss* was rotten to the core, and I'm still pissed. How'd you find me, anyway?"

"What I did on the *Mississippi Miss* was save your ass because you were scared green, and if you're pissed, too bad. As for finding you, that ten-thousandth customer thing was a stretch, and so was the bizarre conversation last night and—"

"That led you here?"

"And Sally sent me. She didn't think you had a flashlight and you'd get lost in the woods. How did you find the way?"

"Cell phone light." She picked up the phone and turned it off. "Sure hope it didn't speed dial anything when it hit. Roaming charges can eat you alive if things connect." She slid the phone into her pocket. "I'm going to look around. Mind if I borrow your light?"

"Look for what?"

She spread her arms wide. "If I knew that, I wouldn't have to look, would I? There's some reason Conrad's turned into Prince Charming. I've got to find a glass slipper around here with Thelma's name on it; then I'll know what this is all about. Wanna help?"

"Christ Almighty, woman."

"Forty-five minutes. That's all we need, if you help. Come on. The woman raised you; you owe her big time."

He ran his hand over his face. "All right, all right! For Thelma. And if we don't find anything, you'll give up this stupid idiotic idea of Conrad having some ulterior motive for getting it on with Thelma. Right?"

"You take the upstairs; I'll take the downstairs. This place is full of antiques. There's got to be a candle here somewhere I can use. My phone's dead."

He came to her and put his hand hard on her shoulder and looked her square in the eyes. "Forty-five minutes, Effie. That's it."

Maybe, she told herself, but said to Ryan, "Then quit standing here yapping at me like some fishwife and get your rear in gear."

Moonlight shone through the beveled sidelights on either side of the front door, spilling into the hallway as Ryan went upstairs mumbling swearwords. Effie made her way into the living room and found a candelabra on the mahogany sideboard beside a crystal decanter and tumblers. Matches, and a little gun in the drawer. Yikes, they play hardball in the South. Maybe forty-five minutes would be enough time.

The warm glow flickered off expensive Orientals—almost museum quality—then two Victorian chairs with balloon backs, circa mid 1850s if her art history class served her right.

Good Lord. Grant could have sat right there on one of those pieces. No wonder he haunted the place.

She spotted a governor's desk with a slant top and opened it. Yesterday's newspaper. This was a waste of time. No one in their right mind would leave something important in the living room, and Conrad was definitely in his right conniving mind. She passed the dining room and entered a small library. A cherry desk with carved

Queen Anne legs sat in the middle. She riffled through it—nothing but a bunch of unpaid bills. She had twenty minutes left before the warden dragged her kicking and screaming from the premises and had come up with nothing.

She put the candles back on the sideboard, snuffed the flames between her thumb and index finger so as not to blow wax everywhere and headed upstairs. She spotted a faint light in the far room and headed in that direction. Ryan sat on the edge of the raised Victorian spool-turned four-poster bed, his light shining on a folder as he pored over the contents.

She grinned into the darkness. Yes! The old boy came through. Ryan found something, she could tell. She'd seen him deep in concentration often enough to know when something was important.

"What's up," she asked as she drew up next to him.

"Hastings Dry-dock is flat broke."

Ryan tapped the folder. "This is a financial statement from his lawyer, Arthur Billings, giving Conrad the bad news. In the last paragraph it mentions alternative options to Conrad's situation."

"From the bills I saw downstairs I'd say Conrad is broke period, and whatever those options happen to be they sure aren't in place yet. All his credit cards are cancelled. Doesn't that guy ever listen to Dr. Phil?"

Ryan closed the folder and put it back in the top drawer of the end table next to the bed. He clicked off his flashlight, leaving them in the dark with moonlight casting shadows across the room. "Conrad might be busted, but that can't have anything to do with Thelma. She's not exactly an heiress who can bail him out."

Effie found two steps beside the bed and hitched herself up, sitting beside Ryan. "Sally or Rory didn't say anything about Conrad's financial circumstances. They don't seem to be public knowledge. Guess he's keeping it quiet, maybe waiting for this option to kick in."

"Hastings Dry-dock has been around for a long time. His family made a huge success of it. Every barge operator from New Madrid to Greenville took their tows there for repairs. Conrad's led the life of leisure. Him without money is hard to imagine. Him working is even harder to imagine. The man's never broken a sweat a day in his life."

"Except putting in that patio out back. He had to sweat plenty doing that. And all because he's trying to impress Thelma."

"Yeah." Ryan raked his hair. "Everything keeps circling back to Thelma, and I can't figure out why or—"

A car roared into the drive and came to a gravel-spitting stop. Ryan stood and looked out the window. "Oh, shit!"

The front door banged open. Laughing and giggling echoed in the hallway with, "Conrad, you are such a bad boy. Give me back my blouse."

"You'll have to come and get it, Surfer Girl."

More giggling, then yelps of laughter followed by running up the steps. Ryan grabbed Effie and pulled her under the big bed a breath before Conrad and Thelma charged into the room and collapsed onto the mattress. Effie pressed her back to Ryan's front, both keeping perfectly still. Thank God for high antique beds. She looked up at the sagging springs, where more giggling followed howls of fun.

"Fuck!" Ryan whispered in her ear.

And that's exactly where this scenario was headed, and she and Ryan would be present for the whole blasted show!

Ryan watched the springs sag and roll six inches from his face. Okay, he loved sex, he truly did. Two consenting adults giving each other pleasure was one of the best things about life. But he didn't want to listen to those adults doing the horizontal hula right above him, especially when one of them was Thelma, the woman who nearly raised him.

He gritted his teeth, his eyes shut at the thought. Effie had her hands over her ears, obviously liking the situation as much as he did. The bed squeaked and moaned. Dang, if the above occupants didn't pace themselves, he and Effie could get squashed like pancakes when these old slats gave way and collapsed right on top of them. More heavy breathing followed, then grunts.

Oh, God. Not grunts. He didn't want to even think what grunting meant.

He needed a diversion, fast. Something to get his mind off the antics going on. Effie rolled over, her nose now touching his, the expression on her face the same as if she'd swallowed a pickle whole. She cupped his ear with her warm hand and whispered, her breath flowing onto his cheek and down his neck. "What should we do?"

His gut tightened; his dick did the same and rose to the occasion. If he and Effie did down here what was going on above, they couldn't think about what was going on above, right? Hell, it was worth a shot! He hooked his finger under Effie's chin, brought her lips to his and kissed her.

Her eyes widened in disbelief that he could consider such a thing. He pointed upward and whispered in her ear, "It's me or them."

Then he kissed her again, and this time her eyes warmed with passion and her lips softened under his. Her mouth opened, letting his tongue take hers in a sultry summer dance guaranteed to keep their minds on just the two of them.

She threaded her fingers through his hair, and her body snuggled close. Considering the amount of heat being generated in this room, Ryan imagined the whole place going up in a burst of flames any minute.

His right hand slid under Effie's blouse, connecting with

her soft damp skin. He reached to her smooth sleek back and unsnapped her bra. She gasped, but he muffled the sound with his own mouth as his fingers freed the material from around her and he cradled her perfect breast in his palm. So firm, so warm, so incredibly luscious. God, he loved luscious.

Conrad mumbled something, but Ryan was too busy with his own agenda to think about it. That was the whole point, wasn't it? Then Effie took his bottom lip between hers, sucked him deeply into her mouth, and Ryan knew he'd want this if World War Three was exploding around him or nothing at all. Some things were too good to pass up, no matter what!

His dick swelled and throbbed against his jeans. Effie's clever fingers undid the snap, lowered the zipper and held him tight. He drew in a quick breath as she stroked him . . . slowly, purposefully, making him hard as the floor beneath them.

He pushed up her blouse and licked her hardening left nipple, feeling her tremble, her breasts filling with desire as his tongue circled the sensitive tip. He did the same to the other, and her fingers held his engorged penis a bit tighter, stroking him faster, bringing him close to the brink. He unbuttoned her slacks, then slid his hands down her smooth abdomen and connected with the soft curls between her legs.

Slowly he eased his hand into the cleft, and she spread her thighs for him, as best she could in this space, letting his fingers glide easily into her warm wetness so ready for him. His fingers probed deeper, one finger, then two. Her eyes clouded, her breaths came faster, hotter, and his dick felt as if it would burst.

God, he wanted to be inside her. Every time he was with Effie he enjoyed her more and more. Usually he tired of a woman, got his fill. He couldn't seem to get his fill of Effie.

She enticed him, intrigued him, tempted him beyond words. Drove him freaking nuts.

He simply wanted more, even here under Conrad's bed . . . until the phone rang?

Good God, not now. He was so close to getting Effie off. A few more strokes, his fingers a little deeper, more pressure, more teasing . . .

Then again, the damn phone ringing could be a blessing in disguise. Effie yelling his name in a fit of climax was not the way to stay hidden. Though the way the two above were going at it they wouldn't notice.

"Don't answer it," Conrad wheezed.

"There might be a problem with Bonnie," Thelma huffed. "I'd never forgive myself."

The bed shifted, and the phone stopped ringing. Conrad groused, "Hello?" He paused, puffed out an audible lungful of air, then said, "Thelma, it's business. I've got to take it. I'll just be a minute. There's champagne and glasses chilling in the fridge. And strawberries."

"Oh, Conrad." She chuckled. "You do know what I like. You take your call, and I'll get the champagne and turn on the Jacuzzi. I know what you like, too."

The bed moved again as Thelma slid off. A soft glow of some small light suddenly bathed the room. Thelma grabbed Conrad's shirt from the floor, probably to use as a robe. She went into the bathroom. Momentarily the soft hum of the Jacuzzi began flowing into the room. Her bare feet headed for the hall.

Reluctantly Ryan slid his fingers from Effie as she let go of his erection. She looked as frustrated as he felt, and that was one hell of a lot of frustration.

Conrad didn't say a word for a few beats, then whispered, "Why the hell are you calling me now? Things were just getting good here. How do you expect me to romance the pigeon if—What do you mean, three days? I thought we had more time. I can't—Fuck! All right, all right. I'll think of something. I just hope Ryan and that broad he's with don't get wise to what's going on. I don't trust either of them. I've got to go. She's coming. I'll see you tomorrow."

The phone dropped into the cradle as Thelma entered the room. "I see you've finished your business. Now we can take care of other . . . business." She laughed wickedly, like a woman in love who wanted to be made love to. "Why don't we take the champagne into the Jacuzzi? It should be hot by now."

Conrad said, "You do know how to show a boy a good time."

He slid from the bed, and four feet shuffled across the bedroom to the bathroom, accompanied by an assortment of sounds Ryan didn't want to think about. Effie made to scoot out, but he held her back in case Thelma or Conrad returned for some forgotten article. But when they didn't, he let her go and scooted out behind her.

He zipped his jeans, not an easy task considering his present condition. Effie reattached her bra. Damn, he liked it so much better taking it off. They crept—top speed for a throbbing hard-on—toward the hallway, the Jacuzzi drowning out old creaking boards. He followed Effie down the stairs, then to the back door.

He looked across the yard to the trees where they had to go. So near, yet so damn far. "I can't run," he whispered.

She looked at him as if he'd lost his mind. "We don't have time for a night stroll, Ryan. We've got to get out of here."

"Hey, you're the one who got me in this . . . state. I expect a little more understanding."

"And how understanding are the police going to be when they haul our butts off to jail."

He snagged her hand, gritted his teeth, opened the door

and sprinted across the yard to the trees, thinking pain, pain, pain with each step.

In seconds the trees swallowed them up, and they stopped in the shadows to get their breaths. "Hope I didn't damage something important."

Her gaze met his, her eyes bright with devilment. "Wanna find out?"

"Here!"

"We weren't exactly playing patty-cake under that bed, Ryan. Can't be worse than a wheelhouse."

His dick swelled larger than before, more painful than ever. She unsnapped her slacks, the material gaping around her waist, and his body went rigid with anticipation. "God, you make me crazy."

She kicked off her shoes, one flipping over his head, settling into the bushes with a soft swoosh; the other ricocheted off a tree limb with a solid thud. Her pants, then her panties landed in a chinaberry bush beside him.

"I don't believe this. Grant, eat your heart out."

She put her hands to her bare hips and twitched her pelvis, the gold ring at her navel catching a ray of moonlight. "You are so damn sexy."

She swaggered to him and slowly wound her arms around his neck. "I can't wait, Ryan," her voice was suddenly ragged and broken.

He took a condom from his wallet, covered himself, then slid his palms against her firm bare derriere, cupping each cheek. "Lean against the tree and wrap your legs around my waist."

"I'm too heavy for you to lift."

"Oh, sugar, this won't take long." He looked her dead in the eyes. "I promise."

He braced her against the trunk and held her as her sweet silky thighs circled him. He kissed her, and in one thrust he drove into her, taking her whimpers into his mouth. She held onto his shoulders, her fingers digging into his flesh as he plunged into her again, then once more.

Her body opened wider each time, allowing him to be more fully, more completely, a part of her. She trusted him, gave herself fully to him, and every cell of his body reveled in the sensation. Then she arched, tensing in climax, yelling his name into the woods as his own release followed.

Every time with Effie was better than the last, and that was impossible because every time was perfect. Her head sagged to his shoulder. He could feel her hot breaths through his shirt, scorching his skin underneath. He kissed her hair. "What you do to me."

"I think it's what you just did to me."

He slid himself out of her and let her stand, her body sagging into his arms. Moonlight danced in her hair. "Are you okay?"

"That was astounding."

A light came on in the house, and they cut their eyes in that direction. "We've got to get out of here. The cops patrol the area. That dirt road is a favorite make-out spot with the local teens. If they spot our cars . . ."

Effie nipped his chin and smiled. "What if they spot us?" She stepped back and snagged her pants from the bush. "We have to get back to Sally and fill her in on what happened."

"Not everything that happened."

She laughed as she slipped into her gym shoes. "I need a cold beer."

"Thought you were a white wine girl."

"Yeah, well, this is the Landing, and things are different here." Her eyes met his, and she said in a low voice, "We're different. But what happens between us when we leave here, Ryan? What do we do then?"

Chapter 14

Effie watched Ryan's eyes darken. "What do you mean, what happens? We go back to being architects, just like before. That's what we both want, right?"

He wrapped the condom in his handkerchief, buttoned his jeans, then took her hand, pulling her into the woods as he clicked on his flashlight. "Follow me. Least this time you won't have to use your cell phone. How'd that work?"

About the same as this relationship. "Crappy." She tagged behind him, thinking about what he said . . . architects like before. That meant when they got back to Designs Unlimited he'd be back to his flavor-of-the-month antics and she'd be back to having the hots for him from afar.

But shouldn't she be over that? She lusted after Ryan for sex, and since they'd been at the Landing she'd had sex, sex and more sex with that man. That should satisfy a lifetime worth of fantasies.

So why didn't it?

"Well, here we are," Ryan said as they pulled up next to their cars. "We made it. No interruptions from Grant. I'll meet you back at Slim's."

He gave her a quick see-you-around-baby kind of kiss

and got in his car. She did the same, and they pulled onto the two-lane, heading for town.

The moon sat in the treetops; the stars winked in the clear sky. She darted around an opossum crossing the road and skidded into the curve by the big hawthorn that must be a million years old. Everything unique. No two things the same on the Landing. No trees alike, no houses alike, no two people alike. No cookie-cutter Starbucks on each corner or predictable Dollar Stores on every block. No Banana Republic, Gap, Limited, Williams-Sonoma. Here there were stores that people owned and named and ran where they knew each of their customers and their families by name. This wasn't the big city, and she felt more at home here than she ever had in San Diego.

She parked the car beside Slim's as Ryan came her way. "What's going on?" he asked as he drew up beside her. "You look like you've got something on your mind."

"Thinking about San Diego."

"Well, don't get too homesick. We shouldn't be here much longer. Rory's PI's been snooping around; he's bound to turn up something soon. Then Dad will find Mimi, and we can head back home."

She spread her arms, taking in the town. "Don't you think of the Landing as home? It's where you grew up, where you know everyone and everyone knows you and your family. Don't you feel something?"

He glanced around, then shrugged. "Once upon a time this was home, but I'm a city slicker at heart." He smiled down at her. "Just like you. Come on, I'll buy you a beer."

They walked into Slim's and sat at the far end of the bar. Sally scurried over and put up two beers as she leaned across the bar. "Holy cow, you two were sure gone long enough. Scared me to death. Any minute I thought I'd hear that Sheriff Spade had you both locked up tighter than a lid on a jelly jar."

She looked from one to the other. "Well don't just sit there slurping free beer, give. What happened?"

A fun tune about Doctor Feelgood wailed, drowning out their conversation from the others and setting Effie's toe tapping to the tune as Ryan said, "You're going to love this. Remember how Conrad always had the best of everything. The most expensive train sets for Christmas, the coolest clothes, a new Mustang when he turned sixteen and we were all so jealous we saw green for weeks. Conrad's broke."

Sally did a low whistle. "Never thought I'd see the day when he wasn't loaded. He's been flashing his money around as long as I can remember."

Effie added, "And most important we overheard a phone conversation where Thelma somehow plays into Conrad's plans of getting himself unbroke."

Sally frowned and popped open a beer and took a long gulp that was not very Wall Street-like. "Thelma? What did she do, win the lottery or something? She doesn't have any money."

Effie said, "But she needs to know Conrad's not playing square with her. That he's got an agenda and she's part of it."

Ryan held up his hand in protest. "But we have no idea what that agenda is. We can't open our big mouths and dash her romantic dreams without knowing what's really going on. What if we're jumping to conclusions and make accusations when Conrad's trying to work things out. Besides, the only thing we heard from our side of the conversation was he didn't trust me and Effie. Big surprise there. Unless we get more information we should butt out and wait."

"I hate waiting," Effie muttered as she drummed her fingers on the bar. "I can't just sit here. But . . . but . . ." She smiled at Ryan sweetly and batted her eyes.

He wagged his head. "Whatever it is that you're cooking up, the answer's no because it's going to involve me and I don't want to be involved."

"Just tell Conrad you've heard about his financial situation by way of the grapevine and you want him to tell Thelma about it because it would be better that way. Tell him you're looking out for her. That way Conrad will know we're on to him, and he'll think twice before hurting Thelma. But if he and Thelma do get serious and wind up together, we haven't alienated him altogether. Kind of the best of all worlds, don't you think?"

"Maybe for you." Ryan set his beer on the bar with a solid thud and glared. "But if Thelma gets wind of me doing this, she'll string me up by the very sensitive parts of my anatomy for interfering in her life. You've never been on the receiving end of rampage-by-Thelma. It ain't pretty, and I don't want any part of it. Not just because of the life-threatening consequences, but because, like I keep saying, we're butting in someone else's life. Doesn't this bother you a little?"

Sally shrugged. "What do you suggest? We stand around looking at each other while Thelma gets her heart stomped flat by a user? Friends don't let friends date assholes. You should have seen them coochie-cooing tonight. I tried everything to keep them here longer, but nothing worked. Good thing you two didn't get caught."

Ryan grinned at Effie. "Well, it was close."

She glared back, and Sally pointed at Ryan. "Don't try and change the subject. We're not that easily put off. Promise us you'll talk to Conrad or at least warn Thelma to go slow."

A voice from behind Effie said, "You causing problems, again, Sally girl?"

Ryan and Effie turned around as Sally looked in that direction, her eyes rounding by half. "Oh, Demar, you big gorgeous hunk of man!" Her face glowed. "Ryan, Effie, this is Demar Thacker, my very handsome man from Nashville who doesn't get here nearly often enough to be suiting me."

Demar grinned and cocked his head, the look of a man in charge, confident . . . a little too confident. He shook hands with Effie, then Ryan, and said, "So, you're the new daddy in town all the way from San Diego. Heard you got yourself one mighty cute baby. How'd she wind up here without you?"

Ryan said, "The mama didn't see me as prize parent material and herself no better. My dad, on the other hand, loves being a grandpa, and he's damn good at it. Heard you're building new houses and breathing some life into this river town."

Demar leaned against the bar and picked up Sally's hand and kissed the back. "Among other things."

Sally blushed. Still looking at Demar, she said, "Daddy's got that forty acres right behind here he's never done any-thing with except let the dogs run. Demar's developing it. Kind of a partnership between him and Daddy, and it'll give people work around here and bring in new folks and their money."

Effie asked, "You're an architect?"

"Contractor." Demar looked from Effie to Ryan, his eyes a bit less friendly. "How long you both going to be here? Taking Bonnie back with you, I suppose?"

Prickles of unease danced up Effie's spine, and Ryan said, "Plans are up in the air right now."

He slid from his stool. "Sorry to cut this short, but I bet-ter get back and relieve Dad from grandpa duty." He nod-ded at Demar. "See you around, I'm sure. You and Sally have a good night."

Ryan pushed the door open and headed for his parked car as Effie caught up with him. "You don't like Mr.

Demar Thacker any better than I do. Now we've got ourselves two to save and don't try and deny it. I saw that look in your eyes when he was making over Sally."

"Hell. Maybe I'm having a knee-jerk reaction to him being a contractor. They're the ones who screw up our plans, put windows where doors belong, put airshafts across open atriums and forget to put in rest rooms and stairways. Maybe we're jaded and Demar's a great guy."

"Maybe Max will learn to fly."

He looked at her, paused, kicked a rock so it skimmed across another and swore. "Least you don't need saving." His eyes met hers, and his face relaxed. He slid his hands in his pockets and rocked back on his heels. An easy grin fell across his face. "Except maybe from me."

"When we get back to San Diego everything's going to be just like before."

"But we're here now, Ef, and can take advantage of it. A little fooling around can't hurt."

Then why did she feel hurt? Especially since they'd left the woods. Because she was getting attached to him, that's why. Dammit all, she liked him. And soon it would all be over.

Well, if that was the case, there'd be no more fooling around. No more getting in deeper than she already was. No more Ryan sex. From here on out it was Sister Mary Effie. She headed for her car. "We have a mall to work on. See you back at the house. Sharpen your pencils, it's going to be a long night."

She could feel his eyes on her. "And from the sounds of it, not the kind of long night I'd like to have. What's wrong now? Are you okay?"

What could she say? I'm a stupid fool for falling for you and knowing it's never going to last? Why go there and create problems that would follow them to San Diego. They already had enough problems. "I'm flipping terrific.

Everything's flipping fine. In fact, if I was any happier I'd be twins!"

Noonday sun blazed overhead as Thelma placed another brick in the sand along the grid Conrad had strung out over the patio to keep the pattern even. Sweat slithered down her back into the waistband of her jeans. At least she worked in the shade. Conrad had worked in the blazing sun for the last three hours. She yelled over to him. "Am I doing this right? Think it's straight?"

He glanced up and grinned. "Looks great."

But he didn't look so great. Face too red, breathing too labored. She got up off her knees, dusted dirt from her pants and walked over to him. Though truth be told it was more a limp mixed with a hobble from crawling around on the ground and bending over.

She kissed him on the head as he studied the section of freshly laid bricks. She touched his sweat-soaked hair. "Time for a break, dear."

He shook his head. "I want to finish this section and see how it looks all together."

She sat down right in front of him, stopping his progress. "This work will be here later, and I want you to be here later, too. I don't want to use the rest of these bricks to build your tombstone. We need a break, Conrad, especially you working so hard in this heat. You get so involved in your work you forget to take care of yourself." She stroked his cheek. "I suppose that'll have to be my job."

She took his hands and pulled off the gloves and dropped them to the ground. "Let's eat lunch. We've got all summer to finish this patio. We can do it after the sun swings to the front of the house and the backyard falls into the shadows."

He picked up another brick. "Thought you wanted this done so we could enjoy it."

She took the brick and put it back on the ground. "I'd much rather enjoy you. I don't want you hurt or anything to happen to you."

"But—"

"What I'm trying to say, Conrad, is . . . is I love you." She smiled and suddenly laughed, the words surprising her as much as Conrad. "I know this is a strange time to tell you that, and I hadn't planned on saying it right now, but I'm so glad I did. I never told a man I loved him before. But it's true. I love you to pieces, with all my heart."

Conrad's mouth opened to say something, but she put her forefinger across his lips. "Let me finish. I want to get this out while I still have the nerve. I've never met anyone like you. You're just wonderful to me. The sun and moon and stars all rolled into one. I've waited all my life for you."

He blinked as if he didn't understand her. "You think I'm wonderful?"

She wagged her head. "I don't think so, I know it. I'm not a young chippie. I know people, and you are the kindest, gentlest, most thoughtful man I've ever met." She threw her arms around him, knocking them both backward, her landing on top of him.

"And," she added in a fit of giggles, "you're handsome. Oh, lordy, are you handsome! Should be a law against someone being so handsome."

"Honey, my hair's thinning on top, and I'm getting a little thick around the middle. I'm not all that handsome. I think the heat's got you."

"Nope, you're the one who's got me." She kissed him again. "You have incredible eyes, and I love your laugh and your smile. I love you. I love being with you. You make me so happy, Conrad. You make me feel good about me. In fact, you make me feel like a kid, like I can do anything when I'm with you."

He wrapped his arms around her, drawing her closer. "I

. . . I love you, too, Thelma." He grinned, his brown eyes dancing now. "I've never met anyone like you either." He laughed. "No woman—or man for that matter—ever laid patio bricks with me. Hell, I've never laid patio bricks, and incredible as it seems, I like it. I like fixing up this house, least with you here I do. I don't think anyone loves this place as much as I do . . . except you."

"Hastings House is fabulous. I've thought so since your father gave me one of his cookies." She grinned. "He was a wonderful man, Conrad. You were so lucky to have him as a father. I'm not rich or from a prominent Southern family or have ties to the business world like the other women you've gone with, but you should know that no one could love you or appreciate you more than I do." She kissed his forehead. "You give me Good Vibrations."

He laughed, and she added, "And not just in bed or in the shower."

She sat beside him and placed her hand over his penis, feeling it harden under her palm. Conrad said in a low growl, "What are you doing to me, girl?"

Her breath caught, and her sex started a slow pulsing between her legs in anticipation of what she wanted more than anything at the moment. "If we weren't so hot and sweaty, I'd beg you to take me here and now."

"That can be arranged." He sat up, and his lips claimed hers in a hard kiss. "Race you to the shower?"

"And the winner gets to do anything to the other that they want?"

"Oh, honey, you are so on. I think lunch will have to wait 'til it's dinnertime."

"Good thing I brought a change of clothes."

His finger ran down her neck, stopping at her cleavage at the Vee in her T-shirt. "You won't be needing clothes for what I've got planned."

She stuck her lower lip out in a coquettish pout. "But I just bought a new red feather boa and matching garter belt and black fishnet hose, Conrad." She batted her eyes. "If you win, I just might let you take them off any way you like."

She batted her eyes again. and Conrad jumped up and tore for the house. She laughed, This was one race she intended to lose. She got up, headed for the house and opened the door. Conrad's shirt lay on the floor, his shoes in the hallway, his jeans on the steps. A man in a hurry . . . for her. Lord Almighty! Just for her!

She smiled as she picked up the clothes and headed for his bedroom. The shower was running full blast. "Oh, Thelma," he sang out, her name echoing off the tile. "I'm waiting for you. I'm ready for you."

She dropped his clothes on the floor, then nearly ripped off her own and tossed them onto the pile. She opened the door to the shower stall, steam spilling out around her, and leaned against the frame, taking in Conrad's fully aroused state.

He winked. "Why don't you come here and let me give you a proper big old Southern-boy welcome."

Droplets of water cascaded over him, slicking his hair to his head and running down his middle and around and over his fully aroused penis. "My oh my, you sure are ready, but I think you need a little lathering up?"

"Sugar, if I get any more lathered up, I'm a cooked goose." He snagged her hand and brought her in, closing the door behind her. She kissed him, backing him to the wall, his erection pressing into her belly, setting her on fire head to toe. She found the soap on the rack and made a lather of slippery suds while Frenching him deep and often. And when she took the suds to his throbbing erection he let out a long hiss between clenched teeth.

"What are you doing?"

"I'm doing you." She rubbed his slippery length, his shaft gliding through her fingers.

"You're killing me, girl."

"You better not die on me. I want you." She let go of him, the fine warm spray rinsing the lather from his dick. She flattened herself against the far wall and hiked her left foot onto the little bench. She crooked her finger in a come-here fashion. "I think I'm ready for that promised Southern welcome now, Conrad."

In a split second his hard shaft slipped into her. "God, we fit good," Conrad breathed onto her lips. Then he kissed her, his tongue imitating his actions below. She spread her legs wider, and he took her harder and deeper with each stroke 'til she thrust against him once, then again, bringing them to climax. She called his name, the sound of her voice mixing with Conrad's.

He sagged against her, pinning her to the wall, his head cradled on her shoulder as hers rested against his. "Holy shit, woman. I didn't think I had it in me to do it like . . . that." He kissed her neck, taking her skin into his mouth, undoubtedly giving her a hicky, a brand. "You really do bring the beast out in me, Thelma."

She kissed the droplets off his chin. "Maybe we should hang around here and see if there's any beast left?"

"Honey, I think the beast is dead, least for a bit. I have an appointment with my attorney this afternoon." He drew his lips together and frowned.

She chucked him under the chin. "What's wrong? You don't like being with your attorney?"

"Oh, girl, not half as much as I like being with you."

And Conrad knew in his heart it was the absolute truth. He liked being with Thelma more than Arthur, more than his friends at the country club or the ones in Memphis or any woman he'd ever met. And not just because of the in-credible sex. He listened to Thelma's laughter fill the shower. She had a great laugh, the kind that made him laugh, too. She said, "Bet that beast will be raring to go later on tonight."

"It's a date. But I better get going or Arthur will come

looking for me, and then we'll have three in here. I don't want to share you with anyone."

She opened the shower door. "See you tonight, big boy." Her eyes danced.

"Well, it isn't so big now, but give me a little time and maybe—"

She eyed his dick. "I don't think you need any time at all, Conrad Hastings. I'll bring raspberries tonight. Playing hide-and-seek with them could be real interesting. That'll give you something to think about while you're with Arthur and make you hurry right back to me." She stepped out of the shower and closed the door.

He looked down. Well, dang! He was ready for her again. He never recouped this fast . . . 'til now. The raspberries suggestion did it. Dang! Did he have to wait 'til tonight? He could already taste her nipples, her navel, her sweet sex. He went into the bedroom and watched as she slipped into her bra and T-shirt.

"Conrad, you're dripping water on the hardwood. You'll ruin the finish."

"I . . . I really love you, Thelma."

"All the sweet-talk in the world isn't going to get me in bed, Conrad. You have an appointment about your business, and that's important."

"I'm a fast driver."

She stopped dressing, and her eyes lit with fire as she stared at him. She put her hands to her shapely hips that fit so well against his. "How exactly do you mean that driver part?"

He nodded at the bed. "Let me show you. Showing's always better than telling."

"Blast you, Conrad. One little look and a few flattering words and you got me and you know it." She yanked off her T-shirt and bra, naked and ready. "I think you could talk me into anything, you bad boy."

She laughed and scrambled into the bed as he followed. His dick slid into her fast, hot and hard as a roaring sound filled his ears, and he climaxed with the intensity he hadn't felt in years.

"Conrad." She breathed his name in a long exhale. "How can you keep doing this to me?"

"It's us, and I think we do it to each other. If I don't get going, that us could include Arthur."

He stood and looked down at her, loving the tousled look of Thelma's hair and the lingering pink glow on her cheeks. "I want to stay, you know."

"Me, too."

He threw on his clothes, only taking time to steal a few more kisses before he left the house and headed for Hastings Dry-dock. He turned off the two-lane and followed the gravel down to the river's edge and parked next to Arthur's Volvo, the only other car in the lot.

Conrad remembered when his daddy had added parking spaces to accommodate all the workers, and built new dock spaces, and bought new machinery for the extra business. But not now, not with him in charge.

" 'Bout time you showed up," Arthur grumbled as he got out of his car.

Conrad looked at the scarred building that served as the office. "Isn't the place open; it's the middle of the day? Where are my office managers?"

"Probably still off in Vegas with the rest of the fucking loser friends you hired, running you further into debt. How the hell could you be so bad at business when your daddy was so good." Arthur took his perfectly folded handkerchief from his back pocket and blotted perspiration from his forehead. "Where the hell were you?"

"With Thelma."

His eyes brightened, and his mouth turned up at the left

corner. "Plucking the pigeon? You are the man with the ladies, Conrad. So, how soon before you get that dowdy bitch to the altar?"

Conrad's gut tightened in anger. He thought of Thelma working hard on the patio beside him. He thought of her all warm and loving and giving as they made love and how she trusted him . . . how she loved him. Dowdy bitch? His gut tightened more. "I . . . I'm not sure."

Arthur's lips thinned into a hard line, and his brows drew together. "Well, you damn well better get sure and do it fast. You've got to marry her and get your finances together before those signature experts get done. You're running out of time here, in case you didn't notice." He nodded at the Ferrari. "You haven't even sold your god-damn car."

Arthur's eyes turned beady. "What's wrong with you? You've got to get your hands on the bitch's money or that precious family house of yours goes on the auction block along with everything you own."

Conrad raked his hair. "I know. Thelma likes that house as much as I do. Getting her to marry me shouldn't be that much of a problem."

"Well, damn, now you're talking with some sense. You got her, boy." Arthur slapped him on the back. "Sell the damn car tomorrow, get her a stupid cheap ring and marry her tomorrow night. There's no waiting period in Tennessee, just do it. Hand her some cock-and-bull story about not wanting to go on another day without her."

"What if she suspects something when I show up without the Ferrari? What if she refuses to go along with this quick marriage?"

"It's your fucking job to make sure she doesn't suspect anything and make her believe she wants to marry you more than breathe. Keep her happy and make her feel like the queen bee. She's just some brainless bimbo who wouldn't know what to do with two million bucks, and she's going to save your gold-plated ass. Marry her now, dammit!"

"She's smart, Arthur, real smart. And she's not a damn bimbo."

Arthur swore. "You sure as hell better not be backing out on me, Conrad. Thelma McAllister is nothing but trailer trash, we both know that. I'm counting on my share of the take to get a nice condo in Memphis where I can live like I want when I'm not with Dolores. My sexual prefer-ence doesn't bother her much as long as I keep making the big bucks, but she'll raise a stink if I take our savings to support my lifestyle. Her keeping quiet about it is what'll save my business. My clients are conservative. Me being gay won't sit well with them, not well at all."

Arthur looked him in the eyes. "You better not fuck around with me on this, Conrad. I'm counting on you. If you don't deliver what I want and follow the plan, you could be damn sorry you didn't."

Conrad put his hands to his hips. "You threatening me, Billings?"

"I don't know what the hell's going on with you. Maybe you're falling for the bitch, going soft, discovering a con-science or having second thoughts on screwing her out of the money."

Arthur put his face to Conrad's. "You fuck this up and make life miserable for me, you can count on me returning the favor, you got me? Think about that. Think about your big fancy house on the hill getting sold . . . or worse. And there is worse, Conrad. Trust me."

Arthur yanked loose his tie and got back in his car. He drove off, leaving Conrad in a cloud of dust, with a sick feeling deep in his gut. What the hell had he gotten himself into, and what the hell was he going to do about Thelma? "Fuck."

Chapter 15

Thelma said good-bye to Conrad, then hung up the phone. She sat at the kitchen table and continued feeding Bonnie cereal and wondered what was wrong with the man? Something sure wasn't right. He sounded . . . different.

"Wow, what do you have cooking for dinner?" Effie asked as she came in. "Something sure smells good around here."

"Pulled pork's in the oven, sourdough bread rising on the stove, chocolate cake for dessert."

Effie groaned and kissed her head. "You're my hero. I should name a building after you. Thelma Towers sounds good. If Trump gets that honor for being rude, obnoxious and having bad hair, heaven knows you deserve it for being nice and pretty and an incredible cook."

Thelma offered Bonnie another spoonful of cereal, and Effie asked, "What's up? You don't seem your usual chipper self?"

"This baby is the worst eater on the planet, and I just got off the phone with Conrad and something's not right. I can tell. He was all serious like. I left him a few hours ago, and he was fine." She remembered making love with him in the shower and in his big bed and knew he was more than fine then.

"That is some blush you have going there, Thelma McAllister, and I doubt if it has anything to do with Bonnie not eating cereal and everything to do with Conrad."

She grinned. "Well, maybe a smidge, not that I'm admitting anything. I'm not a kiss-and-tell kind of gal. But something's changed from this afternoon to now. Conrad wants me to come over to the house as soon as I can."

She put down the spoon and looked at Effie. "We were supposed to meet later on, but he says it's important and he wants to see me right away because this can't wait and . . ." Her eyes widened, and she swallowed. She stood and stared off into space, not really seeing anything as the most likely reason for Conrad wanting to see her hit home. "Oh, my stars, I . . . I think Conrad wants to ask me to marry him!"

"Marry? Has Ryan talked to you about Conrad?"

"Why?" She gasped. "Did Conrad go to Ryan and ask him for my hand?" She giggled. "That's it, isn't it! Isn't that sweet of him! So traditional. Isn't Conrad the best!"

"Where's Ryan now?"

"He asked me to pretty-please make the pork and cake, then took off with Rory to Memphis to talk to that PI fellow."

She came around the table and put Bonnie in Effie's lap. "I need to get over to Conrad's right now." She bit her bottom lip. "I can't wait another minute. I'm going to be Mrs. Conrad Hastings. Isn't this wonderful? I'm so excited."

She hugged Effie and laughed, then nearly cried. "I'm so happy I could bust. I love that dear man to death."

"But Thelma, you . . . I . . . You need to take things slow, Thelma. Talk to Conrad, ask him right out why he's marrying you."

She beamed. "Because he loves me, that's why! I'll call you."

"We have to talk, Thelma. You and me. Right now."

"I don't have time. I'm getting married to the man I love most in this world." Thelma turned and waved as she snagged her purse from the sideboard in the hallway and hurried out the door, skipping all the way to her car. She hadn't skipped since . . . kindergarten. Life was wonderful. Life was great. Life was full of incredible surprises, and marrying Conrad was the biggest and best surprise of all. She laughed as she slid into the Sunfire and tore for Hastings House.

The sun dropped toward the levee. The Landing never looked more lovely than it did today. She slid in a CD of the Beach Boys, cranked it full volume and sang along to "Do You Wanna Dance" because that's exactly what she felt like doing. She pulled up behind Conrad's Ferrari and continued singing as she boogied her way inside without knocking. There wasn't time for formalities. The man she loved, the man she'd waited for all her life, was waiting for her. "Conrad? Oh, Conrad, darling, where are you?" She danced around in little circles in the hallway. "Where are you, my big hunk of wonderful man?"

"I'm right here, Thelma," Conrad said as he came into the hallway. "What are you doing?"

She snagged him around the waist. "I'm dancing with you." She kissed him. "Because I love you more than anything on earth."

Except he didn't look like a man in love. In fact . . . She stopped dancing. "You look awful." Her heart sank, her insides shriveled. "What's wrong, Conrad?"

He took her hand. "I need to talk to you, and it's really important. I need to tell you—"

"That he's been playing you like a well-tuned fiddle," said a man with a loose-hanging tie who walked toward her out of the kitchen.

Conrad snarled, "Get out of here, Billings. How'd you get here in the first place?"

"Came up the back path and waited in your kitchen. I thought you might try something like this, something underhanded, and I am not going anywhere 'til I have a little talk with Thelma here."

He turned to her, making her breath freeze in her lungs from his icy stare. "You should know—"

"Don't do this, Arthur," Conrad demanded. "I'll get your stinking money for you and—"

"That you're an heiress," the man continued, paying no attention to Conrad. "Two million dollars, to be exact, and Conrad here was courting you to get his hands on it. Fact is, I'd say he was asking you here now to propose. You see, Conrad's flat broke, and all he wants from you is a meal ticket and a cushy life."

Thelma felt all the blood drain from her face. "I don't believe you. Conrad loves me, he said so."

Arthur gave her a pathetic look. "What he loves is your money."

"Shut up, Arthur," Conrad hissed.

Arthur shrugged. "I came here to warn you. I didn't know what Conrad was up to 'til I heard him making plans with someone at our office and thought it my duty as a partner in the firm to save you from him."

Arthur looked at Conrad. "Now that Ms. McAllister knows all about you, my mission is complete."

Thelma shook her head. "I . . . I don't believe you at all."

"You don't have to," Arthur continued. "In two or three days you'll get the legal notification that Clyde Pierce was a multimillionaire and left his fortune to you for your great kindness when he was ill. He wrote his will in his own hand and put it in his safety-deposit box that was opened after his death. The will had to be authenticated by several experts in Washington, but that should be complete very soon."

Arthur turned to Conrad. "It gives me great satisfaction to know that Conrad will not succeed at his little ruse. I'm deeply sorry about this, but at least you have your inheritance and know the truth."

Numb, Thelma studied Conrad as Arthur retreated back down the hall, the rear door closing after him with a soft click. She wanted to laugh, tell Conrad she didn't believe a word that this Arthur guy just said, but the stricken look on Conrad's face told her every word was gospel truth. "Why? For money. All this over money?"

"It's not the way Arthur said, least not all of it."

"What did I ever do to you for you to hate me this much, to hurt me so . . ." She suddenly couldn't speak.

Conrad spread his arms and pleaded, "I'm sorry, Thelma. God, I'm sorry. I asked you over here to tell you what Arthur just told you. I wanted you to hear it from me and plead for your forgiveness. This was all his idea. He knew about the inheritance and I am truly broke and he wanted a cut if I could pull this off. But something happened along the way. I fell for you. I . . . love you. I truly do, and when Arthur realized I wasn't going through with the plan he got revenge by telling you first."

She scoffed. "What a load of crap, Conrad. Why should I believe any of it? You've done nothing but lie to me from the beginning. The very beginning."

"It's the truth. I swear."

She forced herself to pull in a deep, steadying breath. "I'm not going to cry, Conrad."

"That's good. That's really good. I don't want you to cry over something I did."

She walked to the sideboard, and Conrad said, "A drink is a good idea. I can pour you one, and then we can have a long talk and work this out."

"I'm not looking for alcohol. I'm looking for a gun."

"Gun!"

"All Southern homes have firearms in their sideboards. I know that, and so do you."

"A . . . a gun?"

She snagged a derringer and held the cold bit of steel in her palm as she turned to Conrad.

"Damn, Thelma, you can't shoot me. I'm not worth going to prison over."

She laughed, and it sounded very controlled, surprising the hell out of herself. "Honey man, no jury in the grand state of Tennessee would ever convict poor little old me after learning what a total bastard you are. Hell, Conrad, they'd probably give me a goddamn medal."

She took aim and pulled the trigger as Conrad dove behind the settee, the blast sounding like a cannon explosion instead of a derringer as the bullet shattered a vase on the cherry piecrust table. "Oops, I hope that wasn't Ming."

"Thelma! For Christsake!"

"Come out from behind there, you lily-livered, dirty rotten son of a bitch. I don't want to hurt another priceless antique trying to make you look like a piece of Swiss cheese. Come out right now."

"Thelma, stop!"

"I don't think so." She rounded the settee and caught his ashen face in her crosshairs as she took aim between his beady little eyes. "Kiss your sorry ass good-bye, Conrad. Because now it belongs to me."

"Shit! Thelma! Shit!"

She aimed and pulled the trigger and put a hole in the floor beside him. Then she dropped the two-shot derringer to the floor and strutted away. "Those misses were on purpose. To pay you back for what you did to me. Now you know what it feels like to be the prey. I hope I scared the hell out of you, Conrad," she called to him. "Because you sure as hell had it coming."

Then she closed the big front door of Hastings House behind her, got in her car, put the Sunfire in reverse and backed into the Ferrari, leaving a little love dent in the fender before she drove off into the blazing sunset.

Effie paced the front porch, not only to help coax a burp from Bonnie, but because of what Thelma could be facing at Conrad's right this minute. Proposal? Marriage? Elopement! Oh, Lord, not elopement. It all sounded great on the surface, but trouble was brewing. Something wasn't right, and Thelma was a babe in the woods when it came to men, especially a conniving, sophisticated asshole like Conrad Hastings.

That man could take advantage of Thelma and she'd never suspect before it was too late. But why would he? What was this all about? If Effie knew that little tidbit of info, she could put a stop to it before Thelma got hurt.

Obviously Ryan thought all was fine here in Happy Valley! Why didn't he warn Thelma?

The Sunfire turned into the drive, spitting gravel in all directions, pulling to a stop in front of the house. Thelma got out and kicked a stick across the yard. "Damn that man! I hope his sorry hide rots in hell for all eternity!"

Cradling Bonnie close so as not to jar her, Effie hurried out to the car. "Oh, God, what happened?"

"Lots." Thelma swept back her hair. "I'll give you the good news first. Seems that I'm an heiress, two million dollars' worth to be exact. The bad news is I didn't put a hole right between Conrad's eyes for trying to swindle me out of it."

"You're kidding."

"Nope. Missed. Didn't have the guts to do him in. 'Tis a pity."

"Holy crap! You pulled a gun on him?"

Thelma shrugged. "It's the South, dear. We do things a tad different than in California, like settle trouble ourselves and call the sheriff later and say 'Oh, my, whatever have I done? Lordy me.' Then do a Southern swoon. The swoon is a nice touch."

Thelma leaned against the car and let out a lungful of air. "How do women go from man to man? This was just one in my life, and he done wore me out. Sucked the life's blood right out of me, damn him. You know, it's not the years that turn a woman gray; it's the damn men."

"Amen." Effie thought of Ryan and how much easier her life would be without him complicating the hell out of it. She looked down at Bonnie. "Are you taking notes on this, little girl? You should. Save yourself a ton of heartache."

Rory's Suburban turned into the drive and pulled to a stop behind Thelma's car. Ryan got out, then Rory, and they strolled over. Rory took Bonnie in his big arms. "There's my sweet pea."

Thelma said, "Any news on Mimi?"

Rory tucked Bonnie into the crook of his arm and kissed her head. "PI guy never showed. Called, said he had a lead and would meet us here tomorrow night with pictures of guys flashing Mimi's photo around towns along the river. We're not the only ones looking for her. We need to get these guys and find out what the hell's going on."

Ryan looked from Effie to Thelma. "What's going on with you two? You both look like you could chew nails."

Effie lifted her left brow. "Well, let's see. Where to begin? Thelma fired two shots at Conrad, missing both times, and at the moment we're not sure if that's a good thing or a bad one." She peered hard at Ryan. "Thought you were going to talk to Thelma about Conrad or Conrad about Thelma or something."

Ryan's brows disappeared into his hair, and he gaped at Thelma. "Good God! You shot Conrad?"

She shrugged. "At Conrad. Seems I inherited a potful of

money from Clyde Pierce." She wagged her head. "Who
would have thought? Sure wish he'd bought himself a decent home to live in rather than leave his money to me.
Anyway, Conrad knew about it and tried to marry me to
get his hands on it because he's broke. I probably would
have done it, too—married him, I mean—until some guy
named Arthur showed up and clued me in before Conrad
could pop the question."

Rory said, "Well, dang, girl. You did have yourself some
kind of day. Thank God you didn't marry the scalawag.
Didn't think Conrad had that much meanness in him.
Least he didn't rob you blind."

"No thanks to Ryan," Effie added, glaring his way.

Ryan folded his arms. "Hey, how the hell was I to know
Conrad would pull a crazy stunt like that? The man's done
some crummy stuff in his time, mostly conceited, arrogant
stuff, but never anything like this. And, for some reason, I
honestly felt he was changing."

Effie poked him in the chest with her index finger and
gazed into his eyes. "Thelma could have eloped with him
tonight; then she'd have been in way too deep and never
believed he was up to no good."

Bonnie started to fuss, and Rory held her up and blew
bubbles on her tummy. "Least then Thelma would have
been ready for him and not missed when she got him in her
sights." He winked at Thelma. "Shotgun?"

Thelma sighed. "Derringer."

"Can't do much damage with a peashooter like that.
Wanna borrow the Winchester? She's in my closet ready
for action."

Effie noticed that sadness had replaced the anger showing in Thelma's eyes a few moments ago. Effie hooked her
arm through Thelma's. "We're heading over to Slim's.
This is one of those nights to drink our dinner and talk
girl talk."

Ryan came up beside her. "I'll join you."

Effie looked him dead in the eyes. "If there's one thing you're not, Ryan O'Fallon, it's a girl."

It wasn't that he hadn't told Thelma about Conrad that had her mad at him, because butting into someone else's business was risky business. But what bothered her most was that she liked Ryan so much it hurt, and he didn't return the feelings—except the sexual ones—one bit. She didn't need him hanging around tonight.

Thelma scratched her head and looked confused. "What should I do with two million dollars?"

What the heck am I going to do to get over Ryan O'Fallon? Not stay around here! Effie spread her hand over the landscape and turned her attention to Thelma. "Two million is a nice tidy sum. I see lots of pretty clothes, and a vacation, maybe a cruise and utility stocks, bonds and a smattering of small cap investments."

Effie started down the driveway with Thelma in tow. Not a breath of air stirred; the heat was like a giant Tennessee sauna as they headed for Slim's. Effie gave Thelma the ten-minute version of investing with caution 'til they got to the parking lot, only half-full now, the usual crowd not pouring in 'til later.

They went inside and "Lost Lover Blues" drowned out talk of money. What she wouldn't give for a little Rod Stewart right now. Thelma hitched herself onto a barstool, and Effie did the same as Sally came over and looked from one to the other. "Good God, what the hell happened now? You look like you could hunt bears with a ball bat."

Thelma pointed to a bottle across the bar. "Conrad tried to swindle me out of a two-million dollar inheritance that Clyde Pierce left me, and Effie's ready to strangle Ryan for not cluing me in. But I really think something else is getting to her and she's just not saying."

"Oh, sweet Jesus," Sally sighed, then snagged the bottle

of Wild Turkey and three glasses. "Gonna be a long night, I sure can see that."

Sally poured, and Thelma held up her glass. "And I shot at Conrad with a derringer."

Sally's eyes bulged. "Well, son of a bitch! A very long night. Should have used a shotgun, you know."

"So I've heard." She tapped her glass to Effie's and Sally's and they tossed back the whiskey.

Effie felt it sear a path clear down her throat, and she gasped, expecting fire to shoot from her mouth like a dragon. Her eyes watered, and her hair fell out . . . least it felt that way. She finally managed, "Damn."

Sally grinned. "Well, well. I think we have a virgin here, Ms. Thelma." Sally poured another gulp into Effie's glass, Thelma's and her own. She raised it in salute. "To virginity lost."

Effie looked on as the other two tossed back their drink, not sure if she'd survive another hit of Wild Turkey.

Sally coaxed. "It's just like sex, girl. The first time is always a total surprise. But the second time"—she nodded at Effie's glass—"ah, the second time is pure delight. It's . . . orgasmic."

Effie coughed, and her eyes bulged. "Orgasmic?"

Sally chuckled, and Thelma offered, "I think that hit a little too close to home. What have you and Ryan O'Fallon been up to?"

Effie picked up the glass and tossed back the firewater. This time it only partially burned out the lining of her esophagus. Her brain did a fast spin. "I can't feel my whips . . . I mean lips."

Sally said to Thelma, "So, did you hit the little bastard?"

Thelma wagged her head, and Sally poured another round of drinks. "Damn shame, that, 'cause it means you like the moron no matter what and all the booze in this place isn't going to make you change your mind."

Thelma threw back another mouthful and grinned, her eyes not quite focusing. "I want to hate Conrad Hastings with every bone in my body."

The three of them touched glasses and drank another shot of booze. Effie felt her eyes roll around in her head and saw her brain. It looked . . . pickled. "I think I'm dwunk."

Sally patted Effie's hand. "Honey, you're just getting started."

"Started on what?" Demar asked as he sat down next to Effie. Even in her inebriated state she didn't like him. He took Sally's glass, splashed in a mouthful of whiskey and downed it. "So, what are we celebrating?"

Effie hiccupped. "Thelma's recent inheritance."

Demar grinned. "Well, congrats, Thelma." He nodded to her. "Does that mean you'll be leaving the O'Fallons' and getting a place of your own?"

Thelma looked at him dumbfounded. "Hadn't considered that. Been my home for twenty-five years. Can't imagine living anywhere else. And who'd take care of little Bonnie 'til Rory finds her mama."

Sally retrieved another glass, and Demar poured more whiskey. "How's he going to do that?" He knocked back the whiskey, and Thelma and Sally followed. Demar nodded at Effie's glass. "No guts?"

"If I keep it up, I think that's exactly what will happen."

Thelma, Sally and Demar thumped their glasses on the bar, chanting, "Eff-ie, Eff-ie."

"All right, all right. I'm caving in to peer pressure. A new low in my very controlled, goal-oriented life." Effie drank the booze, and Demar asked Thelma, "Where'd you say Bonnie's mama's gone to?"

"Wish I knew." Thelma's eyes turned glassy. "Got a PI coming here tomorrow to show pictures around. Somebody's asking about Mimi. She might be in a pack of trouble, and Rory's got to save her. Can't have his baby with no mama."

"Is . . . Is that right?" Demar did a fast glance around, then nearly knocked over his drink, sloshing the contents onto the bar.

Sally giggled. "You best be careful with that stuff, my man."

Demar grinned. "I know a better way to get a taste of good whiskey around here." He kissed Sally long and deep. Effie remembered kissing Ryan like that, and her stomach did a little flip. But something suddenly felt like it happened and it shouldn't have, and she couldn't figure out what. It wasn't just Demar or her wanting to kiss Ryan. Something said? This conversation? Why couldn't she think?

"Whoa," Thelma huffed and fanned herself. "Now, that's what I call a humdinger of a lip-lock."

Sally blushed, her eyes sparkling as she stared at Demar. "Me, too," she said on a dream sigh. She stroked his chin. "You are some man."

He tucked a strand of hair behind her left ear, his fingers lingering there. "I'm mighty glad you think so, sugar. But I got to be going."

Sally huffed and pulled back, the fire in her eyes fading. "But you just got here, Demar. I can't believe you're leaving me already."

"Business, babe, business. You know how it is. Just wanted to stop in and say hey. If we want to get that housing project going, I got to step on it. Want to break ground and get some plans together before the winter sets in, and that'll take some doing."

Effie nodded, feeling her head loosening from her neck. Was that possible? After three, or was it four, shots of Wild Turkey anything was possible. "Getting a housing project together takes some planning." She looked at Demar. "How many units are you planning per track?"

"Track?" Demar grinned, but he looked . . . confused? "See, now that's exactly what I mean. Lot's of stuff to figure out. I'll stop back in tomorrow if I get a chance."

Sally winked at Demar, and he quick-kissed her and did a sexy shuffle for the door, every woman in the place watching him. Sally sagged onto the bar. "Sweet heaven above, what a hunk."

Thelma giggled. "And here comes another right on his heels."

Effie glanced at the door, and as Demar left Ryan entered, the two men exchanging greetings at the door. Effie turned to Sally. "Do you have a back door? I really don't want to face Ryan at the moment." No amount of booze would make her forget about him, but she had to figure out how to handle this . . . attraction.

Sally nodded to the wall behind her. "Door next to the ladies' room takes you to the back alley. Sure you can walk that far?"

Effie shrugged. "I'll soon find out."

She slid off the stool, stumbling as her feet touched the floor. She steadied, then made for the exit. The aroma of barbecue from the back porch wafted into the hall, filling the air with heavenly scents. She stepped outside into night muck. Two men were in the shadows talking. She heard Mimi's name, took another step and lost her balance and tripped down the steps, landing against, "Demar?"

"Hey, girl," he said in a surprised voice as he managed to catch her. He held her upright 'til she got her balance. "You okay?"

"Think I'm plastered. Never had Wild Turkey before." She looked around. "Where's the other guy you were talking to?"

Demar shrugged. "No one but me. Just checking out some ideas for rehabbing the place."

"Thought I heard—"

"What the hell do you think you're doing?" Ryan asked as he stepped out the door.

Chapter 16

Effie watched Ryan's eyes harden and his lips thin as he looked from Demar to her, and she said, "Oh, no you don't." Frustration suddenly cleared her brain. "You give me the there's-nothing-between-us-but-good-sex speech and then you get all cavemanlike because I've got my hands on another guy. Well, you can't have it both ways, Ryan O'Fallon."

He came down the steps and yanked Demar away from her. "Except this man belongs to Sally."

Demar held up his hand. "Hey, this isn't what you think, man. I was here looking the place over for renovations, and Effie tripped out the door, and I caught her because she's a little inebriated."

He nodded to the doorway. "Like you said, I got me a woman inside, and I'm sure as hell not in the market for another. Lord above, one's all I can handle at a time, all any man can handle."

Effie grinned up at him. "And I want to thank you for helping me. I'm usually not like this. See, this is why we need a Starbucks around here."

"I'll keep it in mind." Demar grinned and then walked away as Ryan came over. "Well, hell. How much whiskey did you drink in there?"

"None of your beeswax."

"I swear, half the time you sound like you're from the Landing more than I do." He took her chin between his thumb and forefinger and held her face to his, gazing into her eyes. Even in a stupor he looked good to her. Wonderful, in fact. But looking and the occasional bout of salivating was all the farther this attraction went, no matter how much she wanted more. If she had to buy a chastity belt, she was not getting any more into Ryan O'Fallon.

He said, "You've consumed more alcohol since you came here than you ever did back in San Diego."

"Brought on by the company I'm keeping and I am not referring to Sally, Thelma, Rory or Bonnie. Gee, I wonder who else there is?"

"We're together in California and you don't drink like a fish there. At the moment you could be a poster girl for AA."

"I'm here to get drunk with my friends. It's been that kind of day."

"Mission accomplished. And you need to be sober so we can finish the mall project and fax the prelim plans to the customer tomorrow. You're no good to me drunk."

She stared at him. "Tell me, am I good to you any other way?"

He took her hand. "You're a good architect. I'm a good architect. We have really good jobs that we've worked our butts off to make even better. We could get corner offices by the end of the year, parking passes, gym memberships, a Christmas bonus. We don't need to be screwing all that up because of some summer fling that will never last."

Ryan was right, though the screwing part had definite appeal. She picked her way down the shadowed alley so as not to stumble and embarrass herself more. Was that even possible at this point?

Early moonlight slanted through the trees, guiding their way. "I wonder what Demar was doing in that alley."

"Hell, what were you doing there?"

"Getting fresh air and I'd never move in on Sally's man. You know me better than that. He was talking about Mimi to someone. Doesn't that seem odd? There's something about that man in general that seems odd."

Ryan considered the question and decided Demar was the least of his worries because Ryan couldn't stop thinking about having sex with Effie, no matter how hard he tried or what the hell he did. He was the master of getting over women. Here today, gone tomorrow. No problem. Except Effie Wilson was a huge problem.

If he stayed away from her, he thought of having sex with her; if he was near her, he thought about it. In the car with Rory, burping Bonnie, steering a barge, day, night, through all those things what he really wanted was Effie! The woman was an addiction—not that he'd ever tell her that—and he had to get over her before they returned to California so they could get on with their lives.

The best idea was to stay away from her now, get her out of his system. But when they reached the house it took every ounce of willpower he had not to follow her up the hall stairs to her room. Instead he snagged a six-pack from the fridge, went outside and sat on the top step of the porch, hoping the night heat would sweat the image of Effie all hot and ready for him out of his system.

He studied the six-pack. Beer was a hell of a substitute for sex.

Fireflies twinkled in the trees; the scent of water drifted off the Mississippi. Max parked down beside him, and Ryan scratched him behind the ears. Why couldn't dealing with women be as simple as dealing with dogs? You always knew where you stood with a pet, no second-guessing.

A black truck that Ryan didn't recognize pulled into the drive and coasted to a stop in front of him. Conrad got out, paused as if sizing up the situation, then headed for the steps as Ryan said to Max, "Well, there you go, boy. A little evening snack. Meals on Wheels. Go for it."

Max stood and stretched, and Conrad stopped. "Is your dog going to eat me?"

"I'd say you've got about a fifty-fifty chance. What the hell do you want?"

"I need to talk to you. About Thelma."

"Give me one good reason why I shouldn't just get a shotgun, that seems to be the weapon of choice tonight, and fill your ass full of lead."

"I can imagine what you think of me—and that's okay, I deserve it—but the fact is I love Thelma and I want to get her back and don't know how to do it. I want to make her happy. I swear it's the truth."

He ran his hand over his face. "Look, I started out to swindle her, but then things changed. I changed. I don't want her money, I want her and I intended to tell her everything when my attorney beat me to it."

"Why the hell would your attorney do that? Isn't the idea of having an attorney that he works for you?"

"He suspected I was weaseling out of our deal. He was supposed to get a cut of the inheritance when I married Thelma. He swore if I ruined things for him, he'd return the favor. He kept his promise."

Ryan nodded at the truck. "Slumming?"

"Sold the Ferrari to a guy in Memphis who's had his eye on it for a while now. I'm going to rebuild Hastings Drydock. Get respectable and win Thelma over if it takes the rest of my life."

"I think you're underestimating."

"She won't talk to me right now. Went to Slim's and she had him toss me out on my butt."

Conrad tried to smooth back his hair, but it wouldn't

cooperate. First time that had ever happened. "If you can just tell her all that for me, maybe she'll talk to me. Just talk. Five minutes is all I'm asking."

In all the years Ryan had known Conrad Hastings, he'd never seen this Conrad. Mussed hair, wrinkled pants and shirt, sweat stains under the arms, bleary eyed, a truck. Conrad in a Ford boggled the mind. If he was putting on an act, this was an Oscar-winning performance. Besides, Ryan knew firsthand how women could scramble your brain, and Conrad seemed to be suffering from the same affliction as Ryan . . . frustrationitis.

Ryan nodded to his other side. "Take a seat."

Conrad eyed Max, then parked as Ryan asked, "Wanna beer?"

Conrad exhaled a ragged breath, suddenly looking tired to the bone. "God, I'd love a beer."

Ryan pulled a can of Coors from the plastic webbing holding the six together and handed it over. Conrad clumsily pulled at the tab, the actions of someone not familiar with the ordinary process of opening canned beer. Ryan snapped his can and drank deep; Conrad did the same. He swiped the back of his arm across his mouth and burped. Conrad Hastings, ordinary guy. Who would have thought?

"Why haven't you shot me yet?"

"Blood on the steps? Thelma would have my ass in a sling. Besides, she already did the shooting thing. If she wanted you dead, she wouldn't have missed. Not my business to undo what she set her mind to do. And I've got to admit, you're not the only one with woman problems. I know how it goes in the female department. Can't live with 'em, damn tough to live without 'em."

Conrad took another gulp. "If I get a chance to talk to Thelma, what do I say?"

"Besides you're a dumbass? How do I know you're not planning on taking her money and divorcing her? That was the original plan, right?"

"It was. But now . . . The only thing I can come up with is wooing her with a business proposition. Investing in Hastings Dry-dock."

"Got all the earmarks of investing in swampland in Florida."

"Not if I sell Thelma something she really likes."

"That's a hell of a lot of Beach Boy albums, Conrad."

"I was thinking of Hastings House and the surrounding land for half the appraised value."

Ryan stopped the can halfway to his mouth and gazed at Conrad. "You love that house. It's your family home."

Conrad nodded, studying the steps. "Thelma loves it, too. I want to prove to her that I want to make it all work, that I want to make us work. Think she'll go for it? Give me a chance?"

"Get it written up, use a different attorney. Hell, ask her. Got nothing to lose . . . except your house and business . . . and . . . Damn, Conrad, you sure about this?"

He downed the rest of the beer and crushed the can in his hands. He wasn't quite the wimp Ryan thought. "What if she refuses? What if she doesn't want anything to do with me ever? Not that I blame her."

He raked his hair again and looked at Ryan. "I can't imagine life without Thelma. She believes in me, least she did. It was never about how much money I could spend on her or what I could buy for her. It was always about us, the things we did together, the fun and excitement. She cared for me. I still care for her. Dammit, Ryan, I want Thelma back."

Ryan pulled off another can, popped the top and slipped it in Conrad's hand. "All she can do is tell you to go to hell, and from what I see you're already there. Make it business and prove you're a different man. Then you can start courting her again and see what happens."

Conrad nodded. "It'll take a while. I've got to get her to trust me." He chugged back the beer, then studied Ryan.

"Why the hell are you being so damn helpful? Thought you'd hate my guts after what I did."

"Only some of your guts. Thelma hasn't completely given up on you, and that's good enough for me."

Conrad looked at him from the corner of his eyes. A twinkle of hope sparked. "She . . . She told you that?"

"Hell no. The fact that you're still drawing breath is what tells me. But if I were you, I wouldn't cross her again . . . unless you've got a death wish."

Conrad nodded slowly as if considering the statement. "Mind if I sit a spell and wait for her? She's got to come home sometime, and she's bound to be a little sloshed. Maybe I can get her to listen to me if her reflexes are down."

"Least it'll give you time to duck when she swings." Ryan stood and toed the rest of the beers over to Conrad. "If you're serious about saving the dry dock, I bet Dad knows a couple of guys who might be willing to give you a chance if he says so. Your family had a good name on the river for a long time, Conrad. That counts for something. The *Mississippi Miss* needs her hull gone over and gaskets replaced. I'll bring her around in a day or two."

"I appreciate it."

"Thelma's the one I'm thinking about here."

Conrad gave him a tired half grin. "Me, too."

"Well, now's your chance because she's heading this way." He nodded at Conrad. "Good luck. You're going to need it."

Conrad took another long drink as the screen door banged closed behind Ryan. Thelma came up the drive and stopped at the bottom of the steps. She gave him a defiant stare, hands fisted, ready for a fight. Not a great beginning to redemption by Conrad.

"What the hell are you doing here dirtying up my steps?"

"Waiting for you."

"I almost blew you to kingdom come once today. Wasn't that enough warning for you to stay away from me?"

She had a sassy jut to her hip, but hurt lingered deep in her eyes. He could see it even in the dark. His insides contracted. He had put that hurt there, and by God, he'd take it away no matter what. How could he hurt Thelma? She was a lot of things—lover, companion, cook—but most of all she'd been his best friend, not wanting anything from him except just being himself. "I have a business proposition for you."

She smacked her palm to her forehead. "Dear Lord, please save me from that! You're nothing but a con man." She started for the side door around back.

"I want to sell you Hastings House for half its appraised value."

She stopped and turned. "Why in the world would you do a thing like that?"

"Because you love that house as much as I do and I know you'll take care of it. And I need the money to rebuild the dry dock. I can borrow some, but I need cash up front. Will you buy it?"

"And where the heck will you live?"

"At the dock. My grandpappy lived there when he first started out, and I can, too. There's a little apartment over the office that we use for storage now. I can live there; it's all I need."

Her brow furrowed. "I don't trust you, Conrad. I don't trust you one smidgen. You've got something up your slimy sleeve besides your slimy arm. You're determined to swindle me out of my money no matter what it takes."

"Please, Thelma." He came down the steps. "I'm sorry. I'm sorry for everything. I'm going to rebuild the business, and then I'm going to ask you to marry me."

"Right." Her tone was sarcastic, but her eyes glazed with tears.

"I swear to God it's true. Every word. It's going to take a little while. I already fired my office managers who were bleeding me dry. Now I've got to get the business back that I've lost. Ryan's bringing over one of his tugs, and if I can get good workers and do a first-rate job, the word will get out. Slowly, but it will happen."

He shrugged. "I used to help out at the docks when I was in high school. Bet I can still handle a welding torch."

"And burn the place to the ground." She glared. "And even if you didn't, then what? You marry me and get your big house back?"

"It's yours forever. If you're not in it, I don't want it. I'll sign any papers you want. Do whatever it takes to make you trust me."

Her brows drew together. "You're really going to weld?"

"Watch me."

"Finish the patio?"

"Absolutely. Your chin's quivering. Don't cry, Thelma. No one else would notice that you're going to cry, but I do. I've gotten to know you so well, maybe even better than you know yourself. While some part of me wanted your money, the rest of me fell head over heels in love with you. Every wonderful inch of you." He wagged his brows. "I think some part of me's always been attracted to you. That's why I was willing to go along with Arthur's idea in the first place."

"You are so full of bull crap."

"I'm going to make you believe in me as much as I believe in you. I'm going to impress you, steal your heart, and we're going to live happily ever after."

He planted a quick kiss on her cheek and started for his truck, feeling more content than he had in years. He had a purpose, a real goal. He wasn't a jerk with a credit card running around trying to impress everyone. He had Thelma waiting in the wings. What more could he ask for?

"I think you're a horse's ass, Conrad Hastings," Thelma called after him.

"I'm sure you do, my dear, but I'm going to change your mind because we love each other and we belong together. I messed it up, and now I'm going to fix it."

Effie finished printing out the last of the proposal for the mall as the sunset faded from gold and blues to grays and blacks outside the dining room window. She took a sip of iced tea and sat back in the mahogany chair, the fax machine grinding through the stack of papers, shipping the proposal to San Diego. "Thank the Lord for electronic devices and time zones. Nine here, six in California. What a deal."

Ryan sat across the dining room table littered with blueprints and notes. "It took all day to finalize the project on time, but we did it. You know this was a good thing. Made us remember how much we like our jobs and don't want to risk losing them."

He meant it as an explanation for not taking this fling any further, she was sure of it. The reason why they'd always be just business partners.

Everything for the job. But some part of her wondered . . . what if? What if Ryan was the man she saw here all the time? What if he wasn't the job? What if he was a son, a brother, a friend and a musician part of the time and work didn't rule his life? What if work didn't rule hers? What if the job wasn't everything? "Do you ever consider staying here?"

He took another long drink of iced tea. "Never crossed my mind. What would I do? I'm an architect. I design malls, airports, office buildings, the big stuff. Nothing like that's happening on the Landing. Nothing period happens here. Bonnie's the biggest news since Grant quartered troops at Hastings House."

"Is that bad?"

"Not if this is what you want to do with your life. Run tugs, marry, have kids. Suits Dad, not me or Keefe or Quaid."

"Sally likes it here well enough."

"She got burnt out on Wall Street. Was promised a big promotion with an investment firm, then got passed over. The bastards lied to her to get her customers, then cut her out of the picture. They used her to get what they wanted. The stress nearly killed her, so she moved back. Who knows how long she'll stay."

"She looks content, and Rory's happy here."

"He made O'Fallon Transport what it is. This is his home, and he'd like it even more if he could find Mimi."

Ryan stood and walked to the window. "That PI should be here any minute. Hope we have some luck finding those guys looking for Mimi. Then we can ask them why they're looking for her. I wonder what she's gotten herself into. If she's half the woman Dad and Thelma say she is, she wouldn't have left Bonnie unless things were bad."

"Then we better be careful there's no connection between the mom and babe. That could put Bonnie in danger." Apprehension settled like a boulder in her stomach. "Last night Sally and Thelma and I might have mentioned Mimi and Rory and Bonnie."

Ryan shrugged. "Thelma knows the score, and I think Sally's put two-and-two together by now. It's not like you told anyone who wasn't already in the know."

Effie bit her lip. "Demar was there."

Ryan's eyes met hers through the dim light. "Shit."

"I didn't think about it 'til now. Fallout from Wild Turkey and a short-circuiting brain. And then he was outside in the alley talking about Mimi."

"I'll tell that PI guy what's going on. Just because we don't like Demar doesn't mean he's trouble."

"Except he was talking about Mimi."

"Damn. Not good. Sally doesn't need another person

using her, and this sounds like trouble for Dad. Maybe Demar will show up tonight. I'll find out what's going on."

"I'll help Thelma with Bonnie tonight. With Conrad out of the picture she can use a little company."

A car door slammed outside, and Max went into barking mode. "Bet that's your PI guy," Effie said. "You save him from Mean Max, and I'll get Rory."

Ryan left the room as Thelma came in, and Effie asked, "How are you doing? I haven't seen much of you today with working on the mall project."

"I've got a situation. Conrad wants to sell me Hastings House cheap so he can rebuild the dry dock. I'm thinking about turning the place into a bed and breakfast to cover taxes and upkeep. Ida Landon's done that with Ivy Acres down the road. Course, she's not doing all that well because the woman can't boil water. But I think I could make it work."

"If you serve up pecan pie, you'll make a killing. What does Conrad think of your idea?"

Thelma batted her eyes and rolled her shoulders. "Honey, I don't rightly know what that man thinks, and I don't care. Conrad's got his life, least for the moment, and I got mine. Besides, it's the only way I can afford Hastings House, cheap or not. The upkeep and taxes will eat me alive. I figure with Demar's company fixing up the town and building a residential area more folks will be coming here and needing a place to stay. Besides my pies I see homemade scones, Southern Comfort tea and ghost tours in the woods searching for Grant." She grinned. "'Bout time that Yankee did us some good around here." She winked. "So what do you think?"

Rory hurried into the dining room and handed Thelma the baby monitor. "I think that child of mine has the temperament of a grizzly. The only thing that sounds good is that blasted monitor not making any noise. I got her down, but Lord knows for how long. Try giving her a bottle if she wakes up and take her for a walk down by the river. The stroller's around by the side door. I had to tighten a wheel that wobbled loose." He stopped and grinned. "Sweet Pea sure loves the sound of the river."

"Just like her daddy." Effie kissed Rory on the cheek and took his hand. "Good luck on finding Mimi tonight."

"I've got to find her fast. Things are getting worse instead of better." He left the room, his footsteps sounding in the hall. The front door opened, letting in a triangle shaft of light from the porch light, then closed.

Effie studied the carnage on the dining room table. "What a mess."

Thelma set the monitor on the table and picked up a blueprint. "I'll roll these and put them into the tubes. You sort through the papers and figure out what you want to do with them. You must really like being an architect to put so much time into it."

Effie picked up a handful of paper, noticing Ryan's notes on the side. She knew his handwriting as well as her own. "While other girls played with Barbie I played with her dream house. Added a bath, porch, sunroom Jacuzzi and solar panels for heating. Melted the plastic roof off."

Thelma laughed and turned on more lights as night claimed the earth. She picked up another blueprint as the baby monitor suddenly squawked to life. "That child never sleeps and has one powerful set of lungs on her." Thelma said to Effie, "You get a bottle. I'll head upstairs."

Effie made the trip from fridge to nursery in record time and handed Thelma the bottle as she rocked a wailing Bonnie. "Here you go, little bit," Thelma said over the bawling. "Yum, yum."

Bonnie slurped, and Thelma wagged her head. "I swear that child has some appetite. Reminds me of Ryan and Keefe when they were babes."

"What's Keefe like. Just like Ryan?"

"Ever hear of *Sins and Secrets*? He's Lex Zandor, the sexiest, hottest hunk on daytime television. The network had one of those reality contests where a woman won a weekend with him? Caused a riot right there in New York City when some of the women thought they should get picked and didn't. Called in the police and riot squad. Lord have mercy! I think he's coming home next week to escape."

Effie chuckled. "I can't imagine Ryan on a soap."

"Keefe's loved theater all his life and is having a grand old time in New York . . . 'til that contest came along. All those gals running after him? And the press, I don't know how he puts up with it all."

She burped Bonnie. "We'll go for that walk now. A full tummy and the sound of the tows should put little bit here back to sleep soon enough."

Effie yawned. "Don't know about you, but I could use an early night."

"Because of the work or the man? What's going on between you two anyway?"

Effie leaned against the crib and looked out the window to the near moonless night. "Absolutely nothing."

"You haven't been just designing malls since you've been here. I can tell that much. So, what in the world's keeping you two apart?"

"The mall, a corner office, gym membership, a Lexus, a healthy 401K."

Thelma hoisted Bonnie to her shoulder, then carried her downstairs, and Effie followed to the side door as she continued, "And you need those things? Seems to me you're pretty content with wearing my old blouses, rolled-up shorts, your hair pulled back into a ponytail and walking more than driving while you're here."

"Things are different here. I'm different. So is Ryan."

"Is this a good different we're talking about or a bad one?"

"It's bad for business and careers but . . ." Effie opened the side door and held the stroller as Thelma strapped Bonnie in. Thelma stood and faced Effie. "The answer's plain as the nose on your face, Effie Wilson. You gotta stay here and get Ryan to do the same."

"That is not ever going to happen. Living on the Landing is the last thing on his to-do list." Effie pushed the stroller down the walkway, bumping over the bricks 'til they headed into the grass toward the dim light coming off the dock below the cliff. "Dark as a graveyard out there."

"See, now you have to stay here. You're starting to talk river talk. If you go back to California, they'll make fun of you, ruin your self-esteem." Thelma glanced back at the house. "Wasn't that front porch light on when Rory left? He always leaves it on."

"Burnt out. We'll change it tomorrow."

They headed deeper into the shadows. "Where's Max? He's always wanting someone to throw that yellow ball of his." Thelma stopped. "Things aren't right. All of a sudden I got a real bad feeling crawling up my back."

They both looked to the house, and someone darted across the drive and hid behind the magnolia by the porch. Effie felt ice form in her veins and whispered, "We've got visitors and not the good kind."

Another man ran from behind an oak tree and stepped up onto the porch. He opened the front door and went inside. Effie grabbed Thelma's arm as she sucked in a quick breath. "I think he's got a gun. Burglars?"

"Never had burglars at the Landing before. Nothing to steal. And I bet twenty-to-one he's tracking mud into my clean house." Thelma nodded to the end of the drive. "A car I don't recognize. What do you think they all want? What's going on here?"

"We did this, last night at Slim's. We let it slip in our drunken state that Bonnie was Rory's and Mimi's, remember? And Demar was there."

"After many, many shots of Wild Turkey remembering is out of the question, that's the point. Besides, the Conrad issue sort of occupied my brain, what was left of it. But I believe you. They're after the baby. But what's Demar got to do with this?"

"Good question." She nodded at the house. "They must not have seen us come out the side door. We can't go to town for help. Whoever is in that car will see us. We'll go to the docks. There's a phone."

"When they realize we've gone they'll start looking around. Somehow they knew we were home alone."

Effie swore. "I hate when guys think I'm the weak little woman and they can steamroll right over me."

"Look around, girl. We are weak little women . . . though truth be told I'm not so little."

Staying in the shadows of the oaks, they made for the road that led down to the docks. Thelma stopped. "I hear a whimper. Max?"

Shiny eyes glowed in the dark, Max lying on the ground. "What's up, boy?" Effie petted him, her hand suddenly sticky with . . . She held it up in the faint moonlight slicing through the tree. "Blood." She hissed, "Those sons of bitches shot our Max."

Chapter 17

Thelma whispered, "Suddenly I'm not feeling all that weak. Those assholes are after my babe, shot Max and tracked mud all over my carpets. Fact is, I'm feeling pissed as hell."

Effie bent down and scooped her arms under Max and grunted as she lifted him. "You're okay, boy."

She stood, got a better grip and blew a strand of hair out of her eyes. "Let's get out of here."

Walking fast, she followed Thelma to the road. "Keep to the side and tiptoe."

"And just how am I supposed to tiptoe on gravel?"

Frogs did their nightly serenade, and the river gently lapped the shore as Effie followed Thelma to the first bend, a dim overhead light illuminating the road. Effie thought of better times, and at the moment there were a ton of them, but kissing Ryan at this very spot got top pick. What a kiss. What a guy.

Max whimpered, and she told him to think about steak bones and chasing balls. A crescent moon reflected off the water, stars twinkled. A few lights here and there lit the dock, and three tows bobbed gently at their moorings.

Thelma said, "So far so good. The perpetrators don't even know we're here."

Effie stared. "Perpetrators?"

"Always wanted to use that word. Doubt if I'll ever get a better chance."

"I hope not. I'd so much rather be at Slim's ruining my arteries." They headed for the office boat when Bonnie let out an ear-piercing bellow that rivaled any barge horn. Thelma stopped dead. "Oh, sweet Jesus. Not now, little bit."

Bonnie bellowed again, and Thelma turned to Effie, who said, "Maybe they didn't hear?"

"Honey, folks in New Orleans heard. Those guys know we're down here. The phone's too far away, and by the time help comes we—"

"The boats." Effie nodded to the *Mississippi Miss* next to her.

"Hide there?" Thelma's wide eyes shone against the darkness. "Too obvious."

"Hide on the water." Gauging the swells, Effie carefully stepped from the dock onto the deck and put Max down, then helped Thelma as she cradled a howling Bonnie. Effie said, "I'll take the baby. You cast off the lines and get us out of here."

Thelma stepped onto the deck. "Come again?"

"You can't steer this boat with a baby in your arms, so I'll stay down here and—"

"Wait a minute!" Thelma gave one big wag of her head and said over another ear-piercing yell, "What makes you think I can run a tow?" Her eyes rounded to the size of a full moon.

Effie pointed at her. "The fact that you've lived with the O'Fallons for most of your life. Surely you've—"

"Cooked and cleaned and kept house and minded babies. I hate heights, and I'm not too fond of water, if you must know. Didn't Ryan show you something when you were running the other day?" Thelma gave her a cocky look. "Probably showed you plenty, none of it doing us any good now."

"I live in a condo, drive a Volvo. The only big machinery I operate is an automatic elevator."

"Someone's on the gravel road. There's a fishing boat behind the office at the far end. We could try that."

Bonnie let out another yell. "We'll never make it."

Effie jumped back to the dock, threw off the lines, then headed for the steps, not bothering to be quiet. What was the use in that with bellowing Bonnie on board? Effie's lungs threatened to explode when she got to the wheelhouse and opened the door. Least that's what she wanted to do. Locked! "No!" She banged her head against the glass door.

She spotted a cone from a flashlight on the bend in the road, and voices trailed her way. Thelma yelled, "Hurry up."

"What do you think I'm doing? Where the hell did Ryan hide that damn key? How'd I wind up on a towboat on the Mississippi with bad guys after me? I'm a damn architect!"

She felt over the doorway, and her fingers connected with a key. Shaking, she jammed it into the lock, turned and wrenched open the door. She flipped on the lights and looked at the control panel. Oh, Lordy! Why had it looked so much simpler when Ryan was here?

She pushed down the black button, and the engines powered to life, the familiar rumbling gyrating clear into her bones. Thank God. "Now, which stick-thingy works the back of the boat, the front, and gets us the hell out of here?"

She flipped on all the switch-marked lights, and a floodlight came on. Least she could see the dock if she screwed up big time and plowed into it.

She shoved the long bronze stick left, pushed the

chrome handle forward that added power and prayed she didn't mow over the other tows tied up and probably take down half of Memphis along the way. "Hope everyone's got their insurance paid up."

Flashlights played against the docks as men ran toward the *Mississippi Miss.*

"Oh, shit! Oh, shit!" She gave the engines more power and steered out into the river, leaving the dock and the bad guys behind. If her heart beat any faster, it would pop right out of her chest, and if there was a Mississippi goddess, she just smiled on Effie, until the monitor on the console started to beep. Beeping monitors were never good, on land or sea. At least on land she could call the IT department.

A black blip meaning boat ahead showed on the screen. The beeping grew louder; it was headed her way. She picked up the mike contraption that looked like a fat cell phone, pressed the button on the side and yelled, "Help! Somebody out there on the river. Help! Oh, I think I'm supposed to say Mayday. Uh, yeah. Mayday, whatever the hell that means, this is the *Mississippi Miss* and I'm Effie Wilson and I've just pulled out from O'Fallon's Landing with Thelma and baby Bonnie and a wounded dog that some creeps shot and who are now chasing after us. I don't know how to steer this boat, so you all out there in radio land will have to steer around me. And if someone can call Ryan O'Fallon at Slim's and tell him to get his butt out here right now, I would really appreciate it. Dammit, where is that man when I need him? Just ignore that last part."

She let go of the mike, and it came to life with, "Uh, *Mississippi Miss,* this is the *Jenny O.* What the hell's going on over there?"

Effie pressed the button. "I've got Rory O'Fallon's baby on board, and some men, least I think they're men, that's kind of sexist, isn't it?" She was clearly losing her mind.

"Some people are trying to get Bonnie because they're after Mimi, that's Bonnie's mother, and they think if they get the baby, Mimi will show up to get her back and they can grab her, for what reason none of us knows. What if they get a boat and come after me?"

"*Mississippi Miss*, this is *Jenny O*. I'm not sure what in blue-blazes you just said, but it sounds like you got more troubles than a dog's got fleas, so I'm thinking you should hide out."

"Uh, this is a really big boat, *Jenny O*; and all I see is a bunch of open water."

"Kill all your lights and cut your engines. There's only a spit of a moon, and you'll fade into the night, least for a while. The other tows can spot you on their radar, and I'll put out the word you got problems. You just sit tight now, you hear. Whoever's after you will lose you in the dark, and we'll get someone to help. It takes two miles to stop the *Jenny*, and I'll be long past you to do any good."

Effie shut down everything, casting the tow in total darkness, the only sound the approaching *Jenny* some ways off and to her left. Was that the port or starboard? And why in the world didn't they just call it right and left in the first place?

An eerie quiet hung over the *Miss* as it swayed with river swells and flowed south with the current. Quietly she backed down the stairs, letting her body move with the boat so as not to fall. When she got to the bottom Thelma said, "Why are we stopping? You were doing real great. I was impressed all to pieces."

"How's Max?"

Thelma grinned, her teeth white against the darkness. "Used my bra to stop the bleeding. Nothing like a full-fig-ured cup size and a lot of spandex to do the job right. Why'd you turn out all the lights?"

"No one can see us. Not that the bad guys could come after us anyway unless they find the runabout."

"I was feeling pretty good 'til you threw in the run-about. What if Bonnie yells again?" Thelma kissed the baby's forehead. "This one's like a homing device."

"Take her into the deck cabin. That will muffle the sound a little. I'll stay out here and keep a lookout."

"You should have a weapon."

Effie unsnapped an orange buoy ring from the side of the deck cabin, and Thelma said, "You're supposed to incapacitate evildoers, honey. Not save them."

Effie measured the weight in her hands. "It's solid and heavy. I'll hide behind that big coil of line." She nodded to the thick rope she'd measured when out here with Ryan. "If they come on board, wham." She made a swinging motion with the buoy. "I'll get them right in the gut and over they'll go into the river. Ta-da!"

"I think you've been reading too much *Huck Finn*."

"Wait 'til you see me play poker and smoke cigars."

"Oh, sweet Jesus!"

Ryan bought one of the *River Rat* deckhands he knew a beer and showed him the pictures of the guys asking about Mimi down in Memphis. The answer was the same, never seen them before. Least whoever was tracking Mimi hadn't gotten to the Landing . . . yet.

Demar sat at the other end of the bar, talking to Sally, but when Ryan looked his way he seemed to be glancing back, as if more interested in what Ryan had to say than Sally.

Rory parked next to Ryan as Howlin' Wolf's "Goin' Down Slow" purred from the jukebox. Rory took a long drink of his beer and leaned his elbows on the bar. "Well, I'm having squat for luck. Nobody here knows these guys from Adam. You doing any better?"

Ryan hunched his shoulders. "The same." He flicked the picture. "But I bet they're headed here. They're on to something. When they show up we'll get them and find out who and why—"

"Hey," Sally said as she hurried over to Ryan, her brows arched. "We got a little problem. Dad just got a ship-to-shore call for you from the *Jenny O. The Mississippi Miss* is in the middle of the channel at marker one sixty-eight, and Effie Wilson's at the helm along with an injured Max, Thelma and Bonnie. Someone's after her, and she needs help fast. Holy crap!"

Ryan exchanged looks with his dad, who slid from his stool and hustled his way past the tables, heading for the door, saying, "Christ-in-a -sidecar, boy. Get a move on."

Ryan ran after his dad, not catching up 'til halfway to the Suburban. They jumped into the car, and Demar suddenly appeared at the passenger side window and poked his head inside. "Hey, we need to talk."

"No time," Rory said as he fired the engine. "We got ourselves a crisis situation."

"I'm a cop, working with the Tennessee Attorney General's Office." He thrust a silver badge their way. "I'm looking for Mimi; her real name's Jolie Bains. Whoever's after your baby might know where she is."

Rory scowled at Demar. "You saying my Mimi's into something bad and you expect me to help you find her? Like hell!" He put the car in gear.

"I'm saying she's in a heap of trouble and somebody needs to find her fast."

"Damnation!" Rory slammed his hand against the dashboard, then hitched his chin to the back. "Climb in. But if you think my Mimi's done something illegal, I'm not buying it."

Demar took a seat. Rory headed for the dock as Demar added, "All we know is that she worked for River Environs and they're under investigation for using inferior materials on levees and docks. She contacted the Attorney

General's Office about a year and a half ago saying she suspected wrong-doing. Then suddenly she disappeared."

"Well, dangit," Rory snapped. "That proves straight out she wasn't involved or she wouldn't have blown the whistle. The woman's innocent as the driven snow, I'm telling you, and sticking her neck out to do the right thing proves it."

"Could be, but right now a whole passelful of not very nice people are hot on her heels, and that isn't conducive to a long life. Last night Effie and Thelma and Sally let it slip that Bonnie was yours and Mimi's, not Ryan's, and I'm guessing some others picked up on that as well. Whoever they are, they want Mimi bad."

Rory swore and skidded into the parking area by the dock. He got out and trotted toward the office, then stopped and peered into the darkness. "Our runabout's out there on the river. Can tell the hum of that old engine anywhere."

Ryan swallowed. "Meaning someone's gone after the *Mississippi Miss*."

"That'd be my guess." Rory raked his hair. "Shitfire! And my precious baby girl's right smack in the middle of this whole mess."

Another runabout hummed through the darkness, approaching from downstream, hugging the shore. It glided up to the dock, and Conrad Hastings gave a little salute. "I was at the dry dock working and listening to the radio chatter when I picked up a call from the *Mississippi Miss*. Called Slim's, looking for you all, and Sally said you were headed here. Jump in, we gotta go. The girls are out there."

Rory grinned. "The girls. Well, I'll be damned. Whoever thought Conrad Hastings would save the day?" He stepped into the runabout, and Ryan followed, then Demar. Conrad turned the runabout for the river. "Dark as the ace of spades out here. Can't see a damn thing."

Rory rubbed his eyes. "Used to be I could see as good at night as in the day, but no more."

Ryan made his way to the bow and studied the darkness, shapes suddenly forming as his vision acclimated the same way it had years ago when he ran tows. Once a river man, always a river man. "*Mississippi Miss* is dead in the water, to port, about three hundred yards out. Whoever is in our runabout overshot, but looks like they're doubling back and heading right for the *Miss*. They won't overshoot this time. There's another tow closing in on the *Miss*. Line hauler to port."

Rory said, "Sounds like the *Jenny O*. Should pass close. Hells bells," Rory bellowed.

Conrad opened the runabout engine full throttle, sending the little boat skimming precariously over the surface in the direction Ryan pointed. The hull thumped against the swells. With luck they wouldn't hit a piece of drift and flip like Thelma turning flapjacks on a hot griddle.

"See anyone on the *Miss*?" Rory asked, his tone laced with worry.

"Too dark for that." Ryan could barely get the words out around the fear lodging like a softball in his throat. Effie was smart but no match for these thugs. "Our runabout's pulled up to the *Miss*'s stern, Conrad. Give her the gas! I think someone's getting out. Fuck!"

"I'm closer to the bow," Conrad said. "I'm heading there." He slid next to the shallow deck and killed the engine as Ryan tossed a line around a cleat, securing the runabout to the tow. Two men walked down the side of the deck toward the stern as Rory leaped on board, followed by Conrad, who got a ring buoy in the gut along with a, "Take that, you bastard."

What the . . . "Effie?"

Conrad grunted, stumbled and fell back into the water with a splash, and the men stopped in their tracks. Demar hopped on board the *Miss* and drew a gun, pointing it their way. "Police! Freeze!"

"Fuck you!" someone said. Then the two men jumped into the water. Ryan pulled off his shoes and followed. Not to save them, but to retrieve Conrad, who was gasping for air. The buoy had nearly drowned the man, and Thelma would be none too happy if that happened, no matter how many times she'd shot at him herself.

Ryan swam as Demar yelled, "Where the hell did they go?"

Ryan dove and snagged Conrad's shirt and held on 'til they broke the surface. "Hey, I got you, man. Take a deep breath, okay," Ryan said while treading water.

"What . . . What happened?"

"An overanxious architect." Ryan held on to Conrad and swam for the tug. From the corner of his eyes, he watched the two figures hoist themselves into their boat at the stern and head off into the dark river as Demar ran up the deck, yelling, "We got to get 'em. They're getting away. We got to find out what they're up to."

Rory said, "They're heading into the wake of that line hauler. That's a piss-poor place to be in a runabout in the middle of the night. Rollers get ten feet and more. They'll be lucky to survive."

Effie bent down and snagged Conrad's arm. "I thought you were a bad guy."

"Reformed," Conrad said as Rory helped her pull him on deck. Gasping, he flopped over on his back like a landed fish. Effie reached out her hand to Ryan. He took it, their grip holding tight, gazes fusing across the darkness as she said, "What took you so long to get here?"

Rory took Ryan's other hand and helped Effie hoist him on board. "Hell, woman," Ryan said as he stood, dripping water onto the deck. He swiped his face. "We came as fast as we damn well could. Why'd you take the *Miss* out into the river in the first place?"

She put her hands to her hips. "Because swimming across it didn't seem like a real great idea."

Thelma came out of the cabin, Bonnie in her arms. "What's all the commotion?" She looked from Rory to Demar to Ryan, then the deck. "Who's that?"

"Conrad," Rory offered. "Brought us here in his boat to save you. He had a little dunking in the river, but he'll be okay."

Thelma handed Bonnie to Rory and headed for Conrad. She knelt down beside him. "Are you all right?" She smoothed back his hair.

Even in the darkness, Ryan could see Conrad's broad grin as he said, "Fit as a fiddle, sugar, now that I know you're safe. You had me real worried."

Rory bounced Bonnie in his arms, making her giggle. Then he kissed her on the cheek. He knelt down beside Max. "Seems everyone's okay." He nodded to Ryan. "Why don't you bring this tow home where it belongs? We need to be getting Max to the vet. Thelma's got him all trussed up like a Christmas turkey in her brassiere, and I think the poor animal's suffering terrible from basic male humiliation."

Ryan gazed out on the water. "Trouble is, after all this crap we're still no closer to finding Mimi than before."

Rory stood beside him. "And now whoever's after her knows we're on to them, and they know Bonnie's mine and Mimi's and not yours."

Ryan sat in his dad's favorite leather wing chair, alone in the dark living room. The grandfather clock in the hall chimed three times; the low moan of a river tow drifted over the cliffs and across the dewy grass. He gazed out the open double doors that led onto the front porch. He'd opened them, needing fresh air, humidity and all, instead of the chilled recycled stuff.

The summer curtains stirred, then floated like ghosts on

gentle puffs of the night breeze. He swirled expensive brandy in a crystal snifter, the warm, sweet aroma filling his head, easing the tension that had eaten at him for hours.

"Since when do you drink brandy, Ryan O'Fallon," came Effie's soft voice from the entrance.

"Since you scared the living hell out of me tonight and I needed time and a slow drink to unwind." He looked up, not all that surprised to see her there. They hummed on the same wavelength, connected on some level that defied description, and not just as architects or working partners, but something more, much closer, far more intimate.

"You looked pretty cool to me."

"Thanks to a swim in the Mississippi." A dim light from the kitchen spilled into the hall, framing her silhouette in the doorway. Tall, long, loose hair billowed around her shoulders, shirt falling mid thigh . . . and nothing else.

His insides stirred at the sight; desire to have her right then made him hard.

"Thanks for coming after us."

"You did good tonight, Effie Wilson."

"We did good." She came toward him. "And now you're keeping watch to make sure the evildoers don't return."

"And enjoying Dad's brandy. Haven't had it in years, but tonight, for some reason . . ."

"Did I really scare the hell out of you?"

His gaze fused with hers through the dimness. "What do you think?"

"When it comes to us, Ryan, I swear I don't know what to think, especially since we got to the Landing. And now we're leaving. Thelma's safe from Conrad, least as safe as she wants to be." Effie straddled his outstretched legs, her ankles to his. "And everyone knows Bonnie is Rory's and not yours. There's no real reason for us to stay."

"And you're here now because . . ."

She took a step closer, her knees now caging his thighs. "Guess."

The warmth of her skin penetrated through his jeans, the sexy vee between her bare legs disappearing under the soft denim of the shirt . . . his shirt. She slipped the snifter from his fingers, cradling it in her palm.

"If you've never had Napoleon Cognac before, I wouldn't advise starting now. It's potent."

"I'm in the mood for . . . potent." She gave Ryan a wicked smile that made it difficult to breathe. Then she tipped the glass, and her soft pink tongue licked the contents.

"Oh, sugar," he exhaled.

The bouquet of brandy mixed with a whiff of river and the scent of a woman, this woman.

She put the glass on the table and leaned over, framing his face in her soft palms, the shirt gaping, giving him full view of her sweet body.

"Make love to me, Ryan," she breathed in a sultry voice, smooth as the cognac in the glass. "One last time."

Chapter 18

Effie kissed Ryan, the taste of brandy on her smooth lips and silky tongue. He whispered against her mouth, "I need to keep watch. It's been an unusual night."

"And it's not over." Her lips smiled against his, making him smile, too. "And who said anything about leaving here?"

She straightened and crossed her arms over her chest, then whisked off the shirt and dropped it to the floor, leaving her naked as the day she was born . . . though she sure as hell didn't have that body then.

"What if someone comes in?"

"Everyone's dead to the world." She put her hands to her slender hips and smiled. She nodded at his crotch. "Well, not everyone."

The faint moonlight fell across her firm breasts, her nipples beaded with passion. She knelt on the cushion, his thighs between her knees, then sat on his lap. Her hot sex nestled his dick through his jeans, making his heart hammer and the temperature in the room rise ten degrees.

"Effie."

"Ryan, it's so hot in here. Terrible hot." She took the snifter from the table and dipped her finger in the brandy. She dragged it across her top lip, outlining the fullness, then the bottom, pulling gently at the soft flesh, exposing her warm inviting mouth.

He swallowed, least he tried to.

She dipped her finger again and trailed the liquor down her throat, then between her breasts. She slipped the tip of her finger in her mouth, slowly pulled it out and licked it. "Would you like some . . . brandy?"

A puff of air stirred through the room and played in her hair. He watched her for a moment, not wanting to break the spell that saturated the room. "I can't get enough of you." He wound his fingers into her golden hair and brought her face to his and kissed her, the taste of brandy on her moist lips an incredible aphrodisiac. "If we sat here all night, I'd still feel that way." This time his voice sounded throaty and rough.

He kissed her neck, and she trembled . . . or was that him? He added more kisses, taking his time, savoring the taste of fine liquor mingled with Effie's own distinct essence. No elixir, no potion, more seductive.

Holding onto his shoulders, her head arched back, she offered him her delectable breasts and swollen pink peaks. He licked her cleavage, then her left nipple, the nub a morsel of pure heaven against his tongue. Her breaths quickened, and her fingertips pressed hard as he took her right breast and slipped his finger into her silky, slippery heat.

She shivered. "You feel so good, but I want you in me, Ryan. Us giving each other pleasure."

His finger probed a bit deeper, and her face turned to his. Her eyes clouded, her breaths were erratic.

"Just looking at you like this, wanting me as much as I want you, gives me more pleasure than you can imagine." He gently, reluctantly, withdrew his fingers then leaned forward and tumbled them onto the Oriental carpet, breaking their fall with his left hand as he held her with his right. They landed in a soft thump, him on top, her under, their legs intertwined.

She smiled. "Hope we didn't wake anyone."

"If we did, they're in for one hell of a show." He knelt over her, a leg on each side, taking in the sight of Effie, his body throbbing with desire. He yanked off his shirt and tossed it beside the one she'd worn. He took a condom from his back pocket, opened his jeans and made himself ready for her.

"You're perfect." Then he slid into her, going slow, taking his time to remember the feel of Effie under him, around him, making love to him like no one else ever had before.

Effie wrapped her legs around Ryan, his sweaty, bare back against the inside of her calves, and then the inside of her thighs as he thrust deeper. She arched her back, giving more, the feel of him inside her a bitter-sweet paradise, knowing she'd never get this chance to make love with Ryan again.

And, she realized, that's exactly what it was . . . love. She loved Ryan O'Fallon with all her heart.

He whispered in her ear, saying she was wonderful, incredible, lovely beyond words. And then he climaxed just as she did, and for a moment she felt as if they were united, one in spirit and body. She held him tight even after their releases, not ready to let him go as they lay together, the hall clock ticking out the fleeting minutes.

Ryan stirred, then raised his head and braced himself on his elbows. He grinned. "Dear God, you're terrific."

"You taught me . . . everything, Ryan."

"What you did to me . . . for me . . . tonight was all you, sugar. You should write a book. Be a best-seller in no time. You'll have to use a pseudonym, of course. Shoot your career to hell and back if you don't. Maybe when we get back to California."

Her insides froze. California. San Diego. Going . . . home, the end of . . . everything. "Maybe we should stay here for a while and help Rory out. Make sure everything's all right before we take off."

Ryan's brows arched. "Palates, your laundry, Wally. Besides, Dad can take it from here. Demar's on the job, and Keefe's coming in. We need to get back to work, iron out the kinks for the mall before we call in the contractors."

He gave her a quick kiss. "I'm going to clean up. Be back in a minute."

He left, but she didn't move. She stared up at the ceiling, thinking about the mall, her job, San Diego and her life there. What life! Somehow it all seemed so far away, and not just in mileage but . . .

She felt Ryan's footsteps on the wood floor and sat up as he parked beside her. "You're not talking. What's up? Something wrong?"

She raked her hair, lifting it at the nape to cool off against the summer heat and Ryan. Just being near the man made her hot all over. But making love made her . . . sizzle. "Everything's fine. Too fine . . . maybe." She looked at Ryan. "I'm not going back to California. I'm staying here."

The words just spilled out by themselves in a big rush, surprising her almost as much as him. Except to her they felt right. From the look on Ryan's face she could have told him she designed flying broomsticks for a living and he wouldn't have been more astounded.

His mouth opened, then closed, then opened again. He craned his neck toward her. "What did you say?"

"I'm not going back to California."

"You must have whacked your head when you fell out of that chair. Take a couple deep breaths and think, 'There's no place like home.'"

"You're right and I feel more at home here."

"This was just a break in the action, well, sort of because we had the mall to deal with and guys chasing you and the Conrad chronicles. But now it's over. Your whole life's in California. Parents, work, friends. Hell, two weeks ago you weren't sure how many *s*'s were in Mississippi and couldn't find Tennessee on the map."

She picked up Bonnie's bunny rattle from the floor and shook it, then smiled, thinking of the baby. "I don't really like who I am in San Diego. I don't want to go back to that person."

"Sure had me fooled. You looked real comfortable at Designs Unlimited."

"I'm a robot, doing what I'm supposed to be doing, going through the motions of living a life I thought I wanted because that's what I knew. But I came here, remembered another life I once had when I was a little kid, and I like it."

"You want to make mud pies and run around barefoot?"

She held out her hands. "For the first time in a long time I think I know who I am. I'm happy here, really happy."

"Trust me, Effie. If you get the corner office and partner, you'll be beyond happy. You love being an architect. You couldn't be as good as you are at it and not love it."

He took her hands in his. "We'll be nominated for some terrific awards if this mall turns out half as well as I think it will."

She smiled. "Won't that be great?"

"Then why the hell are you leaving the firm?" He gave her a squinty-eyed look. "Is this some woman thing you're going through?"

She gave him a squinty-eyed look in return, and he held up his hands. "Okay, okay. It's not a woman thing. But where is this all coming from? This isn't even your home."

"It could be."

"Come back and visit. This is a great place to visit."

"How about I visit California and live here. The mall plans are done. I'll make you a deal. You can have all the credit for the mall if you clean out my office and send me Wally. My parents aren't really cat people unless you count that little medallion that sits on front of their Jaguar. I'll come back in a month or so to sell the condo and straighten things out with my family."

He looked totally bewildered. Handsome went well with bewildered on Ryan O'Fallon, gave him a vulnerable quality that made her love him even more. Yeah, that's just what she needed!

He asked, "What the hell are you going to do?"

"I don't know. I'm figuring this out as I go. For the first time in my life I don't have a five-year plan. Heck, I don't have a five-day plan. Since Demar's really not a contractor maybe I can cook something up with Slim. Sally knows the business angle."

"You're certifiably nuts."

"I don't think Designs Unlimited will care about me not giving them a two-week notice. They have you and the plans, and I'm only a phone call or e-mail away."

"What about us?"

She stared at him, her chest tight, not enough oxygen in the room. "When we get back to San Diego everything changes, we both know that. We really don't even like each other very much back in San Diego."

She slipped on her shirt, stood and walked to the sideboard. She took a sip of the brandy, hoping it would chase away the sudden chill that had replaced the fire blazing between her and Ryan minutes ago. "You're all business in San Diego and have your harem for diversion. I'm all uptight and fretting over my hair not being just right or my suit having a speck of lint or if I should take palates or yoga or have my nails done. I'm not the same person in San Diego, and neither are you. We do okay here."

"Okay?"

She turned and held the glass up in salute. "We do great, flipping terrific. The problem is you wouldn't be happy staying at the Landing, and I get that. Your dream's in California. You have to go."

He stood and came to her, stopping a few feet away. "We do a lot of competing, but when it comes down to it we're a team, you and me. Your strong suit is design; mine's the infrastructure."

"Your success never hinged on me. We only started working together eighteen months ago with the mall project, and you were well on your way to partner before that. I know from personal experience there's a ten o'clock flight out of Memphis. You'll be back in San Diego tomorrow, and your whole world will fall back into place and be better than ever. Women will probably line up at the airport, form a motorcade. I'll UPS back the office equipment."

She came to him, tiptoed and kissed him lightly on the lips, already feeling him slipping away. She turned for the hallway, not trusting herself to keep her cool with tears so close. "Thanks for bringing me home, Ryan O'Fallon."

"This isn't your home, dammit."

The stairs squeaked, and footsteps sounded. Rory shuffled into the living room, shotgun over his shoulder militia style. "What the hell's going on down here?"

He looked from one to the other. "Hasn't this been a long enough day? Why don't you two just go find a bed somewhere and leave me in peace?"

Ryan snagged his shirt from the floor. "That's not happening any time soon. Effie's staying on, ditching an incredible career for the shores of the Mississippi."

Rory yawned. "And what about you?"

Ryan met his dad's gaze across the dark room. "This isn't where I belong, you know that."

"What I know is this is your home, boy, always was, always will be. But if you think you'll be happy as a pig in mud back in San Diego, then go and don't let the door hit you in the ass on your way out. Kids!"

He turned to Effie. "Least I managed to hold onto one of you. The other?" Rory nodded at Ryan. "Hell's bells. He's smart as a whip and a damn fine architect, but if he goes and leaves you here, in my book he's got shit for brains."

Ryan added the mug with *Architects Know All the Angles* to the box filled with personal stuff from his office. He picked it up and hauled this last load down the hallway to his new corner office and plopped the box on the mahogany desk. He looked out the window that faced the pristine courtyard fountain of the office complex.

Okay, this was it! He'd arrived! It took only three weeks after he—make that he and Effie—submitted the plans for the mall. The client went ape-shit over the specs and wanted Ryan to redesign two more malls. That kind of revenue for Designs Unlimited made him an immediate shoe-in for partner. A success he'd dreamed about since he started snapping Legos together when he was a kid.

He took in the contemporary office furnishings. All new. He'd picked out the sleek desk, bookshelves, chairs, lamps . . . everything. He waited for the feeling of supreme accomplishment to rush through him . . . except it didn't, least not like he thought it would. It sort of crept through him at a snail's pace.

He wasn't expecting the Alleluia chorus and angels to appear and do whatever angels do, but there had to be something more than a damn snail.

"Mr. O'Fallon," a woman's voice came from the open door. It was the senior partner's private secretary. "Mr. Delroy and Ms. Compton would like for you to meet them for dinner tonight at Mille Fleurs at eight." She smiled knowingly. "I'm thinking congratulations are in order."

"Because they . . ."

"The partners voted this morning. Your name will be

added to the letterhead next week." She smiled sweetly. "Course, you didn't hear that from me. Have a wonderful dinner." She closed the door behind her as she left.

Mille Fleurs. Ryan sat on the edge of his desk. Probably the most expensive restaurant in the country, and he knew that's where the seniors would take him for dinner if he made partner. He'd dreamed of this moment, down to the details of what he'd order—salmon tartare with Wassabi caviar and crème fraiche.

He smiled as he started to unpack his items, feeling more euphoric than a few minutes ago. He couldn't get excited before because it all hadn't been finalized yet. That was it. That's why no angels sang and he got the snail treatment. But now . . . Hell, now he was deliriously happy, right!

He picked up the mug about architects and angles Effie had given him for Christmas and felt his delirious state vanish like . . . like fog over the Mississippi.

Dammit-all! She should be here. She should be going to dinner with him and moving into the big office across the hall. What the hell was wrong with that girl? This was the good life, why the two of them had busted their butts for a year and a half to draw up a set of plans that came in under budget, was mindful of the environment and was incredibly beautiful.

And where was Effie now? In some mangy river town. The woman was fucking insane, he was sure of it. What the hell was Effie Wilson doing there?

"What the hell am I doing here?" Effie asked more to herself than Sally while studying the blueprints spread out on the bar at Slim's. "I forgot to put in the electricity. I'm losing my flipping mind."

Morning sun and fresh air poured through the open windows and doors as Sally bustled about, airing the place out and getting the bar ready for the day's business soon to follow. Blind Boy Fuller's "It Doesn't Matter, Baby" hummed low and sweet from the jukebox.

Sally stopped drying a glass and leaned over the plans for the town renovations and proposed residential housing. "All I know is whatever you're doing it looks great to me. I really love the fountain and park in the middle of town and the white frame houses with touches of steamboat Gothic architecture and all overlooking the river."

"We'll add lighted footpaths down to the bank and put in docks for fishing and picnicking. That the Landing is on a cliff and not at river level saves us from flooding."

"If I market this right, we'll have no trouble selling houses. We're only an hour from Memphis, and I've been talking to the banks about special financing."

Effie tapped her pencil on the plans. "I need to start interviewing contractors. We want this right, no hackers."

Sally sipped her coffee. "So if everything's looking great, why are you in a tizzy?"

"Infrastructure."

"Meaning?"

"I'm not great on laying out water lines, sewers, electricity." Effie dropped her pencil onto the sketch and parked her chin in her palm, her elbow braced on the bar. "Ryan O'Fallon, on the other hand, is the king of infrastructure. He's the one who makes all these designs work flawlessly. And since we're presenting these specs to the town tonight at the high school gym, it would be nice to tell them they'll have electricity and sewer. I hate figuring that stuff out, takes me forever. Ryan waves his magic pencil, and everything is hooked up, powered up and flushed away."

"You'll get it nailed down by next week when I go to Nashville and talk to the suits to get us grant money for rehabing the Landing. You don't have to worry about putting infrastructure on the plans for tonight."

"Think Nashville will give us the grant? The Landing's not rich enough to afford renovations on its own."

Sally fluffed her hair and tipped her head. "Girl, you've never seen me in my Chanel black power suit and Harvard MBA mode. The grant is as good as ours."

"Going to stop by and see a certain detective while you're there?"

Sally stopped fluffing and fumed, "That man thinks he's Dick Tracy when he's really just a plain old dick."

Thelma walked in and sat down on the bar stool beside Effie. "You talking about Conrad?"

Sally wagged her head. "Not this time. I was ragging on Demar."

She looked from Effie to Thelma. "Aren't we a sorry sight. We should get awards for doing the worst job of picking men on God's earth. I fall for a lying, scheming, opportunistic jackass of a cop who used me and my friends to get the information he needed. Heck, if I wanted that kind of treatment, I could have stayed in New York and gotten paid for it."

She nodded at Thelma. "You go loopy over a guy trying to swindle you out of your money, and Effie here's nutty about a man who's clear across the country and chooses the perfect job over the perfect woman."

"Well," Thelma sighed. "Then I must be the sorriest sight of all because I love Conrad, warts and all. I really do and . . . and we're engaged."

Effie snagged Thelma's left hand. Diamonds and rubies in a vintage filigree setting of what had to be platinum sparkled in the light. "Ohmygosh. It's gorgeous." She hugged Thelma. "You're gorgeous. I've never seen you happier. This is so exciting. I'm thrilled for you."

Sally took Thelma's hand. "Let me see! Let me see! Oh, my Lord, it's beautiful. I take back everything I said about the jerk . . . I mean Conrad. I think the man's truly trying to redeem himself. Not only does he rescue you from those gun-toting punks who were after Bonnie, but he sold you

Hastings House at a real steal and now he's given you this. Mercy!"

Thelma beamed. "It was his mama's. We haven't set a date. Conrad's working like a maniac down at the dry dock and won't even talk wedding 'til he's got the place in the black and making money again."

Sally winked. "That's okay as long as he's moved in with you and keeping your big soft bed warm at night."

Thelma put her hands over her face and moaned, "Oh, I so agree, but he won't do either 'til we get married. Says he doesn't want to ruin my fine reputation and wants to keep me respectable."

She looked between her fingers. "You all are looking at the horniest woman east of the Mississippi."

Effie and Sally laughed, and Sally said, "I know that feeling. Nothing like a good man at your side, but for me and Effie it's not happening this time around." She looked at Effie. "Do you miss him?"

Effie almost said, I miss Ryan putting in the ductwork, pipes, lines and electricity, and that's all. Except that would be a huge lie. Instead she said, "After presenting the renovations and proposed residential housing to the town tonight at the high school, I'm going back to San Diego."

Chapter 19

Sally sighed. "I knew this would happen. I knew Effie would cave and go back with Ryan, especially with Keefe home. Nothing like one twin to remind you about the other."

Effie rolled her shoulders. "Trouble is I don't need reminding. I think about him all the time. I have to give it a try, see if we can make things work. We're so different there than here but maybe, just maybe . . ."

"You love him," Thelma stated.

Effie shrugged. "And I can't help it. I've tried to get over him but . . . I'll fly back here once a week to check on the renovations and new buildings. Get a local architect to help out and keep in touch with him to make sure our project goes smoothly. I can draw up the plans, but I have to do them in San Diego."

Sally patted Effie's hand. "We understand." She looked at Thelma. "Don't we?"

Effie turned off her computer from the power point presentation as the high school gym began to empty, and Thelma walked over. "Well, we had some turnout. Everyone wanted to see what was going on."

"They sure had enough questions, and now they understand that the updates won't change the Landing and the construction will create jobs, get cottage industries and start-up businesses going and keep people here instead of them leaving for work in the city. Notice how everyone wanted to add their two-cents' worth."

"And you did a bang-up job convincing them to leave their paws off your work."

Effie pointed at Thelma. "So, you heard it, too."

Thelma's eyes grew large, and she suddenly busied herself getting papers together. "Heard what, too? I didn't hear anything, too."

"A cat. Meowing from somewhere in the back."

She tisked and waved her hand as if shooing off a fly. "Now, who would bring a cat to a meeting? Makes no sense at all. You must be hearing things, and at your age, too. Who would have thought?"

"You're the one who said paws. I'm just following through."

"I'm heading over to Slim's as I suspect most of the others are. We need to tell Sally how things went."

"And you're meeting up with Conrad?"

Thelma grinned and gave a sassy smile. "You bet. Come with me. I'll buy you a farewell beer since you're hell-bent on leaving us tomorrow."

She shoved her papers into her briefcase and closed her laptop. "It's not that I want to leave; it's just that—"

"You want to leave," Thelma finished as they headed out the door. "I understand, and so do Sally and Rory and Slim and everyone else around here."

"I can't stay here with Ryan there," Effie said as they crossed the road, heading for Slim's. "The two of us may not ever get together permanently, but I'll be near him, spend time with him, and that's got no time beat by a mile. You know, I thought I'd get over him."

"And then you didn't."

Effie pushed open the door to the bar, and Sally waved a

telephone at her from behind the bar, pointing to it and mouthing Ryan. Effie stopped and said to Thelma, "This is the first time he's called. Least he still remembers me. Think it's a good sign?"

"It can't be a bad one."

Effie took the phone as Rod Stewart played from the jukebox. "You better get Rod off there or this place is going to mutiny, and it won't be pretty."

Sally groused, "Will you just answer the damn phone and quit with all the suggestions?"

"Don't be so grouchy." Effie took the receiver. "Hi."

"Hi yourself. What are you doing? I hear you don't like to figure in power plants and sewers in your plans."

"Somebody tattled." She laughed. It felt so good to laugh with him as she listened to his banter and teasing. She missed him, missed him more than she thought possible. "Guess what, I'm coming to San Diego. I'm leaving the Landing. Staying here was a . . . mistake. You were right. I'll be—"

"You don't want to come to San Diego."

Her heart stopped. She couldn't breathe. She covered the phone with her hand and said to Sally, "Oh God! He's found someone else!"

"What?"

"That's why he called. It's like that show where the guy calls the gal that's his best friend to tell her he's getting married. Ryan's getting married."

Sally took Effie's hand from the receiver. "Talk to him."

Effie swallowed, then said to Ryan, "You've fallen for someone, haven't you? A woman?"

"It's not a man."

Her heart dropped to the floor. She'd waited too long. "I . . . I . . ."

"Turn around."

"Why in the world should I—" Sally turned her head, and she gasped. Ryan sat at the end of the bar. He grinned and pointed to the blue pet carrier. A familiar meow drifted her way. "Wally?" she squealed.

She dropped the phone and ran past Ryan to Wally and petted him through the metal grating on the front. Then she faced Ryan, who had a dopey smile on his very handsome face.

"You never make things easy."

"Me? You scared me to death. I thought you were marrying someone—"

"Else," he finished as he snagged her into his arms. "God, I missed you. I love you, Effie Wilson."

She bit her bottom lip, and her breath caught. "You . . . You do? You really do?"

"Yes, and now would be a great time to say, 'I love you, too,' so I didn't kiss off a really good job for nothing."

"You quit the firm? That was your dream."

"You're my dream. I really need that I love you."

Laughing, she threw her arms around his neck, knocking him off balance and into Conrad, who said, "Effie, for crying out loud, tell the poor man you love him so we can get rid of this sappy godawful music."

She laughed and looked into Ryan's wonderful blue eyes that she'd missed so much. "You played this music just for me?"

"Like anyone else around here would appreciate it?"

She kissed him. "I love you. I was on my way back to California to be with you."

"And I was on my way here when Sally called and told me what you were planning. Why would you come to San Diego? We're terrible there."

"At least we'd be terrible together. I don't want to be without you, Ryan. Ever. For any reason."

"Then marry me, Effie Wilson. Say you will and we'll figure out the future together." He brought his lips to hers. "I didn't know what happiness was, 'til there was you."

Hi, Romance lovers,

You've just read about Ryan, Effie, steamy nights, the wail of a soulful sax, moonlight on the Mississippi River and a baby left on a doorstep in the first installment of the *Four O'Fallons and a Baby* series.

Now soap opera star Keefe O'Fallon's on his way to the Landing hounded by the tabloids and Callie Cahill in *The Way U Look Tonight*. Keefe wants no part of the press invading his privacy until the resourceful Callie offers him the deal of a lifetime, along with fulfilling sensual fantasies and proposing a few surprises of her own.

Return to O'Fallon's Landing with Keefe and Callie where fun, sass and a whole lot of romance are just around the bend.

See you there,
Dianne

Visit me at Dianne Castell.com
E-mail *DianneCastell@hotmail.com* for bookmarks and newsletters

Please turn the page for a sneak peek at
MaryJanice Davidson's hilarious
THE ROYAL PAIN,
available now from Brava . . .

Shel Rivers looked down at the small foot wedged in his doorway, then up at the ridiculously good-looking woman attached to said foot. She didn't look mad or pissed or haughty. Just had a patient look on her face, like, 'you're gonna get this thing off my foot, right?'

Finally, he said, "That's a good way to break something," after a moment that felt longer than it was.

"Not before you get shot," she replied, and shouldered her way past him. A good trick, since he had, at best estimation, four inches and thirty pounds on her. He got a whiff of lilacs as she brushed by, and he almost reached out to see if her black, shoulder-length hair was as silky as it looked. "Dr. Rivers and I will be right out," she added, and closed the door on the protests of everyone else in the party.

The princess (princess! in his lab!) looked around the small, cluttered room for a moment, her small hands on shapely hips. Then she glanced back at him. He actually forgot to breathe when those crystal blue eyes fixed on his.

"I don't think we've been properly introduced," she said pleasantly.

"And I don't think your security team is going to like this at all."

"I'm Alexandria Baranov—"

"I know."

"I'm talking now, please. And you're Dr. Rivers. You're also rude and annoying, which is fine, but *nobody* slams a door on me."

"Especially when your family built half the aquarium," he snapped, trying not to look at her breasts.

"Irrelevant. I wouldn't tolerate that behavior if *you* were funding *my* work. What a disaster area," she continued, turning in a circle to take in the whole room. "How do you find anything in here?"

"None of your business."

"I think we could find some paperwork to prove that isn't true. What's so important? What are you working on?"

"Is playing twenty questions part of the tour?"

"No, it's part of being relatively pleasant. And why did you dodge the tour? You don't even know me."

Because she was rich. Because he was busy. Because she was a princess and he was a lowly Army brat. Because she was too beautiful. Because she was trouble with a capital T, and he'd had enough of that to last five lifetimes.

She was waving a hand in front of his eyes. "Dr. Rivers? Hellooooo? Is anyone in there? Is it lunchtime already?"

He jerked his head back and gave her a good glare. "I've got more important things to do than play tour guide for a stuck-up VIP."

He was sure she'd get pissed, but instead, those amazing blue eyes crinkled at the corners and she grinned. "I bet you don't," she said, and turned to reach for the door handle.

"Okay, okay," he said, grasping her elbow. She took his wrist and pulled it away, almost absently, and in the bottom of his brain a small red flag popped up. "I'll give you the damned tour. But no annoying questions."

"You're a fine one to talk about annoying," she retorted.

"And no potty breaks."

"I went on the plane."

"And I'm not going to be doing this all day, either."

"You can't," she pointed out. "I'm having lunch with Dr. Tomlin in three hours."

"Another rich fat cat," he muttered.

"Did you just call me fat?"

"Hardly. In fact, when was the last time you had a meal?" She was gorgeous—she more than lived up to her moniker as one of the most beautiful women in the world—but too skinny. The planes in her face made her blue eyes seem enormous. "Or even a milkshake?"

"I don't know," she said absently. "It's probably on the schedule somewhere."

Another red flag popped, and he was so intrigued he almost forgot about his experiments. "Well, there's a snack bar on the second floor. Maybe we can grab some fries or something. Although, once you have to watch Dr. Tomlin eat, you're gonna lose your appetite. Assuming you ever had one."

"That's all right, Dr. Rivers."

"Shel."

"Shel. You don't have to worry. I'm not even hungry. And I'm Alex, by the way."

He shook her small, cool hand. His wrist was almost twice the width of hers. Definitely needed a few milkshakes, among other things.

"It's nice to meet you, Alex."

"What a lie, Dr. Rivers."

He smiled in spite of himself.

And don't miss JoAnn Ross's
sizzling "Cajun Heat" in
BAYOU BAD BOYS,
coming in December from Brava . . .

It was funny how life turned out. Who'd have thought that a girl who'd been forced to buy her clothes in the Chubbettes department of the Tots to Teens Emporium, the very same girl who'd been a wallflower at her senior prom, would grow up to have men pay to get naked with her?

It just went to show, Emma Quinlan considered, as she ran her hands down her third bare male back of the day, that the American dream was alive and well and living in Blue Bayou, Louisiana.

Not that she'd dreamed that much of naked men when she'd been growing up.

She'd been too sheltered, too shy, and far too inhibited. Then there'd been the weight issue. Photographs showed that she'd been a cherubic infant, the very same type celebrated on greeting cards and baby food commercials.

Then she'd gone through a "baby fat" stage. Which, when she was in the fourth grade, resulted in her being sent off to a fat camp where calorie cops monitored every bite that went into her mouth and did surprise inspections of the cabins, searching out contraband. One poor calorie criminal had been caught with packages of Gummi Bears hidden beneath a loose floor board beneath his bunk.

Years later, the memory of his frightened eyes as he struggled to plod his way through a punishment lap of the track was vividly etched in her mind.

The camps became a yearly ritual, as predictable as the return of the swallows to the Louisiana Gulf coast every August on their fall migration.

For six weeks during July and August, every bite Emma put in her mouth was monitored. Her days were spent doing calisthenics and running around the oval track and soccer field; her nights were spent dreaming of crawfish jambalaya, chicken gumbo, and bread pudding.

There were rumors of girls who'd trade sex for food, but Emma had never met a camper who'd actually admitted to sinking that low, and since she wasn't the kind of girl any of the counselors would've hit on, she'd never had to face such a moral dilemma.

By the time she was fourteen, Emma realized that she was destined to go through life as a "large girl." That was also the year that her mother—a petite blonde, whose crowning achievement in life seemed to be that she could still fit into her size zero wedding dress fifteen years after the ceremony—informed Emma that she was now old enough to shop for back to school clothes by herself.

"You are so lucky!" Emma's best friend, Roxi Dupree, had declared that memorable Saturday afternoon. "My mother is soo old fashioned. If she had her way, I'd be wearing calico like Half-Pint in *Little House on the Prairie*!"

Roxi might have envied what she viewed as Emma's shopping freedom, but she hadn't seen the disappointment in Angela Dupree's judicious gaze when Emma had gotten off the bus from the fat gulag, a mere two pounds thinner than when she'd been sent away.

It hadn't taken a mind reader to grasp the truth—that

Emma's former beauty queen mother was ashamed to go clothes shopping with her fat teenage daughter.

"Uh, sugar?"

The deep male voice shattered the unhappy memory. *Bygones,* Emma told herself firmly. "Yes?"

"I don't want to be tellin' you how to do your business, but maybe you're rubbing just a touch hard?"

Damn. She glanced down at the deeply tanned skin. She had such a death grip on his shoulders. "I'm so sorry, Nate."

"No harm done," he said, the south Louisiana drawl blending appealingly with his Cajun French accent. "Though maybe you could use a bit of your own medicine. You seem a tad tense."

"It's just been a busy week, what with the Jean Lafitte weekend coming up."

Liar. The reason she was tense was not due to her days, but to her recent sleepless nights.

She danced her fingers down his bare spine. And felt the muscles of his back clench.

"I'm sorry," she repeated, spreading her palms outward.

"No need to apologize. That felt real good. I was going to ask you a favor, but since you're already having a tough few days—"

"Don't be silly. We're friends, Nate. Ask away."

She could feel his chuckle beneath her hands. "That's what I love about you, chere. You agree without even hearing what the favor is."

He turned his head and looked up at her, affection warming his Paul Newman blue eyes. "I was supposed to pick someone up at the airport this afternoon, but I got a call that these old windows I've been trying to find for a remodel job are goin' on auction in Houma this afternoon, and—"

"I'll be glad to go to the airport. Besides, I owe you for getting your brother to help me out."

If it hadn't been for Finn Callahan's detective skills, Emma's louse of an ex-husband would've gotten away with absconding with all their joint funds. Including the money she'd socked away in order to open her Every Body's Beautiful day spa. Not only had Finn—a former FBI agent not charged her his going rate, Nate insisted on paying for the weekly massage the doctor had prescribed after he'd broken his shoulder falling off a scaffolding.

"You don't owe me a thing. Your ex is pond scum. I was glad to help put him away."

Having never been one to hold grudges, Emma had tried not to feel gleeful when the news bulletin about her former husband's arrest for embezzlement and tax fraud had come over her car radio.

"So, what time is the flight, and who's coming in?"

"It gets in at five thirty-five at Concourse D. It's a Delta flight from LA."

"Oh?" Her heart hitched. Oh, please. She cast a quick, desperate look into the adjoining room at the voodoo altar, draped in Barbie-pink tulle, that Roxi had set up as packaging for her "hex appeal" love spell business. Don't let it be—

"It's Gabe."

Damn. Where the hell was voodoo power when you needed it?

"Well." She blew out a breath. "That's certainly a surprise."

That was an understatement. Gabriel Broussard had been so eager to escape Blue Bayou, he'd hightailed it out of town without so much as a goodbye.

Not that he owed Emma one.

The hell he didn't. Okay. Maybe she did hold a grudge.

But only against men who'd kissed her silly, felt her up until she'd melted into a puddle of hot, desperate need, then disappeared from her life.

Unfortunately, Gabriel hadn't disappeared from the planet. In fact it was impossible to go into a grocery store without seeing his midnight blue eyes smoldering from the cover of some sleazy tabloid. There was usually some barely clad female plastered to him.

Just last month, an enterprising photographer with a telescopic lens had captured him supposedly making love to his co-star on the deck of some Greek shipping tycoon's yacht. The day after that photo hit the newsstands, splashed all over the front of the *Enquirer,* the actress's producer husband had filed for divorce.

Then there'd been this latest scandal with Tamara the prairie princess . . .

"Guess you've heard what happened," Nate said.

Emma shrugged. "I may have caught something on *Entertainment Tonight* about it." And had lost sleep for the past three nights imagining what, exactly, constituted kinky sex.

"Gabe says it'll blow over."

"Most things do, I suppose." It's what people said about Hurricane Ivan. Which had left a trail of destruction in its wake.

"Meanwhile, he figured Blue Bayou would be a good place to lie low."

"How lucky for all of us," she said through gritted teeth.

"You sure nothing's wrong, chere?"

"Positive." She forced a smile. It wasn't his fault that his best friend had the sexual morals of an alley cat. "All done."

"And feeling like a new man." He rolled his head onto

his shoulders. Then he retrieved his wallet from his back pocket and handed her his Amex card. "You definitely have magic hands, Emma, darlin'."

"Thank you." Those hands were not as steady as they should have been as she ran the card. "I guess Gabe's staying at your house, then?"

"I offered. But he said he'd rather stay out at the camp."

Terrific. Not only would she be stuck in a car with the man during rush hour traffic, she was also going to have to return to the scene of the crime.

"You sure it's no problem? He can always rent a car, but bein' a star and all, as soon as he shows up at the Hertz counter, his cover'll probably be blown."

She forced a smile she was a very long way from feeling. "Of course it's no problem."

"Then why are you frowning?"

"I've got a headache coming on." A two-hundred-and-ten pound Cajun one. "I'll take a couple aspirin and I'll be fine."

"You're always a damn sight better than fine, chere." His grin was quick and sexy, without the seductive overtones that had always made his friend's smile so dangerous.

She could handle this, Emma assured herself as she locked up the spa for the day. An uncharacteristic forty-five minutes early, which had Cal Marchand, proprietor of Cal's Cajun Café across the street checking his watch in surprise.

The thing to do was to just pull on her big girl underpants, drive into New Orleans and get it over with. Gabriel Broussard might be *People* magazine's sexiest man alive. He might have seduced scores of women all over the world, but the man *Cosmo* readers had voted the pirate they'd most like to be held prisoner on a desert island with was, after all, just a man. Not that different from any other.

Besides, she wasn't the same shy, tongue-tied small town bayou girl she'd been six years ago. She'd lived in the city; she'd gotten married only to end up publicly humiliated by a man who turned out to be slimier than swamp scum.

It hadn't been easy, but she'd picked herself up, dusted herself off, divorced the Dickhead, as Roxi loyally referred to him, started her own business and was a dues paying member of Blue Bayou's Chamber of Commerce.

She'd even been elected vice-mayor, which was, admittedly an unpaid position, but it did come with the perk of riding in a snazzy convertible in the Jean Lafitte Day parade. Roxi, a former Miss Blue Bayou, had even taught her a beauty queen wave.

She'd been fired in the crucible of life. She was intelligent, tough, and had tossed off her nice girl Catholic upbringing after the Dickhead dumped her for another woman. A bimbo who'd applied for a loan to buy a pair of D cup boobs so she could win a job as a cocktail waitress at New Orlean's Coyote Ugly Saloon.

Emma might not be a tomb raider like Lara Croft, or an international spy with a to-kill for wardrobe and trunkful of glamorous wigs like *Alias*'s Sydney Bristow, but this new, improved Emma Quinlan could take names and kick butt right along with the rest of those fictional take-charge females.

And if she were the type of woman to hold a grudge, which she wasn't, she assured herself yet again, the butt she'd most like to kick belonged to Blue Bayou bad boy Gabriel Broussard.

And here's the fabulously funny
Gemma Bruce, back with
WHO LOVES YA, BABY?
Available now from Brava . . .

The night was suddenly still. Cas peered into the woods again. He would swear someone was standing just inside the ring of trees, out of the moonlight. He rolled tight shoulders and cracked his neck. What the hell was he doing in Ex Falls, chasing burglars through the woods?

He snorted. His just desserts. He'd chased Julie through these woods more times than he could remember. And caught her. He smiled, forgetting where he was for a moment. He'd been pretty damn good at Cops and Robbers in those days. He'd been even better at Pirates.

A rustle in the trees. *Wind? No wind tonight.* Another rustle. Not a nocturnal animal, but a glimmer of white. All right, time to act, or he might still be standing here when the sun rose, and someone was bound to see him and by tomorrow night, it would be all over town that he had spent the night hiding behind a bush with an empty gun while the thieves got away.

Cas said a quick prayer that he was out of range and stepped away from the bush. He braced his feet in the standard two-handed shooting stance he learned from *NYPD Blue,* and aimed into the darkness. He sucked in his breath.

A figure stepped out to the edge of the trees. There was

just enough light for Cas to see the really big handgun that was aimed at him.

The "freeze" he'd been about to yell froze on his lips.

"Freeze," said a deep voice from the darkness.

Hey, that was his line. He froze anyway, then yelped, "Police."

"Yeah. So drop the weapon and put your hands in the air. Slowly."

Cas dropped his gun. "No. I mean. Me. I'm the police."

"You're the sheriff? A sound like strangling. "Why didn't you say so?"

"I did. I was going to, but you—Who are you?"

"I'm the one who called you." The figure stepped into the moonlight. Not a thief, but an angel. Not an angel, but a vision that was the answer to every man's wet dream. A waterfall of long dark hair fell past slim shoulders and over a shimmering white shift that clung to every curve of a curvaceous body. His eyes followed the curves down to a pair of long, dynamite legs, lovely knees, tapering to . . . a pair of huge, untied work boots. He recognized the boots, they were his, but not the apparition that was wearing them.

He must be dreaming. That was it. It wouldn't be the first time he'd dreamed of Julie coming back to him. Her hair long and soft like this, hair a man could wrap his body in. A body that he could wrap his soul in. Mesmerized, Cas took a step toward her. She stepped back into the cover of the trees, disappearing into the darkness like a wraith. He took another step toward her and was stopped by a warning growl. His testicles climbed up to his rib cage. *Stay calm. It's just a dream.* Strange. He'd imagined Julie as many things—but never as a werewolf.

He barely registered the beast as it leapt through the air, flying toward him as if it had wings. *Time to wake up,* he told himself. *Now.*

He hit the ground and was pinned there by a ton of black fur and bad breath. The animal bared its teeth. Cas squeezed his eyes shut and felt a rough, wet tongue rasp over his face.

"Off, Smitty."

Cas heard the words, felt the beast being hauled off him. He slowly opened his eyes to find himself looking up at six legs: four muscular and furry; two, muscular and sleek—and definitely female. He had to stop himself from reaching out to caress them.

Her companion growled and Cas yanked his eyes away to stare warily at the dog. He was pretty sure it was a dog. A really big dog.

"Never lower your firearm on a perp who might be armed." She waved the muzzle of her weapon in Cas's direction, then leaned over and picked up his .38 from the ground. She looked at it. "And maybe, next time, you should try loading this." She dropped it into his lap and heaved a sigh that lifted her shoulders and stretched the fabric of her shirt across her breasts. And Cas forgot about the dog, as he imagined sucking on the hard nipples that showed through the silk.

She stomped past him, shaking her head. The dog trotted after her.

Cas watched them—watched her—walk away, her hair trailing behind her, the work boots adding a hitch to her walk that swung her butt from side to side and set the fabric, shifting and sliding against her body. And he wanted to touch her, slide his fingers inside the shift, and feel warm, firm flesh beneath his fingers. But mostly he wanted to touch her hair.

Halfway to the house, she paused and looked over her shoulder. "They're getting away," she said and continued toward the house.

After a stupefied second, he pushed himself off the

ground. What was happening to him? He never thought about groping strange women, even magical ones like this one. He licked his lips, stuck his .38 in his jacket pocket and followed after her.

When he reached the porch, she was at the front door. So was the dog.

"Uh, miss . . . Ma'am? If you'd call off the dog, I could take down some information."

He saw a flick of her hand and he had to keep himself from diving for the bushes, but the dog merely padded past her into the house.

"Well, if you're not going to chase the thieves, you may as well come in," she said and turned to go inside.

"Wait," he cried.

She stopped mid-step.

"You might want to leave those boots on the porch."

She looked down at the work boots, sniffed, then wrinkled her nose. "Oh." She leaned over to pull them off.

Her ass tightened beneath the soft nightshirt, and Cas had a tightening response of his own. He shifted uncomfortably and stared at the mailbox until he got himself under control.

This was ridiculous. He should be used to this. For three months, women called him in all sorts of getups at all hours of the night. He was, after all, the town's most eligible bachelor. Actually he was the town's only eligible bachelor. None of them had the least effect on him. But this one knocked him right out of his socks. Made his dick throb, just looking at her. She might not be Julie, but she looked pretty damn good. He might as well find out who she was and what she was doing here—and how long she planned to stay.

"Coming?" she asked and let the screen door slam behind her.

Oh yeah, thought Cas, *I'm coming.*